At Second Sight

L. BETH CAMPBELL

At Second Sight

L. BETH CAMPBELL

ISBN-13: 978-1-960639-11-0

Case Cover Art and Layout by L. Beth Campbell

Jacket Art by Alexia Roberts Anderson

This is a work of fiction. Any similarities to real people, living or dead, are merely coincidental.

lbethcampbell.com

To Kevin and Paula, you are proof of second chances

PART ONE

Boy Meets Girl

Girl

"I'm surprised you're not already going through all your preparations for tonight," my roommate and best friend tells me from the top of the basement stairs. I'm sitting on my spin bike with less than ten minutes left in the long cycling workout I both love and hate to do on Saturdays and holidays. Love—because there's nothing quite like the high of completing a forty-five-minute spin session; hate—because the discipline and grit required to finish a forty-five-minute workout test my resolve in a way I would rather avoid. Like it has every other time, the love overpowers the side of me that wants to quit early.

"I have three hours before I have to leave," I say to her, nearly breathless from the intensity of the interval.

Ever since my roommate surprised me with the ticket to the NYE Masquerade Ball, I've been counting down the days in my head and using an app on my phone as a backup countdown. In addition, I've been scouring my typical discount and thrift stores in the hunt for the perfect black dress. Eventually, I caved and bought the one I had bookmarked online from one of my favorite stores. I have a philosophy that if I've been admiring a piece of clothing or a pair of shoes for more than a month and can afford to buy said item, the financial investment is worth the surge of joy that accompanies the arrival of the purchase. So, I bought the dress and accessories at a discount because I waited for a sale.

"Right, I just assumed you would want to get there early so you can find the best parking," she says before walking away as one would after detonating a grenade.

Parking turns out to be the very topic I need to keep my mind occupied as I push through the final hard and all-out intervals of the workout. Parking is why I don't "get out more" as those older than me encourage me to do. Well, it's not my only excuse, but it is a big one. While the streetcar along Main Street has helped mitigate the downtown parking nightmares of the past, public transportation loses its appeal for evening events in the winter. I want to have easy access to my car when the temperatures are below freezing at the stroke of midnight. Going to a party alone on New Year's Eve is enough to make me want to arrive hours early for a coveted parking space.

She only bought one ticket to the infamous NYE Masquerade Ball tonight, specifically for me. It's not that she doesn't want to come with me, but between the price per ticket and the opportunity to spend the evening with her boyfriend and his family, this will be a solo adventure for me. Given the impending proposal he's planning, I'll have to get used to sharing her with him. Soon, he'll be the one sharing his wife with me.

I ease myself off the bike seat and walk around to accustom my legs to solid ground again before making the arduous trek from the basement to the living room for a cool-down stretch. This is the best part about the near-hour of torture—the endorphins. One banana, a homemade chocolate milk cappuccino, and two slices of whole wheat toast with butter later, I peel off my workout clothes in exchange for a robe and assess my features. I spent two hours yesterday evening straightening my naturally kinky hair. In a perfect world, I would quickly curl it with my bubble wand, but the time on my phone doesn't agree with that prospect. Curling it might take an hour and holds the risk of burning myself as I fry my hair into ringlets.

I opt for the less time-consuming option of French braiding my long bangs and pulling the rest into a low bun. Then, I go through the multiple steps of washing my face and applying the full effect of makeup from primer to mascara. Satisfied with my efforts, I stare at the rare reflection in the mirror. That girl has chocolate brown eyes that can get away with any color eyeshadow and long, dark eyelashes that don't need extensions. Her red lips have the perfect Cupid's bow that can entice any man in her vicinity. She's confident and capable and doesn't need a date to a New Year's Eve party.

Once I'm in my new black dress and sleek heeled black and gold booties, I move my phone, keys, and lip gloss to my pearl clutch that my aunt gave me for Christmas last week. I hold my breath as I gently lift the gold glitter mask from my top drawer. Years ago, I bought the mask with the hope that the day would come when I would need it for a ball.

I park my small blue sedan in the underground parking garage below the recently renovated Barney Allis Plaza.

While parking garages make me nervous, I trust them more than I trust the above-ground parking lots in the Power and Light District. At least the parking garages tend to have some level of security and decent lighting at night. I take a few deep breaths to calm the nerves that always appear when I'm about to enter a new environment filled with strangers. The frigid December air bites my skin as I speed walk toward the elevator that will take me to street level.

Finding the street signs to gain my sense of direction, my mind flashes back to the two times I got lost in this area of the city. Neither time was my fault since I wasn't driving or deciding the walking direction for our group. In the first instance, my dad was at the wheel while I was told to navigate us to the restaurant he remembered seeing on his GPS app. The problem was that the downtown area is notorious for one-way streets that only a native or experienced transplant can expertly maneuver; we were mere visitors then. The second time, I instinctively knew we were headed in the wrong direction simply because the few months I had been living on campus at the university had taught me that certain streets are north-south streets, and the numbered streets are east-west. Had I been consulted on the matter, we would have never gotten lost. A few years later, I can theoretically find my way around without a map. Theoretically.

Limousines line the front entrance of the Grand Hall at Power and Light. From a distance, I watch as their occupants step out of the rented cars and onto the makeshift red carpet for the event. The men sport tailored suits and dress shoes that likely cost more than one semester's tuition at the University of Missouri-Kansas City. Their dates are just as extravagant with their gowns and heels. Although seeing the wealthy class is intimidating, I push forward anyway. I have a ticket to the same event they're attending, granting me the same access. The worker at the door checks my ticket and takes my coat from me with a smile that I interpret as genuine.

Before tonight, I had only seen this event space in photos and videos online. In person, the historical space is exquisite with crown molding dividing the sections of the high ceilings and the delicate details of the railing that lines the mezzanine level. The center of the main level is the designated dance floor with a live string quartet on the low stage at the far edge. There are round tables and chairs set up for guests and rectangular tables intended for food and drinks. Unsure of where to go, I drift toward the table with the complimentary champagne fountain and fill my hand with a flute. Then I move to the side, far enough away from the table to be out of anyone's way.

Most tables aren't assigned seating except for a few designated with reserved signs for those who donated an unthinkable dollar amount to the charities highlighted at tonight's ball. Those seats will be filled with Kansas City's elite, the surnames that are displayed on our performing arts centers and stadiums as well as the professional athletes that play in those stadiums.

The millionaires and billionaires of this midwestern city are forming their usual cliques, finding each other naturally despite the masks. They can smell the money on each other the way they can smell the lack of it on me. These booties are far from Louboutin, and my perfume is a souvenir one of my friends brought back from her trip to Paris. A classic black dress is still a classic black dress though, no matter the price tag. I would rather spend the night in a corner observing them than have to pretend I enjoy small talk with people with whom I have nothing in common besides these fleeting hours. It's better to be lonely and by myself, than be lonely while around someone.

I sip the champagne I would never buy simply because I know it must be out of my budget if this crowd goes back for refills from the fountain. I slip out my phone and take a picture to send to my friends because if I don't leave with proof, they'll never believe me about how ostentatious this affair truly is.

"You know, most people here only take selfies to post to their social media accounts," a deep voice says behind me—too close behind me. I whip around and almost collide with the source of the comment. Dark blue eyes sparkle behind a velvet black and gray mask, hinting at either amusement or mischief. Or a combination of both. His smirk communicates an air of confidence that evokes both the inclination to slap him and the desire to kiss him. At first sight, he is a living paradox to my emotions.

Boy

Something about her draws me in like a magnet. It's the only way I can explain why, of all the girls my age at this ridiculous charity ball, she's the one I decide to talk to. I watch her from the other side of the makeshift dance floor, intrigued by whatever holds her attention. In a room bursting with the types of people my father would love for me to schmooze with, she appears out of place—she's the genuine leather purse surrounded by cleverly disguised knock-offs.

I surprise even myself as I move across the room to her. I don't realize how close I'm standing behind her until she turns around and almost brushes up against me. The near contact sends a shiver through me that she's too shocked to notice. Deep brown eyes framed with gold sparkles inspect mine, and I'm grateful for the masquerade theme hiding my identity. Her eyes are absent of any recognition. This simple mask is enough to protect my anonymity. I've already passed on my father's regrets that he couldn't attend in person to everyone on his typical list, leaving me without responsibilities for the remainder of the evening.

My face morphs into my signature smirk to hide the effect her scent has on me—hints of coconut and something else I can't pinpoint. Her shiny dark hair that belongs in a shampoo commercial is pulled back from her face of light brown skin that's naturally near-tan from an intriguing mix of ethnicities. Although I appreciate what my mask does for me, I can't help but wish that I could see her whole face without the disguise. Her big brown eyes and heart-shaped lips tease that she could be the most beautiful girl I've ever seen. At first sight, she makes me wish I could stay.

"What would be the point in spending hundreds of dollars on an evening gown you'll wear once if you don't at least publish a photo for all the world to see?" She says her reply as a rhetorical question, and her tone is dripping with sarcasm. I want to soak up her voice like a sponge.

"How do you know how much they spent on their dresses?" I ask her, silently praying that she takes me up on my clear invitation to hold a conversation. I shift my body so that we're facing the same direction with a respectable distance between us. She's close enough to discourage anyone from stealing her away while still far enough away that someone could interrupt without it seeming rude.

She barely hesitates before she says, "Most of them are wearing Neiman Marcus. Different dresses from the same collection and easily hundreds or thousands of dollars. And while I don't doubt that they go to enough black-tie events to get many uses out of them, chances are, they don't wear the same dress twice. My dress costs a fraction of what theirs does, and I'll wear this again."

"If it makes you feel better, I think you look better in your dress than they do in their designer gowns," I blurt before my mind catches up to my mouth. It's far from a lie; the simple black silk shows off her curves in a way that should make every other girl here jealous. I didn't know I had a type until I laid eyes on her five minutes ago.

Despite her slight blush at my compliment, she chooses not to acknowledge it. "Do you come to these things often?"

"More often than I would like," I say with no shame in my declaration. "I'm only here tonight because I have yet to figure out how to say 'no' to my father. You, however, don't seem to be here because you're being coerced."

"I've always wanted to go to a masquerade ball," she says, "but I should have reconsidered coming to one alone." She takes a sip from her champagne flute to hide her embarrassment at her admission.

Her words spark an idea, a way to make tonight less unbearable and more enjoyable for both of us. To buy myself time to solidify the details in my head, I offer to refill her glass. She obliges rather than using it as an opportunity to escape my presence, further encouraging the plan forming in my thoughts. By the time I return with her drink and one of my own, I know exactly how to frame my proposition.

"I have a proposal for you," I say as our hands brush in exchanging the glass. That tingling sensation isn't normal.

"Slow down, we just met," she jokes with a cheeky expression that makes my heart race and my blood sing.

Distracted by her response, I ask, "Do you believe in love at first sight?"

And because this girl is as amazing as I first suspected, she ponders her answer rather than letting my question taint the atmosphere with awkwardness. "I believe in chemistry and attraction at first sight," she says as her eyes drift to the immaculate ceiling in search of a further explanation. "My problem with the concept of love at first sight is that it ignores the strength of love that's gone through the mess of life. Love at first sight hasn't seen the imperfections or flaws that show up on day two or day three thousand. The idealized perfection of love at first sight only stays perfect if it's temporary and confined to that one moment."

"You sound like someone who might be too young to be this jaded," I tease with a smile that usually works when I'm trying to win over the opposite gender.

"Do *you* believe in love at first sight?" She doesn't hold back the accusation behind her question. I hope she never holds back anything she's thinking from me.

My previous plan, the one I'd derailed with my earlier question, finds its way back onto the tracks of my thoughts. "Yes, but I also agree with your argument. I have a theory that if you and I spend the rest of this ball together, no names and no expectations beyond tonight, it'll be more than just attraction or chemistry—it'll be love at first sight and never tainted by the so-called mess."

"You think you can get me to fall in love with you in a few hours?" The logical part of my brain buys into her skepticism. As social creatures, an escape from loneliness can be mistaken for love.

"I think—I know—that you're the only girl in this room I want to talk to tonight," I say with false bravado to appear more confident than I feel as I put myself on the line for her. "I'm also extremely handsome and charming and a good dancer. You seem to enjoy talking to me, and there's no way this connection I'm sensing is one-sided."

"Someone has a bit of an ego," she says, but it's flirtatious teasing.

"If you didn't want to be around me, you would have made an excuse to go to the restroom by now."

She bites her bottom lip in thought, mulling over my words. My eyes are immediately captivated by those red lips, wondering if she tastes like the champagne we've been sipping. "If you enjoy my presence so much, why don't you want to know my name or exchange contact information?"

Rather than whip up an excuse, I opt for the truth. "I'm leaving the country tomorrow for an extended trip and can't promise you anything beyond this ball. It wouldn't be fair to either of us to start something after one night when it would have to be long-distance."

One year of living in Italy on our family's land after graduation has always been the plan. I finished college a semester early to jump-start the whole process my father had set up to help me learn to step into his role one day. I hadn't minded the prospect of spending a year in Europe since it seemed inevitable, but meeting her suddenly made me regret my impending departure tomorrow morning. If I hadn't been in such a rush, I could have had one more semester here to get to know her before leaving.

"Okay," she says with a smile that erases whatever I was thinking. "No names and nothing that could identify us. Just two strangers with natural chemistry enjoying a New Year's Eve masquerade ball together before going back to our lives. You have a deal."

Girl

It's because he's tall and wearing a tuxedo, I tell myself as my thoughts battle against each other. He also smells incredible, which isn't helping tame the pheromones. As if his proximity weren't already sending my hormones into overdrive, he holds out his hand to shake on our deal. I reciprocate, immediately regretting the sparks from that skin-to-skin contact. My limited relationship experience doesn't make me an expert by any means, but I know enough to be certain that this isn't normal. I shouldn't want to melt from a handshake.

"Do you know where the restroom is?" I ask him because two glasses of champagne have followed the natural path from my lips to my bladder.

He feigns a hurt expression as he says, "If we hadn't just agreed to be each other's dates tonight, I would think you're trying to get away from me." He follows up his statement by offering me his arm.

"Never," I tease. *I tease.* Who am I right now? I'm usually the quiet girl who observes others from the fringes. I put on a black dress and a mask and suddenly I'm this girl who flirts with a hot stranger who could likely afford one of those reserved tables near the center. Correction: his father could afford one of those tables.

I slip my arm through his and pretend that his nearness doesn't evoke flutters in my stomach. Through the layers of clothing, I can feel the arm muscles he must work hard to sculpt at the gym. The way he fills his tailored tuxedo hints that he is one of those guys with a home gym and personal trainer. Given that I'm a nobody, it wouldn't matter if he saw me without my mask. I'm not sure that I would know who he is without his on either, but there's something about the mystery that makes the idea of an evening with him more appealing. In real life, our paths would never cross. If they do—

"What if we meet again in the future and somehow figure out who the other is?" I ask hypothetically. I'm never going to run into a man who's leaving the country tomorrow. I'm never going to run into a man with more than enough wealth to watch professional sports games from a private suite.

He laughs because he knows the possibility is absurd. "If you and I meet and know it's not the first time, then we'll just have to admit that it's fate. I assume neither of us believes in fate."

"I believe that things happen for a reason," I say in mock defense. "More times than not, that reason is a consequence of a choice or action in the past." His low chuckle—I want to commit that laugh to memory and play it on repeat. It's the

16

insatiable desire that makes this temporary arrangement of ours dangerous, like playing with fire. I'm his Cinderella who won't leave a shoe behind. He's the unattainable prince who won't be around to search for me even if he wants to.

"It peeves me when people want to blame everything else for their lot in life rather than taking responsibility," he admits with his voice low. "Perhaps the reason you might struggle to find a high-paying job is due to your choice to spend thousands of dollars pursuing a philosophy degree because it seemed 'easy.' If you're going to take out a loan to get a college education, at least pursue something like engineering, law, or medicine that has a higher demand and payout in the end. I know some jobs care more about the degree itself than what the major is, but the major and GPA show how hard you worked and a willingness to learn."

My parents would love this boy, as scary as that is to acknowledge. I recall moments when my father said nearly the same thing. "I wouldn't know what it must be like trying to pay for tuition on my own though," I say to him since it's something we likely have in common. "I worked hard in high school and did well on all the standardized tests. Whatever scholarships don't cover, my parents have been more than willing to pay. Neither of them was born in the United States, but they went through all the hoops to be here legally with my mom being a doctor and all. They never would have paid for me to major in philosophy though." Though the previous two generations of my family lived in the Caribbean, aspects of the Chinese culture live on through my grandmother.

"The way my father explained it to me, he thinks it's shortsighted when parents who can afford to help their kids through college choose to let their kids 'get a loan and figure it out,'" he says, stopping in front of the restrooms. Neither of us is in a rush to separate, and his statement demands further expounding. "When you take out a loan, you have to pay all the money back plus interest, which is criminally high for student loans. All that money going toward interest to lenders could have been kept in the family had the parents been willing to help financially. Higher interest rates are one of the things that can hold a family back from building generational wealth. Part of what causes unproductive familial cycles is the idea that things have to be learned from experience. Some life lessons don't have to be learned the hard way."

My brain is busy soaking up the nugget of insight when he lets go of my arm and gestures toward the women's restroom. I walk into the stall on autopilot as the gears in my head churn. Though he can't be more than a year or two older than me, I suspect that his position as the son of a business tycoon of some sort has given him wisdom that others my age can't begin to comprehend. Based on the expectations he appears to live with, I can guess that he's the firstborn, possibly an only child. A man like that is being groomed to handle millions—potentially billions—of dollars. If our interactions together weren't constrained to a few hours, I would pick his brain and write a book with all the life lessons passed down to him from his father.

It's not until I'm washing my hands and looking into the mirror that I stop to admire the bathroom reminiscent of the Roaring Twenties. It would be a dream come true to get married in a space like this. When I emerge from the restroom, he's waiting for me with a goofy smile that I can't help but return. Most guys would have been on their phones, but he's fully present in this moment with me. With a few feet between us, I pause for a minute to fully admire him. His dark brown hair is styled in the "purposely messy but still stylish because it's an expensive haircut" way. It's the type of thick hair that tempts me to run my hands through it. His five-o-clock shadow paints the sharp planes of his jawline, doing nothing to dampen my attraction to him.

He offers his arm to me again and says, "They're going to start serving dinner in roughly ten minutes. We should find our seats."

I wrap my arm in his and relish the feel of the quality fabric and his bicep beneath. He shoots me that smirk of his again, aware of my subtle approval. "Based on your experience at these types of events, where is the best place to sit for dinner?" I ask.

"The outside edge facing the main ballroom," he says without hesitation. "It's the ideal location to keep an eye on everyone and everything. Being on the outskirts makes it easier to leave early or to go to the restroom. It's also easier to find waitstaff on the edges. The reserved tables are toward the center because the most wealthy typically want everyone's eyes on them during charity balls like this. You would be surprised how many business deals are birthed at those tables."

"You don't have a seat reserved at one of those tables?" I ask, unsure if the answer would reveal too much about his identity.

He finds a way to respond without giving away too much. "When my father isn't here, I sit where I want. All he cares about is whether I show up and converse with his colleagues long enough to show face. If the food weren't so good, I would probably leave before dinner. Who would have guessed that you would have catering to thank for our meeting tonight because I wouldn't have stayed long enough to notice you otherwise." I'm not sure whether to be offended or flattered by his statement, so I choose to assume he meant it in a good way.

He leads me to two open seats at a table in the corner with the perfect view of the dance floor and string quartet. Before I can pull out a chair, he releases my arm and does it for me, displaying a rare chivalry. The mellow tones of the violin and cello dance through the air like a love spell being hummed over all the attendees. The atmosphere is thick with romance as he reaches for my hand under the table and intertwines his fingers with mine. To label this an insane connection doesn't sound significant enough for the electricity buzzing from the contact. While the action would normally strike me as too fast and too forward, we're running on a condensed timeline.

"Tea or coffee?" He asks as he lifts our joined hands to inspect them. Maybe this feels as unreal to him as it does to me.

"I thought the waitstaff brings all that out with dessert," I reply as I squeeze his hand. His breath hitches, and I bite my lip to hold back my amusement. He returns the sentiment. Science should do a study on this to figure out how holding hands can generate so much energy between two strangers like this.

Taking photos of each other has to go against the rules of our date, but I wish I could take a photo of that smirk of his. "I'm asking you if you prefer tea or coffee in general. The answer reveals a lot about a person."

"Both," I say, appreciative of a question that allows us to learn something about each other without uncovering too much. "I like coffee, but sometimes I would rather have a cup of English breakfast tea with honey and a dash of milk. Most days, I drink both."

"English breakfast tea," he repeats my words, mulling them over to himself. "Have you ever been to London?" Another harmless question since plenty of people have traveled outside the country.

"Twice, but the first time can hardly count since I was only two. I remember the second time though. Sometimes I wish we had tea time in America. It's nice to take a break in the afternoon and sip some tea while eating biscuits. Honestly, it's a treat whenever I have time to slow down to enjoy my tea or coffee."

The heat of his gaze would start a fire if I were made of paper. "I like you, if that wasn't obvious. Sometimes you say things that leave me speechless, and other times, I wonder if we're two variations of the same person."

"You've talked entirely too much for me to have left you speechless." Speechless, breathless, awestruck. In another time and place that left us with more than tonight, I would allow myself to bask in the extent of his existence. I haven't even gotten to know much about him yet, but merely sharing the same air has somehow convinced me that our souls have discovered all the things we won't have time for. If circumstances were different, he could be my person.

"I didn't mean that literally. I meant that you're intriguing. You might be setting me up for unrealistic expectations in the future with how witty and cute you are. Ready to admit yet that this is love at first sight?" I shake my head and roll my eyes at his question. The table to our right is being served their meals, and ours is next in the queue. A waiter walks over before I can think of a smart response.

"Did you mark beef, chicken, vegetarian, or vegan on your RSVP?" The waiter asks the two of us. Given that all the attendees are wearing masks, they have no way of tracking whether someone gives the correct answer. They only know how much they've prepared of each option.

My date nudges me to go first. "Beef."

"Beef for me as well," he says and waits for the waiter to be out of earshot. "Always order beef because slightly undercooked beef isn't likely to poison you, but undercooked chicken can give you salmonella. And if you're that distrusting of the meat, vegetarian and vegan are surprisingly delicious as well. I know the chef though, and his steaks are perfection."

He must be growing on me because I don't find his comments like that off-putting. To him, fancy steaks and seven-course meals are the norm. He doesn't know what it is to eat microwave ramen for several meals a week to save money on the meal plan to eat at the Chick-fil-A in the Student Union after a stressful test. His personal chef can probably emulate Chick-fil-A's entire menu, or he has an assistant that can go through the drive-thru for him.

22

"Did I lose you there?" He waves the hand that isn't holding mine a few inches from my face.

"Sorry, I zoned out a bit," I say with a smile. Our salads are placed in front of us, and for the first time, I notice the row of forks at each place setting. Inside out or outside in? He lets go of my hand now that there's food in front of us. At least he has his priorities straight. Out of the corner of my eye, he holds up the outside fork for me to see. Any judgment is absent from his eyes as he gives me a genuine smile. In that other universe where he's my Prince Charming, he would guide me through the rules and subtleties of upper-class society.

Even though the salad is just a salad, it's not just a salad. The mixed greens taste better than the organic counterpart I buy at the store. I moan with delight at the mix of dark leafy vegetables and balsamic vinaigrette with olives.

"That's a strong reaction for a salad," he says before taking a bite of his sans sound effects.

"This is a really good salad," I say between bites. "What's the secret ingredient? Crack?"

He covers his full mouth out of politeness as he laughs at my question. "Of course not. It's sugar. They hide sugar in everything to make it taste better." He winks at me in jest.

"Ummm, no, sugar is what they add to cheap food to hide the taste of dirt and chemicals."

"Maybe what you're tasting is a lack of dirt and chemicals," he says with a question in his tone like he's hoping his playful banter doesn't unintentionally hurt my feelings.

I reach out to squeeze his unoccupied hand in reassurance. It's only now that I take note of how perfectly our hands fit together despite how much taller than me he is. Without heels, I'm just at average height for a woman in the US, but my days of playing high school volleyball and overall jeans shopping would argue otherwise. He's probably just above average height; I'm merely a bit mesmerized by him.

Quickly after the salad plates are cleared, the waitstaff serves out plates of pasta. All the plates have two types sharing the dish as halves of a circle. Despite the little time between courses, he holds my hand while we wait, as if he can't stand not touching me. This is entirely too addicting to be easily severed at midnight. He repeats the pattern between the pasta and the main course and again between the main course and dessert. As full as I thought I was before the plate was placed before me, I can always make room for tiramisu.

"Wait," he says as he releases my hand from his again. "I want to feed you a few bites."

My eyebrows rise with incredulity. "That's so sappy. I'm not sure if a year together would be long enough for me to let you try that."

He has those puppy dog eyes. His smile and smirk are effective enough weapons in themselves, but those eyes he's giving me could convince someone to give him the moon.

"You already have money and charisma on your side," I say to him with a mock pained expression, "how is it fair that you can do that too?"

He laughs, and I relent. As I predicted, it's sappy and romantic and I debate whether I can convince him to stay, marry me, and let me have his babies. I must be ovulating, stupid hormones. There is no tomorrow to daydream about. With the desserts devoured and the coffee with cream consumed, he offers his hand to me while gesturing to the dance floor.

I don't have any experience doing this type of ballroom dance, but I follow his lead like a moth to a flame. No normal boy can perform a flawless waltz like this without a history of dance classes. "Did you have to go to Cotillion when you were a teenager?" I ask, hoping I used the correct term.

"Do you think I would know how to dance like this if I hadn't been forced to learn at a young age?" He smiles despite his wry response. "Now though, it's a very useful skill to have to impress the ladies. My nonna especially loves to dance with me at my cousins's weddings."

I laugh at his comment though I'm liquid on the inside imagining him dancing with his grandmother. "Well, this girl is also impressed. I thought you were being egotistical by including dancing in your list earlier."

"I only have a few hours with you, and you thought I would spend it making up lies to impress you? There's no benefit to being anything but myself with you when this is all the time we have together. It can't be love at first sight if I'm dishonest or misleading. As long as it doesn't give away who I am, you'll get nothing but the truth from me."

His confession pulls the switch that controls the walls that guard me. I can be real with him while still hiding behind my mask. There will be no consequences tomorrow for what I tell him tonight. Except for the few details that might matter.

"I should have asked you this before I agreed to your deal, but you are single, right?"

"I would have never started flirting with you if I were in a relationship," he says with complete candor. "Plus, I'm leaving tomorrow for long enough that any relationship I might have been in would have been broken off by tonight. It doesn't make sense to try long-distance with someone unless I believe there's a chance I could marry her, and I've never thought that about any girl that I've dated."

"How many girls have you dated?" That is a question my filter should have stopped before it escaped, but two glasses of champagne are enough to loosen the lips of this lightweight who rarely drinks alcohol. His wince is enough to make me want to take it back.

Boy

Somehow, I'm still taken aback by her directness. Usually, girls tiptoe around the question, sending subtle hints that they think I'll catch. Even when I do, I still wait until they specifically ask me what they want to know in case my assumptions are incorrect. With this girl, I don't have to guess what she's thinking. If she wants me to know or wants me to tell her something she's curious about, she'll say it.

"Let me tell you my side of the story," I say though she doesn't know who I am to figure out the side the tabloids prefer to tell. "I have a reputation for being a flirt, but I'm not trying to flirt with those girls most of the time. People tend to put me in the stereotype of a wealthy, good-looking playboy, so anytime I'm nice to a girl, they think I'm flirting. Sometimes I go along with it because it's easier than trying to change their minds, but it's exhausting after a while. Their idea of me doesn't fit with the closet romantic who wants to find something serious and long-lasting. I don't believe in 'the one' necessarily, but I do believe that there's a girl out there who fits me in all the best ways. I would like to find her once I'm at a point in my career to do so."

She contemplates my confession as I spin her. She's picked up the tempo and pattern of the movements quicker than any other beginner I've danced with.

"You didn't answer my question." And she's right; I didn't. Not technically.

"Three, two in high school and one in college, all of them casual," I say before spinning her again.

Once she's facing me, she says, "Define casual," and I realize my mistake in using that term. In the world of dating, *casual* typically includes sex with very loose, if any, commitment. It's the term that fits the playboy stereotype rather than the boy who went out on a few dates and kissed a few girls. Although she agreed to this convoluted plan of mine, she doesn't strike me as someone who would agree to a casual arrangement.

"Is that what you really want to know, or is that subtext for the real curiosity of yours?" I ask, and she blushes. *Blushes.* It's so endearing. If we weren't on the dance floor, I would kiss that blush of hers.

"Fine. How many women have you slept with?" She can't hide her embarrassment from asking me. Until our conversation took this turn, I hadn't seen the signs. This girl is innocent, but not in a naïve way.

But I'm not the commitment-phobic jerk either. "None, because contrary to what others assume about me, I want sex to mean something. Those girls were fun to kiss, but they didn't mean anything. I'd rather be a closet virgin romantic than try to fit the mold of who the world thinks I should be."

She appears surprised, and I wonder if I've misjudged her. "It's not very often that someone else sees it the same way I do. I would have pegged you differently an hour ago simply because you were so smooth and confident when you started a conversation with me."

"I was intrigued and desperate to talk to a girl in a sexy black dress," I say with a self-deprecating smile. "I've been using all my best lines on you to see if they work."

"They're working." Those words convince me that we've danced enough for the night.

"Do you want another glass of champagne?" I ask her. "There's something I want to show you, and we should grab some now if you want more."

She only thinks about it for a second. "You're intoxicating enough to the system without adding more alcohol to the mix. Plus, I shouldn't have more than the two glasses from earlier. I do have to drive home tonight. Maybe just a glass of water."

Resisting the urge to kiss her before midnight, I lead her to the water station since I don't want to leave her side for anything but a restroom break, which is next on my list before our little adventure. We take turns, holding the other's water while we wait. Then, she follows me silently without insisting on knowing where I'm taking her as if she trusts me implicitly. Any other girl attending this ball would refuse to go with me without knowing the destination and whether others would be able to see her with me.

At this moment, I feel as if I'm racing against the clock. Half an hour until midnight means half an hour left in this fairytale before she vanishes from my life forever. In a world this big, it feels that final. I use my father's key and sneak us onto the rooftop access. Whenever he makes time to come to these events, he likes to get away from everyone for his smoke breaks. Normally, my father isn't a smoker, but even the constant social expectations get to him on occasion. Before I left the house tonight, I asked him if I could borrow the key, and he graciously let me have it as long as I give it back to him before hopping on my flight tomorrow. He'll hold me to my word.

The skyline of the city lights is a welcome respite as we step out into the late December air. She shivers from the cold, and I'm the worst kind of idiot for not thinking of swinging by coat check before bringing her up here. I swiftly remove my tuxedo jacket and drape it around her, hoping that it might somehow capture some of her smell for me to relish later. I know enough about glitter to recognize that any that falls off her mask and onto my suit jacket will be there for years. Glitter is essentially the STD of craft supplies. As strange as that comparison is, it's comforting knowing that in ten years, I'll still have a reminder that this night was real.

"This view is worth the cold," she says as her breath condenses in the winter air. That statement is why she's the one up here with me. Using the cold to my advantage, I wrap my arm around her to "conserve body heat," and she snuggles into my embrace.

"I brought you up here because I thought it would be romantic, but I'm doubting if frostbite is romantic," I say to hear her laugh. I'm rewarded for my efforts, and she reaches for my hand. I revel in the soft, smooth skin of her hand, memorizing every detail I can. This is what will get me through the next year in an unfamiliar country surrounded by girls who are all related to me.

We stand huddled together in silence watching the city around us and stealing glances at one another. Neither of us feels the need to fill the vacuum with conversation because we're comfortable with each other. I wait until about five minutes before midnight to tell her, "I'm going to kiss you at the end of the countdown if that's okay with you."

Initially, I thought about surprising her but decided against it. A closet virgin romantic asks permission before kissing a girl he met a few hours ago. Even if he is too curious for his own good. Kissing her might just make the world explode.

"That's okay with me," she says quietly, and I look over to see her smiling to herself, a slight blush on her cheeks. Absolutely breathtaking.

I use the hand that isn't holding hers to pull out my phone from my pocket to find a countdown. One minute before midnight, everything around us comes awake. It's as if the wind itself is counting down in anticipation for what might be a glimpse of magic. Or it might be my imagination. Even if it isn't love at first sight for her, it is for me. When my screen blinks with ten seconds remaining, I turn to face her and lock my eyes on hers. Our breathing syncs in those last few seconds until the clock strikes midnight.

We both move to close the distance, our lips colliding. My hands cling to either side of her face, and her hands cover mine. My body breathes a sigh of relief while also coming alive like it's taking its first breath in years. If magic is true love's kiss, this is enough to make me believe for a lifetime. Kissing her is more than kissing, more than anything I could ever deserve to share with someone else. As painful as it is, I end the kiss before it can turn into something more.

Girl

"Wow," I breathe as he slowly tears himself away from the kiss. "So, that's love at first sight." He laughs into my hair and pulls me into a hug.

"Told you so," he says, but I can hear the sadness in his voice. The electricity from the kiss had wiped away the finality of midnight, but now I remember that this is the end. I'm not ready for this to be over, and I know he isn't either. But it has to be.

"Thank you for one perfect night," I say to him as he slowly releases me from his grasp. As much as I want to jump into his arms and kiss him again, I know that will only make it harder to say goodbye.

"Love at first sight," he repeats my words as he shakes his head and smiles at me. "That's what I'll remember you as every time I think of this moment from now on. Can I walk you to the general vicinity of your car?"

I nod, and he slips his hand in mine before opening the door that leads back inside. Once we're sheltered from the cold, I stop to hand him his suit jacket. He puts it on, and I help brush off whatever glitter I notice under the lights. His vibrant blue eyes watch me with an intensity that makes me shiver. He grabs my hand to stop me after a few seconds.

"Leave it," he says referring to the glitter. Then, he holds my hand again to stop me from continuing my attempts to clean off the gold flecks. He weaves us through the crowd of people exiting the event space until we reach coat check. I hold his winter jacket as he helps me into mine, and he shrugs into his before reuniting our hands.

Outside on the sidewalk, he lets me take the lead toward the parking garage where my car is parked. At the entrance, he leans in to peck my cheek. To my disappointed expression, he says, "I won't be able to walk away if I kiss you again."

"Goodbye," I say as I let go of his perfect hand.

"Maybe one day."

I want to watch him walk away, but he stands and waits for me to enter the parking garage. I take one last look at the tall, handsome stranger before returning to my normal life.

Boy

WHAT IFS

My lips still tingle from that midnight kiss. I wait a few seconds after she's disappeared from my line of sight to turn around and return to the Grand Hall at Power and Light. My father's driver is scheduled to pick me up at the front entrance a quarter after midnight, and he's unnaturally punctual.

I am not punctual; I'm either too early or too late. Right now, I'm not sure where I fall between the two. Am I too early in meeting her tonight, tasting those lips years before I'm supposed to know her? Or, am I too late in realizing now that I shouldn't have let her go without any way to contact her in the future? For once, I arrive at the meeting spot just as the familiar black SUV pulls into the loading zone. Without a word, I climb into the back seat and mentally calculate how little sleep awaits me.

Zero. The answer is zero because I hate packing and tend to put it off until the last minute. At one in the morning, I turn on the light in my bedroom to reveal an empty suitcase and a pile of clean clothes on my bed. Since I've already chosen the masochist option of packing after a New Year's Eve party, I prolong the inevitable by showering first. No amount of soap or water can wash away the lingering aftershock of the sparks. Can time even make something that tangible fade in my memories?

I pack my suitcase on autopilot as the adrenaline from the evening wanes. Her laugh echoes in my subconscious as I finally crawl beneath the sheets of my bed. The memories and dreams of her may remain entirely untainted by the mess of life, but I would have taken her mess in exchange for more time with her. Time is worth the imperfections.

Caffeine helps me function but is not a replacement for a full night of sleep. When facing a nine-hour flight over the Atlantic Ocean, one does not need to be fully rested. I've never flown economy class, but I've seen enough movies and have heard enough stories to know that my father's private plane is a luxury most can't even imagine. After satisfying my dad's inquiries about whether I adequately conversed with his business connections last night, he reverts his attention to his phone. When I'm sure he's finished talking to me, I excuse myself to my small private bedroom to crash while the jet transports us to my life for the approaching year. This time, I'm too exhausted to dream about anything.

MAMMA IS among my family that waits for us at the airport. She flew here a month ago to be with her family for the holidays. My father and I stayed in America because there were too many opportunities to wrap up unfinished business to spend Christmas across the ocean. At the time, I thought it was a ridiculous reason not to join the rest of our family, but I would have never been at the masquerade ball had we not stayed behind until the new year. That one decision changed my whole perspective on "love at first sight."

I witness the moment my mother's attention diverts to my father. It's comparable to the slow-motion moment in movies where lovers are reunited after being apart. Twenty-five years of marriage hasn't dulled the spark between them. Deciding to spend the holidays apart must have been a difficult one for them, but they'll be here together for a month before returning to Kansas City without me.

Within a minute of walking through the door of the family villa outside Treviso, Nonna is covering my face with kisses. "Alessandro," she says my name with the same warm affection she showers on her other grandchildren. Nonna always calls me by my full name, Alessandro. The rest of my family and friends call me Alex. If I hadn't suggested anonymity, I would have responded to either name coming from my mystery girl. The problem is that I didn't want her to recognize me by the name the media repeats in increasing circulation: Alessandro De Luca. This year in Italy was always part of the plan, but now it has the additional benefit of keeping me out of the public eye for an extended period. Here, I'll be around family and work on the farm where my father and mother fell in love.

Mamma pulls me away from the loud gathering of cousins, aunts, and uncles to show me to my room for the foreseeable future. Instead of the small room where I normally stay, she leads me outside to the private guest house.

"Since you're an adult, and you'll be here long term, I convinced Nonna to let you stay out here and have your own space," she explains before I can ask. "Of course, you're still expected to join her for most of your meals unless you want her knocking down your door. Also, we're trusting that you won't have any sleepovers with anyone who isn't family. Nonna will drag you to mass every Sunday if she catches you in bed with a girl."

I groan, "Mamma! I have no interest in any romantic relationships while I'm here." Somehow, she deciphers something in my tone, something in what I didn't say.

"Alex, what's bothering you?"

I wait until she's unlocked the door to the guest house to replay the tale that feels like a dream. I tell her about the girl and the undeniable sparks I'd felt at the smallest touch. Although I'm talking to my mother, I tell her about the perfect first kiss as the countdown signified a new year. Reliving it makes it both more real and surreal.

Mamma pulls me in for another hug and rubs my back in a way she hasn't since I was much younger. It's different now because I tower over her, but the same in how it brings the comforting touch of a mother.

"It might be the exhaustion from traveling, but I'm starting to think that I made a mistake in letting her go," I admit out loud.

She distances herself to look me in the eye as she says, "Alessandro, doing the right thing is never a mistake. A new relationship would have been nearly impossible being an ocean away, especially with how hard you'll be working on the farm. You hardly know her after one night. There's no way to know whether or not she's the love of your life. I have a secret for you that you're old enough to understand now. Some people have more than one love in their lives due to circumstances or unreciprocated feelings. You're so young that the woman you marry one day might be her, or any number of women you meet throughout your lifetime. The sun will still rise."

"Do you think it's possible that I could meet her again?" It's a ridiculous idea considering the unlikelihood. It's why it would have to be fate to cross paths again. Still, the possibility feeds the hopeful romantic in me.

Mamma smiles sympathetically. "Possible, yes. Likely, no. But who am I to say what the future holds?"

People who meet each other and exchange names tend to forget years later without the constant familiarity of seeing faces and repeating those names. I suggested remaining strangers with the one girl I now wish could know me inside and out. I'm the one who kept her at arm's length.

The noise and activity of Nonna's kitchen and dining room hold a striking contrast to dinners with my parents back in the States. Sometimes, my father and I don't leave the office until the sun is well below the horizon, but Mamma waits up for us when my father takes the time to call her and let her know. I've seen my father step out of critical business negotiations to update her on our estimated time of arrival. America's culture of working too hard has rubbed off on him in some ways. Italy's culture of family and community always wins when the two battle for supremacy.

Fourteen. There are fourteen of us squeezed into the dining room meant for a maximum of eight. When I offer to help, Nonna shoos me away and insists that my work starts tomorrow after I've had some proper rest. I know better than to argue with a stubborn and strong Italian woman.

Nonno walks through the door leading to the garden, taking off his shoes before Nonna can yell at him. Fifty years of marriage lie beneath the affectionate softness of Nonno's eyes as he spies his wife in the kitchen. Risotto is a specialty in this area of Italy, and my grandmother likes to cook it for special occasions. Based on the selection of Prosecco and what looks like tiramisu, she's treating the arrival of her son and grandson like a holiday. She swears that our family recipe is one of the original versions of the famous dessert.

I'm surrounded by several conversations in Italian, all in competing decibels with one another. Having spent most of my life in America, my grasp of the language is passable, but I'm not fluent enough to understand half of the questions thrown in my direction. My parents speak some Italian around the house and have taught me the basics; this next year is my opportunity to truly learn the language of my ancestors. Among the familial chaos, I still feel alone in my inability to converse in Italian freely. Mamma squeezes my hand, my anchor when I'm feeling overwhelmed.

Despite the winter months, there's always work to be done at the family vineyard and hours of hard work in the sun left me exhausted every night for the first few days. It takes about a week before my thoughts catch up to me. I could contact the planners responsible for handling the guest list from the masquerade and narrow down the possibilities using the process of elimination, first by filtering out tickets for more than one person and then removing any from the list that I recognize. There's a chance someone else bought that ticket for her, but it would also breach our agreement if I tried to find her now. The whole purpose is to leave it up to destiny to lead us back to each other if and when the time is right as if such a thing exists.

Still, the idea is tempting enough to mull over the intricacies for a few weeks. With my father's company being one of the largest donors to the charity organization, getting the names would be easy. Even with a name, finding her could prove to be difficult if she's not on social media. Unlike me, her name and face aren't posted across the tabloids. It wouldn't change that I won't be back in America for nearly a year. Nothing relevant has changed.

"Cos è male?" Nonna asks when I zone out after eating the panino she prepared for lunch.

"Non ha importanza," I say as I attempt to shake the reminders of the mystery girl from my conscience.

Nonna gives me a disbelieving expression as she sits at the table across from me. "Le soffre le pene d'amore."

Lovesick. I've felt that since I let her get away that night. A girl that I barely know shouldn't have this effect on me, but what I do know about her convinces me that she's everything I never knew I wanted. None of what I'm feeling is logical. Knowing it's illogical doesn't stop the fear that I'll never feel like that again. It doesn't stop the heartbreak that I've lost out on someone amazing.

"Sì, Nonna," I admit to her in surrender.

"Amore non è senza amaro," she says, affectionately holding my hand in hers. "But you are a Marc Antonio, so we can easily find you a nice Italian girl."

Nonna rarely breaks out into English, but it's usually a source of comedic relief when she does. What started as an Italian saying about love not being without bitterness ended with her assessment that I fit the tall, dark, and handsome category. Most Italian men fit the dark and handsome requirements, but "tall" can vary nationwide. Italians are short compared to Americans, but some Italians in the north near Austria have mixed Germanic descent.

I kindly tell my grandmother, "I don't want to think about any girls right now. I'm here to learn from you and work hard, not to get married and start a family. There will be time for the other things later."

As my time in Italy passed by, the pain and regret lessened. Long distance wouldn't have worked with how little time we had beforehand. One day certainly isn't enough to agree to that type of arrangement. There's a seven-hour time difference between Italy and Kansas City. Chances are, our sleeping patterns wouldn't ever overlap, leaving over half the day that one of us is asleep. The odds were always stacked against us. Oceans are too big to cross every day, and technology can only lessen the distance so much.

I will never kiss her again. I will never hold her hand again. I will never see her whole face without a mask obscuring her features. She won't be my wife, and she won't bear my children. I will never know whether her first name combined with my last name would sound like music or a tongue twister. Those dark brown eyes will never sneak a stare at me when she thinks I'm not looking. I will never know the mix of ethnicities that combine to create her striking features. I will never truly know if letting her go was letting go of the love of my life. What I do know is that there's nothing I can do to change it now.

PART TWO

Seven Years Later

Sonnet

~~~~~~

My favorite part of this drive is seeing the downtown skyline accented by the iconic, towering buildings. Although it's not the same view of the city as one would get from the Liberty Memorial and the World War I Museum, it still takes my breath away. The best part is when I'm not trying to drive and admire my city at the same time. It may not be the fastest route from my house to the airport, but we managed to leave early enough that I convinced my best friend to take the scenic highway.

"Sonnet Kincaid, are you sure you don't want me to come with you?" Taylor asks as we pass another exit. "I can call Gabe and have him pack a suitcase for me. I'm sure he won't mind my being gone for ten days."

I tear my focus away from the blur of trees outside to stare at her. "Firstly, you're seven months pregnant. There's no way you'll be comfortable on a tour like this. Secondly, we both know we can't trust Gabe to pack for you. You're the one who makes sure he has everything he needs whenever you go on vacation."

"I know, but I hate the idea of you traveling by yourself," she says, failing to hide the sympathy from her expression. "It was supposed to be a trip for two, not just you. Although, I'm glad you're still going. You deserve a vacation after everything that happened."

Everything that happened. It's how everyone around me refers to the wedding I'd had to cancel when I caught my fiancé cheating on me. One night, I had decided to surprise Rich—or Dick as my friends now call him—only to discover another woman with him in the shower. I had rarely ever used the key he gave me, which might explain why he was surprised to see me. Fortunately, he hadn't even started packing his things to move out of his apartment and into my house. We were waiting until after the wedding to move in together because I wanted and still want to stay celibate until marriage. I thought we were on the same page. I was wrong. The good news: the house was never his, and I hadn't gotten around to giving him a key.

Not only was I left with the emotional shards of witnessing the man who was supposed to marry me with another woman, but I was also responsible for the daunting task of canceling everything I could regarding the wedding that was no longer happening. My mom and Taylor both helped as I called the event space and caterers and sent out "just kidding, the wedding's off" messages to all the guests. I could never get my money back on things like engagement photos and save-the-dates, but I was able to salvage 75% of the deposits I had made. It turned out though that the honeymoon trip to Italy was nonrefundable. The money is gone whether I take the vacation or not, so I'm taking the vacation.

Last night, we had an old-school sleepover with pizza, popcorn, ice cream, and nostalgic romantic comedies from our high school years. All my friends who were supposed to be my bridesmaids showed up with snacks and helped me pack for my solo honeymoon trip. They refused to let me be alone on what would have been my wedding night. I wondered if it was too soon to hide my relief that I wouldn't be spending the rest of my life with a man named Dick, short for Richard though he insists that people call him Rich. I might have dodged a bullet.

Taylor Swift plays from the car stereo because my best friend Taylor is ironic. She's been choosing Taylor Swift a lot more lately when she's in charge of the music, and I suspect it has more to do with her iconic break-up songs than with the romantic ones. Today, "Red" was the first to start playing as we left my house. When a song I've never heard pops up, she quickly pushes the "next" button on the steering wheel.

"Why did you skip that song?" I ask her suspiciously. If I can handle several romantic comedies, I can handle a Taylor Swift love song. I'm about to go on vacation to some of the most romantic places in the world. I'm not as fragile as everyone is treating me.

"It's not my favorite," she says, and I immediately sense that she's lying. I type a reminder on my phone to listen to the song later while I'm waiting to board my flight. "Back to the topic of your trip. If you don't kiss at least one Italian man while you're there, I'll be disappointed. I know it's a tour, and you won't be staying anywhere for more than two nights, but Italians are romantic. Plus, you're a gorgeous American who knows their language well enough to impress one to kiss you."

I stare at her even though she can't do the same to me and keep her eyes on the road. If there's one thing I can count on her for, it's being a good driver. "In case you forgot, I've already done the whole kiss a stranger after one-night thing," I remind her. Over seven years later, that masquerade ball is still branded in my mind as the perfect night.

"You make a good point. A repeat of that on Italian soil with good wine and exquisite food might ruin you for any normal guy who tries to win your heart," she says. More ironic than Taylor listening to Taylor Swift is the notion that a man who is perfect for strictly one night is a greater threat to my possible future happiness than the man who betrayed me after making such a promise. But isn't he? I unconsciously chose not to date for the first two years after that ball. No one could meet the standard I set up for myself until Rich, and that had backfired.

"It's not love at first sight as much as it's knowing at first sight that you could fall in love with the person," I paraphrase from one of the many romance novels I've read and listened to on audiobook.

Taylor is uncharacteristically quiet for the next few seconds. Finally, she says, "Falling in love in the beginning is the easy part. Choosing to love someone every day for a lifetime is what matters. As much as I want you to find that, Dick was never going to be the one to withstand the hard times. You always deserved better than him."

The exit for the airport approaches on the right, and she turns on the blinker. I have just enough time to tell her the revelation I've been mulling over since watching those romantic comedies last night.

"I think I was more upset that Rich cheated on me than I was hurt by his cheating," I say, unsure if my words made sense. To clarify, I add, "As in, it was a bigger blow to my ego and self-confidence than it was to my heart." Hearing it out loud settles it for me.

My best friend chuckles and gives me her "tell me something I don't know" look. Neither of us has time to delve into the depths of that topic though. She follows the road that leads to the departures area of the newly built airport terminal and shifts the car into park. I hop out the passenger side as she unlatches the trunk where my suitcase lies.

"I expect a photo from you every day with updates," she says as she walks around to the rear of the car to hug me. Her baby bump gets in the way of her squeezing me as hard as she would like, but she makes a valiant effort. I hold back the tears that well up at the knowledge I won't see her for ten days. We haven't gone ten days without seeing each other since she went on her own honeymoon. Mine is essentially a honeymoon in reverse.

I roll my suitcase around to the curb and grab my backpack from the backseat. She waits until I'm through the front doors of the terminal entrance before pulling into the flow of traffic. After I've gone through check-in and security, I buy a cup of coffee and settle in the waiting area outside my gate. My first flight is to the Chicago O'Hare Airport with a two-hour layover before the international flight to Rome. With another half hour before boarding starts, I search for the Taylor Swift song my friend had skipped on the drive to drop me off.

The acoustic intro to "Enchanted" plays through my earbuds, a calming contrast to the bustle of the airport around me. I tap the screen to read the words as she sings them, and it's immediately obvious why my friend didn't want me to hear the song. Every line reminds me of him, of that night, of all the feelings that verify my earlier declaration. If I had to assign Rich a Taylor Swift song, even before the cheating and broken engagement, I don't know if it would have been a love song. I deserve someone who would be a love song.

I'm so lost in the rabbit hole of Taylor Swift's love songs through the years that I almost miss when they start boarding my flight. My assigned seat is by the window, and my row companions graciously stand to let me past them. They're a couple, assuming their wedding bands mean they're married to each other, although they could be siblings who don't look alike. The woman is in the middle seat, and I'm unsure whether I'm relieved or dreading the short flight. Some women talk at a rate that makes up the average number of words per day for those of us who are quiet. I open the shade of the window and watch as they finish loading our luggage and complete final checks before takeoff.

"Is Chicago your final destination, or do you have a connecting flight?" She asks me to make polite conversation.

"I have a connecting international flight," I say, silently praying I'm not about to spend the next hour as a third wheel on an arrangement I never asked for. "What about you?"

She beams as she says, "We have a connecting flight to Honolulu to celebrate our first anniversary." Ah, not quite newlyweds, but a marriage still in the honeymoon stage. She glances at him with stars in her eyes. Did I ever look at Rich like that?

"Congratulations," I say because I mean it. I have no problem being happy for people who have found love and made a lifetime commitment to one person. Deep down, I still want that for myself despite the risks of being hurt and betrayed again. When my gaze shifts back to hers, I can sense that she wants me to share where my destination is. "I'm going on a trip to Italy."

Instantly, her face lights up as if a spotlight had turned on. "Oh my gosh, that sounds so romantic. Are you traveling by yourself, or are you meeting your boyfriend there?"

"Babe, you can't just ask someone that," her husband says with an apologetic look in my direction. "Her relationship status is none of our business."

"I'm traveling by myself," I say and add, "and I don't mind her question. It was originally supposed to be a vacation for two, but things changed."

Her face drops at my answer. "Oh, honey, I'm sorry that happened to you. Sometimes being single in a romantic place turns out to be a good thing. Italian men have a reputation for knowing how to treat a woman right."

What is it with this idea that I want an Italian man? Do all women who already have a husband of their own assume that the rest of us will find our matches at any moment? What if I want to go to Italy, enjoy amazing food and art, and maybe get a tan from all the time I'll spend walking in the sun? I don't need to come home with a story involving an Italian man for this trip to be successful.

"It's also perfectly fine to stay single," the husband adds shooting glares at his wife.

She sighs and rolls her eyes at him. "Of course, there's nothing wrong with staying single. But if I were single and traveling to a place like Italy or France, I would enjoy the pickings of the single men there. The worst that could happen is that you get some free food and wine out of it. And you're pretty, so the worst isn't likely to happen to you."

"I would flirt with Italian men if it meant getting free food," her husband agrees with a shrug. "Free ice cream, free coffee...that doesn't sound like such a bad deal to me."

"See, flirting will save you a lot of money while you're on vacation," she says as if it were ironclad logic. This is when I decide that I don't mind talking to them. They're not overly lovey-dovey the way some couples can be, and she seems like a genuine person.

I open up to her and say, "This would have been my honeymoon, so I'm not sure how much flirting I'll be doing. I couldn't get a refund when I had to cancel everything else regarding the wedding, so I decided that I should be the one who gets the vacation since I'm not the one who cheated. It's part of a tour which means I'll be in a group most of the day anyway. I'm hoping the others aren't all couples on vacation though, otherwise, things will get awkward very quickly."

"Imagine being the only single person on a couples retreat," she says with her hand on her heart.

"That sounds like the plot for one of those romance novels you're always reading," her husband says. "I'm sure it'll be a healthy mix in the group. My parents went on one of those tours last summer, and they said there were families there as well as friends traveling together. It sounds like it's a great way to see the major cities and sights." He chooses this moment to slip on his headphones and dismiss himself from the conversation.

"He hates the take-off and landing part of flying," she explains for him. "He always slips on his noise-canceling headphones and plays music until the seatbelt light turns off. You should have seen him when we were flying for our honeymoon; he was an absolute mess of anxiety. The first thing I did when we got home was order those headphones for him. Anyway, have you ever been to Europe before?"

Grateful that she chose not to talk about my broken engagement, I humor her and talk about the family trips my parents took me on growing up. Between having family in other countries and parents who saw value in showing us cultures different from our own, I had a small list of countries I had visited before I turned eighteen. Talking about travel, both in the past and in hopes for the future, fills the hour, and the next thing I know, we're going our separate ways in the terminal in the Chicago O'Hare airport.

My layover is long enough for me to eat lunch before boarding the overnight flight. I order a burger at the Chili's a short walk from my gate and savor the last American food item I'm likely to have for a while. Given my love for Italian food though, I won't miss burgers while I'm there. From my spot in the small food court, I watch the people who pass by on their way to somewhere that isn't here. Chicago is close enough to Kansas City that I've opted for either driving or the train when I want to come here. I wonder what the ratio is between people who fly here to stay versus those who are just here to eat and move on.

The plane headed to Rome is larger, and the waiting area fills up as the departure time grows nearer. Around me, I hear conversations in both English and Italian, my brain picking up on bits and pieces of both. Italy had been my idea, partially because I'm familiar enough with the language to communicate in a situation where someone doesn't speak English. It's also entertaining to eavesdrop when others don't expect you to be able to understand them.

Once on the plane, I sit in the aisle seat I had booked for Rich, grateful that I'll have space between me and the others in my row for the long haul over the Atlantic Ocean. This larger plane has more amenities at the seats including options on the screen that show a map with the estimated travel time remaining. There's a decent selection of movies and TV shows, enough to appease most people and keep them entertained. I find a newer romantic comedy, one Rich had promised to take me to see and never did. It's more heart-wrenching than I had mentally prepared myself for, and I follow it up with music to lift my mood. A few songs later, I fall asleep with my earbuds in.

Alex

My mother always hugs me with all her strength. Even now, I can feel her strong grip around me despite the contrast in our height difference. Belinda De Luca has always been a strong woman. I know she wishes I were going home with her, but she understands my need to stay longer. A week ago, we buried my father on the land now owned by his older brother. I had held my mother for hours while she wept over the loss of the love of her life. Despite the tragic occasion, our family surrounded us and added a liveliness we didn't often experience back in the States.

"Call me if you need anything," my mother says as she pulls back enough to look me in the eyes.

"Mamma, I should be the one saying that to you," I say, even though we both lost someone significant to us.

"Belinda, we should get going," Derek, my father's former best friend and business partner, says to my mother. He flew here with her for the funeral and to deliver the timeframe for my accession to my father's position at the company. Years before his passing, my father had written up contracts approved by the board regarding my transition to CEO in the event of his passing. It was less than an hour after his heart stopped beating that Derek informed me that I had three months. One month has already passed.

My mother kisses my cheek, and I quickly hug Derek, the man who is like an uncle to me. "Text me when you've landed," I say to both of them, knowing my mother is the one likely to forget. Derek nods, and I wait until they've disappeared into the airport terminal to take the car to the hotel on the northern outskirts of the city. Now that my mother and soon-to-be business partner are on their way out of the country, I'm officially on vacation.

My father didn't take many vacations because his trips always involved business. If I'm going to spend the better part of the rest of my life chained to the legacy my father gave his life to build, this is how I'm spending the last scraps of freedom I have left. Although I lived in Italy for a year over seven years ago, I never got to see all the popular destinations that attract tourists here in droves. I experienced the Italy that my family knows, but not the Italy that outsiders frequent. Now, I'm taking the time to see what they see.

I pay the driver to take the scenic route, and I look out the window as iconic Roman monuments appear on the other side of the glass. To those who live in this city, the Colosseum is a historic ruin, but Americans will spend hours standing in line to look inside a structure older than the United States. It's surreal to think of all the lives that have existed in this city since its rise and fall as a world superpower.

Given that my family here lives in the country, the driving style of the city catches me off guard. While I'm nervous sitting in this backseat, I'm also relieved I'm not the one at the steering wheel. Despite the chaos of the swearing and double parking, I don't see any vehicle accidents on the ride from the airport to the hotel. Fortunately, my plans don't require me to risk my life in a rental car.

The cab driver maneuvers the car into the only open spot in front of the hotel. I tip him after he pulls my suitcase out of the trunk, and I watch as he squeals away to find his next willing customer. The hotel lobby is bustling with activity as several men in suits are waiting to be checked in. Given that this is the designated hotel for those going on the tour beginning in two days, most of these men must only be here for one night. My arrival is a day earlier than many of the others with whom I'll be sightseeing in Italy.

The overwhelmed concierge at the desk doesn't spare me a second glance—an action that would offend my father, but one that has the opposite effect on me. I've already contacted the tour guide and asked that my identity be kept under wraps if at all possible. I don't usually have an issue being recognized here in Italy, but at least a fraction of my future travel companions are from the United States where my face is frequently plastered across tabloids and business publications. Even if none of them know my face, my last name is bound to spark recognition.

I wait patiently in the lobby until the businessmen slowly trickle out with their room keys and suitcases. The concierge motions me over.

"Buongiorno, sorry about the wait," he says in English with a strong Italian accent. It catches me off guard because most look at me and see the Italian features passed down to me by my parents.

"Non c'è problema," I respond in Italian to ease his worries. "Ho una prenotazione. Il nome è Alessandro De Luca."

"Un momento," he says as he searches for my reservation on his computer. Within five minutes, I have my room key and a map of the nearby shops and restaurants. My stomach growls to remind me to eat lunch. A quick check on my phone, and I decide on a restaurant a short walking distance from the hotel. The hotel has a restaurant onsite where I'll eat breakfast and possibly dinner tonight, but my legs are itching to get out and explore. Nothing is quite as far as it seems once one knows how to get there.

After satiating my hunger with a sandwich and gelato, I venture south toward the Villagio Olimpico. Roma hasn't hosted the Olympics since 1960, but the name is still used to refer to the district where the events were held. The countryside where my uncle lives is silent compared to the constant honking and shouting that echoes across the streets in the capital city.

Two days from now, the tour guide will be taking our group to the popular sites, however, one day is hardly enough in a city this rich in history. I could easily get lost in the winding streets without a map. In casual clothes and sunglasses, I'm as anonymous as I'll ever be again. When I turn onto one of the more commercialized streets, I catch sight of a billboard displaying an ad I had modeled for two years ago for one of the Italian designer clothing companies. "Most eligible bachelor" as if I were a prize to be won over. The man plastered there for the world to see isn't the same as the man who looks back at me in the mirror.

Sonnet

∽

I wake up as the flight attendant asks everyone for their dinner preference: chicken or pasta. I choose pasta to be safe and stretch out my limbs as much as I can in a plane seat. My eyes are dry and heavy, but I keep myself alert. The flight attendant hands me the pasta and what must be dessert before continuing onto the row behind me.

It's surprisingly not too bad for something that has to be premade and heated on a plane suspended over the ocean. A glance out the open window across the aisle reveals the night sky and the dark vastness of the waters below us. Once the meals are finished and cleaned up, the lights in the cabin dim to allow and encourage passengers to sleep and acclimate to the time change. Losing seven hours while also traveling overseas is no small feat. Jet lag is the main thing I'm dreading about this trip, while a minor price to pay in the end.

With a full stomach, I drift back to sleep for a few more hours. When "morning" arrives, they serve us breakfast, but the coffee is all levels of disappointing, especially compared to the coffee that awaits when we land. I can hardly sit still as the excitement registers in my body. This is the trip I've wanted to take since I was ten.

We land and exit the plane slowly as if we were sardines shoved into a can being released. We are all at least slightly groggy and need caffeine and a nap in whichever order they come. The signs in the airport are in Italian, as one would expect them to be in Italy. Somehow, the line finds customs and immigration where the default answer to get through quickly is "vacation." This must be the typical workday for the Italian customs workers at their international airports. Tourism is a large part of their country's economy.

Despite the sleep deprivation, my brain works enough to translate the signs to find the baggage claim. I want to jump with delight when I see my suitcase because it's one step closer to being able to relax. My eyes scan the pickup area until they spot the sign with the logo of the tour company I booked my trip through. The woman holding the sign appears to be in her thirties with brown curly hair and a friendly smile. I walk up to her with my suitcase rolling behind me.

"Hi, my name is Sonnet Kincaid," I say to her, hoping I've found the right person who can get me to a bed with my name on it.

"Ah, yes, my name is Marisol, and I'll be your guide for the tour over the next ten days," she says, and I sigh in relief. "Will Mr. Morrison be joining us?"

"No, he was unable to make it," I say with a fake look of disappointment. Right now, words can't describe how thankful I am that he isn't with me.

Her expression is neutral as if she's seen this before. "No worries. You'll have all your rooms to yourself. Let me show you to the coach. We're still waiting for a few more who have just landed." I follow her to the tour bus. The driver helps me load my suitcase into the luggage compartment. I climb the stairs into the air-conditioned passenger area and plop onto a seat in the second row behind the driver. If this is the bus we'll be taking from city to city, it's well worth the money I paid. Big windows, comfortable seats, a bathroom in case of emergency, a limited amount of wireless internet—I'm already impressed, and we haven't even left the airport yet.

As Marisol had told me, others begin to wander onto the bus, all looking as exhausted as I feel. We exchange tired smiles in solidarity as we spread out on the bus. Marisol joins us when the last person makes an appearance. She's too chipper to have traveled from another time zone.

Fortunately, most people are quiet during the drive to the hotel, and I can hear the music playing on the radio. If I didn't know better, the songs on the radio would have had me fooled into thinking I never left American soil. All the songs that are played are by artists I know singing in English. It's no wonder that most Europeans can speak English fairly well if this is what's playing across the airwaves in Italy. My curiosity keeps me awake and staring out the window at the architecture of the old city. It's disorienting to pinpoint where we are on a map with the way the highways form a circle around the center with branches veering off in all directions. All roads really do lead to Rome from a satellite vantage point.

I watch cars and vespas weave chaotically through the streets, all narrowly avoiding a collision. Driving in Rome is absolute madness, and our coach driver doesn't seem phased by any of it. A man in a suit passes us on a Vespa, and I note how attractive he looks. In fact, all the men my age I can see through the glass are handsome. Maybe my type all along has been Italian men. I'm going to have withdrawals after ten days of seeing men like this. As much as I try, I don't recognize any historical buildings or landmarks, but they seem to blend into the rest of the city. I can only hope that the Colosseum isn't this elusive.

Despite its historical significance, aspects of Rome have been modernized with billboards and public transit systems. On one street, I notice large apartment buildings that aren't new compared to American standards, but they're certainly not old compared to the city they're built in and on. The bus makes turns onto roads that weren't designed for vehicles of this size, but the driver is experienced and manages to make it work.

Finally, but not soon enough, the bus stops in front of a nice hotel that looks like the photo I had looked up beforehand. A few people enjoy their lunch on the outdoor patio area while they smoke like it never went out of style here. Because in Europe, it didn't. I claim my luggage from the pile the driver unloaded and roll it into the hotel lobby behind one of the couples who was on the same bus. I overhear as the concierge informs Marisol that the rooms aren't ready for us yet. My excitement deflates at knowing I'm stuck in this lobby until I can check in.

Exhausted, hot, and hungry, I slink to an open chair in the business lounge. On the bright side, I can access the hotel's wireless internet and text Taylor and my mom to let them know that I've arrived safely. With the time difference, neither is awake yet, but my mom should be up soon. For good measure, I also text my dad. I glance over at the front desk, but there doesn't seem to be any change in the check-in situation. If I didn't have my suitcase and backpack with me, I would venture out to find food to relieve at least one of my needs. This is a miserable situation.

And then, it gets worse. The businessmen who use the business lounge (imagine that) need this space to conduct whatever meeting they came here for. The only space that's out of their way is the outdoor patio area. Outside is hot and humid with a slight breeze that keeps me from completely melting. I pull a book out of my backpack in hopes that reading will make time pass faster. Instead, I hold the book up while I people-watch everyone who walks by, mostly paying attention to the men in their twenties and thirties. Priorities.

I see one particularly attractive man—a ten in a sea of nines —walk out from the front doors of the hotel. One glance down at myself reminds me that I'm still wearing the same outfit I traveled in. Given the time difference, I've lost count of how many hours it's been since I changed my underwear. It feels like two days, though what little math my brain is capable of calculates roughly twenty-four hours, give or take. Once I have my room key, fresh underwear will need to happen before food can. This inner dialogue is precisely why I will not be initiating a conversation with the beautiful man headed right toward the busier street.

Assuming he's staying at this hotel, the opportunity may come up later.

By the time my room is ready for me to check in, I'm basically a zombie. Fresh clothes only do half the trick. Using the map I downloaded to my phone, I locate a small sandwich and gelato shop a short walking distance from the hotel and set out on my first real adventure. The street curves and descends, but I manage to find the place.

All the sandwiches on display have descriptions in Italian, and the man behind the bar only speaks broken English. I switch to Italian to order myself a sandwich and a cappuccino despite the time of day. I'm clearly an American who doesn't know the rules regarding espresso and milk anyway. He obliges because I'm a paying customer who was kind enough to speak to him in his native tongue.

This. Sandwich. Is. Everything. I think it can't possibly get better until he places my coffee in front of me, and I fall in love all over again. It's frothy and delicious and I'll never be satisfied with Starbucks. THIS IS COFFEE. He even topped the milk froth with a dusting of cocoa, as if it couldn't get any better. It does get better. On my way out, I eye the gelato display I had walked past to get to the sandwiches and coffee. I walk onto the street with a cone of stracciatella gelato in my hands and a smile on my face. When in Rome.

A glance at my watch tells me that I have thirty minutes before the meeting Marisol had asked all tour guests to attend. It's meant to be an informational meeting with pertinent details combined with a chance for all of us to introduce ourselves to each other before we hop on a coach together in the morning. I make the uphill trek back to the hotel slowly because walking while eating gelato is more difficult than I assumed it would be.

I manage to find the room Marisol had commandeered for the mandatory gathering and settle in a seat in the back. Half the chairs are already occupied by others, a few of whom I recognize from the bus ride here. Toward the front is a group of roughly twelve who all look Chinese. Based on the way they converse, they're either related or all know each other. Behind them is a family of four with two parents around the same age as mine and their daughters who are either in high school or college. The older couple who had been in the lobby earlier turn around in their seats to wave at me. I politely return the gesture.

Others trickle in until the only remaining unclaimed chairs are the one next to me and the two in front of me. Rich's absence is very evident at this moment. A second later, Dick's absence is the furthest thing from my mind because an opportunity presents itself. The ten, full stop, from earlier in the afternoon strides in and takes the seat next to me without even a glance in my direction. Up close, his score in my mind doesn't diminish; if anything, he might be an eleven. Apart from the obvious fact that I saw him a few hours ago, something about him strikes me as familiar.

"I'm going to take attendance to make sure I have everyone here," Marisol says loudly to get the attention of those who have been talking. She waits for the voices to quiet down before delving into her speech. English may not be her first language, but her job as a tour guide has ensured she's fluent. She runs through the list of names on her clipboard, and I make a mental note to try to remember which names match which faces.

68

"Richard Morrison—oh right, he was unable to make it," she says and corrects herself when she looks up at me and remembers my explanation at the airport pickup. "Sonnet Kincaid." I raise my hand, and she nods with a smile. "Alex De—," the man beside me nearly jumps out of his chair to interrupt her.

"Just Alex is fine," he says with a voice I wish I could bottle up and wear as perfume or maybe capture in a shell like Ursula does in *The Little Mermaid*. My instant reaction to him scares me. I haven't thought or felt things that immediate or intense about someone in over seven years. It's the reaction of a girl who belongs in a Taylor Swift love song.

Marisol continues, "Now that everyone is here, I'll get started so you can eat and rest before our full day tomorrow. There are a few things you need to know before we kick off this tour. Every evening at whichever hotel we're staying at, I will have a whiteboard displaying the bus departure time and our itinerary for the day. I will also announce these things every evening upon our return to the hotel. Breakfast will be served at all our hotels, and I advise that you eat before we leave for the day. You're going to need the calories with all the walking we'll be doing. On the days that we're checking out to head to another city, you will need to leave your bags outside your hotel rooms for the luggage service to pick up and load onto the bus. I have labels up here for you to put on your bags so they can know the correct suitcases to transport. Lastly, if you would like to join an optional excursion that you didn't sign up for, let me know. I can try to make arrangements for you to join, and it'll be added to your bill at the end."

Because I felt extra at the time I booked this trip, I signed up for all the activities. At least it sounds like I might be able to get my money back on Dick's half of the excursions. With the meeting adjourned, the older couple quickly make their way toward Alex and me before either of us stand from our chairs.

"I'm Jean, and this is my husband Lawrence," the wife of the older couple says to us as she holds out her hand. I shake it first before Alex does the same, and her husband follows the same sequence. "We're going to have dinner at the hotel's restaurant around eight if either of you would like to join us." Neither of them asked for our names as they walked away, but Marisol's run-through of the list may have made it unnecessary.

"That's nice of them," Alex says as if he's considering their offer.

I allow myself a few seconds to subtly look at him now that my attention isn't needed elsewhere. He's tall with dark hair and blue eyes—my ultimate weakness. His features look Italian, but what little I've heard him speak so far suggests that he's possibly Italian-American. Though his clothing is casual, my fashion sense knows that those brands are anything but cheap. Five hundred for the jeans with alligator leather accents and two hundred for the teal polo shirt easily. His wrist sports a Rolex that Dick would drool over if he were here. Alex looks like he comes from money, so what is he doing here on this tour when he could likely afford more private accommodations?

"My name is Sonnet," I say to him, taking advantage of the opportunity before it's gone. "I think Marisol said your name is Alex?" I pretend to ask it as a question even though I know I heard correctly.

"Yes, short for Alessandro," he says as he holds out his hand to shake mine.

I choose to be brave as I shake his hand, fully aware of the warm tingles as a result of the small touch. "Why are you traveling alone?"

A faint smile touches his lips as he says, "Because I'm desperate for a vacation. I'm about to take on a lot of responsibility, and this is my last chance to go on one of these tours."

I dissect his words for any hidden meaning. Responsibility could mean many things, but it's safe to assume it doesn't mean he's about to get married. Surely his fiancée would be here with him if he had one. If he had a pregnant significant other, I doubt he would be here alone. His left hand is bare, not even a tan line like the one I still have from my engagement ring. Whatever awaits him when he returns home, there's little chance it has to do with a change in his relationship status. I give up trying to figure it out for myself.

"You didn't answer my question though," I say. "Why are you on vacation alone?"

He smiles, and I almost forget what I had asked him. That doesn't bode well for intelligent conversation if his smile short-circuits my short-term memory. "Because I didn't want to take a vacation with my mom and share a room with her."

Alex

Whoever Richard Morrison is, the guy is undeniably an idiot. It's clear that whoever he is, he was supposed to be here with her. No smart man would let his girl go to Italy by herself without a ring on her finger. Hers is absent of a diamond, though I notice a faint tan line where one might have been recently. My curiosity gets the better of me this time.

"Why is a pretty girl like you traveling in Italy by herself?" I ask, the question sounding more forward than I intended. I inwardly wince at how brazen I must seem to her. Something about her laugh at my joke made me forget common manners.

There's a slight blush on her face when she says, "Because Richard Morrison couldn't keep it in his pants long enough to make it down the aisle and to his honeymoon." Her wince is outward once she realizes what she's said. One of her dark curls falls in her face, and I resist the urge to tuck it back for her. Her dark chocolate eyes and light brown skin are similar to that of another I've never been able to forget. The thick natural curls on this girl could keep my fingers occupied for hours. I can't begin to estimate how long it must take her to detangle and wash her hair.

"Well, it's a good thing Richard Morrison couldn't make it then," I say, the flirtation in my tone an automatic reaction. It's the effect her unfiltered beauty has on me. "I hope the distancing from Richard is permanent."

"Oh, it's permanent," she says with a smile. "He prefers to be called Rich. Once I had to cancel the wedding, all my friends started calling him Dick instead."

I chuckle at the joke. "It does seem like the most fitting of possible nicknames. I'm glad you decided to come on the trip instead of him. I don't think I could tolerate being in the same tour group as a guy who cheated on his fiancée and left her to deal with all the wedding cancellations. You're much better company." I'm not even trying to flirt, but it sounds that way when the words leave my mouth. I'll sit here all night talking to her if I don't leave now.

I stand to non-verbally communicate my need to leave. She follows my lead, and my eyes trace her curves involuntarily. This is going to be a long ten days. I gesture for her to walk in front of me, and she doesn't argue. Our paths diverge once we're out of the small meeting room. She's heading toward the front entrance, and I turn toward the stairs to my room. I have another fifteen minutes before the time I promised my mom I would call, so I pop in my earbuds and turn on some music.

The wireless internet in this hotel isn't the fastest, but it's enough that the video call has minimal delays or cutting out.

My mom looks tired from the flight home, but she pretends that it's not a big deal. With the time difference, it's morning there. She didn't get home until yesterday evening.

"How is Rome? Did you find any good restaurants? What have you seen so far?" She bombards me with questions faster than I can answer them.

"Rome is full of life, just like you said it would be," I tell her. "Tomorrow starts the official tour. We'll be going to Vatican City to the museum and the Sistine Chapel in the morning. Would you like me to pass along a message to the pope from you?"

She laughs as she says, "You know your father and I have never been Catholic. It's the only thing about our lives that our parents didn't approve of. That'll still be an amazing experience. The art is breathtaking, especially considering that they painted on the ceilings for years to complete it. Make sure you take as many pictures as you can for me."

I feel a sting of guilt at her last comment. I hadn't offered for her to do this with me, but part of me knew it would be better this way. I need the time away from my real life while she needs time to grieve and adjust to life without my father. I might be on vacation, but it's a trip that guarantees many hours of walking and riding on a bus.

"Don't worry, Mamma, I'll make sure you see all my photos when I get home," I say to her. "I'll bring you souvenirs and give you a slideshow presentation if that will make you happy." In all honesty, I would do anything to make her as happy as she's always done for me.

"I'll let you get back to your busy vacation," she says as she stifles a yawn. "Thank you for making time for your mamma. I love you."

"I love you, too," I say before I hang up the call. My stomach growls as if it doesn't know that dinner isn't for another two hours. At my uncle's villa, there was always food in the kitchen to snack on between meals, but I'm going to need a stash of snacks if I'm going to make it to the late dinner time customary in Italy. I remember seeing a grocery store on the way to the sandwich shop I found yesterday.

On my way out the door, I notice the hotel staff preparing the restaurant for dinner. If I hurry, I might return in time to catch Lawrence and Jean. Down a hill and a flight of stairs, I find the grocery store advertised on the street level. Moments like this remind me to be thankful that my family insists on only speaking Italian most of the time. I've been fluent since I was twenty-two and have been literate since I was a baby. Stores like this don't cater much to the English-speaking tourists who wander the aisles on occasion. I almost collide with one as I round the corner.

"Sorry, I didn't see you there," Sonnet says before the recognition glints in her eyes. "Oh, it's you." She has a pack of bottled still water in her hands.

I say, "I'm here to grab a few snacks and to help you carry that back to the hotel."

She doesn't hide her surprise, but she recovers rapidly and says, "I don't need your help."

"At least let me walk with you then," I say because she and I both know it'll be hard for her to make it back with those waters. It's upstairs and uphill from this store. "You'd be doing me a favor."

She rolls her eyes but doesn't walk away. "I'll go pay for these and wait for you. Don't take too long to choose your snacks. I want to get back in time to have dinner with Lawrence and Jean."

I want to get back in time to have dinner with them. I keep that tidbit to myself though because she has nothing to do with my decision on that. I find my favorite snacks and pay before finding her balancing the pack on one of her knees to give her arms a rest.

Rather than push, I ask her, "Ready?"

She nods, and we match pace, mine purposely slower due to my longer stride. Sonnet isn't short, but I have an eight-inch height advantage over her. My height is one of the few things about me that isn't typical for an Italian. Sweat glistens on her face and her breathing is heavier than mine, but she carries on. While I want to help her, I admire her tenacity and stubbornness. She's strong and capable, and it's attractive.

Halfway up the hill, she gives in. "This is harder than I thought. Alex, would you mind carrying this pack of water for me?"

If hearing my name in her voice wasn't enough to get me to say yes, the way she asks would win her many favors. I brace my muscles as she shifts the weight from her arms into mine. We continue walking toward our destination. Without the water to occupy her attention, she's taking obvious glances at my flexed arms. Sonnet is openly ogling me the way I hoped

76

she would when I offered my help. It's a boost to my ego to know that despite her jerk of an ex-fiancé, she still finds me at least somewhat attractive. It means she likely hasn't written off men forever.

I look at her and wait for her eyes to drift up to mine. Her face flushes red as she surmises that I've caught her staring. "I've also been thinking about taking up Lawrence and Jean on their offer," I say to her.

"We should be able to make it," she says as she checks her watch. "If you don't mind helping me carry this to my room?" I don't know why she says it like it's a question rather than a certainty.

"Of course," I say to reassure her. Her hesitation is understandable in full context. I met her an hour ago; it just feels like longer than that to me. It's the type of undeniable connection that's so rare, I was beginning to believe I would never find it again. Instead of leaving home to live in Italy for a year, I'm in Italy on a two-week vacation prolonging what awaits me at home. Either way, the situation is temporary. It would be nice to find this kind of chemistry with the women I have to be around in my everyday life.

I follow her into the hotel elevator, and she pushes the button for the same floor my room is on. Logistically, it makes sense that the rooms for those who are part of the tour would be near each other. It's easier for the luggage service when it comes time to load the bus for the next city on our itinerary. For now, I'm grateful that her room is only a few doors down from mine because it'll mean less time spent dropping off our things before running back down to the restaurant.

We stop at her room first because I'm beginning to show signs of fatigue from carrying her water. I'm not sure how she expected to get them here on her own if I'm feeling the weight of the trip. I set them down on top of her mini-fridge before we hurry to my room to drop off my snacks. Elements of this bring me back to my college days during my freshman year living in the dorms on campus. If I could go back to those days, I would warn my younger self not to be in such a rush to get to the next step of my father's plans. I would warn him that timing is a tricky thing that we often get wrong more times than not.

My mind jolts back to the present as the elevator stops on the ground floor. Sonnet seems lost in her thoughts as well, but she's not entirely on autopilot the way I was. When we walk into the restaurant, Lawrence and Jean spot us and wave us over to their table. The older couple is sitting at a table for four as if they expected both of us to show. That, or they're the type to invite others to join them if we didn't.

"We're so glad you could make it," Jean says to us with genuine excitement on her face. "Most of the time people your age would rather get out and go on an adventure."

"Being in Italy is enough of an adventure," Sonnet says to her before adding, "Plus, I'm too exhausted from jet lag to do anything crazy tonight." I would argue that trying to carry that pack of water from the store to her hotel room by herself is crazy, but I keep my mouth shut out of politeness to our company.

Jean turns to me and asks, "What about you? You don't seem as jet-lagged as the rest of us."

"I've been in Italy for a few weeks already," I say without revealing too much. "I was visiting family in the northern area before I took the train to Rome yesterday."

"See, Lawrence," Jean says to her husband. "I knew he was too good-looking to not be Italian." She winks at me, and I feel the blush heat my face. Jean reminds me of my grandmother, which makes this conversation heartwarming in a way I didn't anticipate. At this rate, I'll be anything but lonely while on this vacation.

Sonnet

~∞~

Dinner with Lawrence and Jean is entertaining and refreshing. Although they seem as if they've been married most of their lives, they share the story about how they met when Jean was twenty-four and Lawrence was twenty and in the military. Their relationship back then was a crazy whirlwind that ended after a few months. They didn't reconnect until over twenty years later after multiple divorces and children each. Lawrence tracked her down, and this time, it stuck. The years taught them a lot from the mistakes they made, but in the years apart, they both found Jesus. This tour is their twenty-year wedding celebration.

"It sounds like a Hallmark movie," I say with a sigh when they describe what it's been like being back together.

"We were crazy when we were younger," Jean says with a shake of her head. "We would have been terrible for each other then had we gotten married. When he came back into my life, I had just gone through another divorce. I don't know that I would have ever tried again if it hadn't been him." Lawrence and Jean's story is a Taylor Swift love song.

I glance at Alex to gauge his reaction to their story. His eyes are liquid blue like two lagoons, a small satisfied smile on his lips. In my head, I mull over the facts I've discovered about him so far. One, Alex comes from money, but he isn't someone who brags about his money. Two, Alex is courteous to a fault. Three, Alex is a softie for a good, romantic story.

The food is delicious—do they have bad restaurants in Italy? —but the people I'm with are what make this one of the best meals I've had in a long time.

"If you don't mind my asking, what happened to the man who was supposed to come with you on this trip?" Jean asks me after we've had our fill of the mushroom-stuffed ravioli. Apparently, Alex wasn't the only one to take note of where Marisol looked when she mistakenly called Richard's name.

"This was supposed to be our honeymoon trip, but we called the wedding off," I say. Repeating it gets less painful each time. My voice is nearly devoid of emotion in this instance.

Jean grabs my hand and holds it gently in hers, "Be grateful you called off the wedding. Divorces are messier than breakups."

Those are the words that assure me once again that I made the right choice in not giving him another chance. Initially, before any cancellations or phone calls had been made, Rich showed up at my doorstep with a bouquet and a remorseful expression. Less than an hour later, he was storming out of my house as we yelled at each other. It was the first and last time we ever yelled when we fought.

After we devour our tiramisu, I question how much food I consumed. "How do Italians eat like this all the time?" I say with a groan.

"They go on walks afterward," Alex says as he holds out a hand for me. "Or they drink grappa. Both can help with digestion. The former is known to minimize blood sugar spikes and will help you get to sleep easier."

I take his hand because standing after that much food is hard. Standing is still hard though due to the electric buzz from his touch. It's the same level of intense chemistry I felt that night at the masquerade ball—the chemistry that set my standards so high. Hindsight, I was right to be picky about the men I dated. Maybe I could have avoided the drama of Dick if I hadn't made compromises on what I'm looking for.

A few seconds after the shock from the contact wears off, I get up of my own volition. Lawrence and Jean tell us goodnight. We escape into the humid, slightly cooler summer air outside. Rome has the same lights and sounds as any major city, but the angry words the drivers yell are in Italian here. Alex is contemplative as he leads us on a path he's likely already explored during his extra day here.

"Do you think it's fate or Providence that they found each other again?" I ask him since Lawrence and Jean are fresh on my mind.

"He did look her up, even if it required more effort back then without social media," Alex points out but not in an arrogant way. He's as curious as I am about it. "I think I prefer the term Providence. Fate has the connotation of still being somewhat random for something that's 'meant to be' while the concept of Providence is that God, an intelligent being, is the one behind it."

I smile at his answer and then ask, "So where does choice come into all of this?"

"Choice is the most romantic part of it all," he says without hesitation. I look at him in the dim streetlights. There isn't a hint of joking or sarcasm in his expression. "Fate or Providence can create the circumstances in which you meet someone whom you could have an incredible future with, but you still have to choose to be with that person. You have to choose to be vulnerable and tell him how you feel. Choice is more powerful than fate. People say that Romeo and Juliet were fated, but the story could have ended differently had they chosen to make a plan B."

I laugh despite the reference to a tragedy. Like him, I've always found the end of that story frustrating. "Why are we humans so silly sometimes?"

"Because Providence likes to laugh," he says with a smile that reflects the light from the storefront nearby. Perfect teeth. I can only hope that I find some faults with this man as this trip progresses. Falling for a seemingly perfect man while on vacation isn't exactly the healthiest way to move on from my previous relationship.

He leads our walk, so I'm not paying attention when he stops suddenly. I look at our surroundings and recognize the hotel entrance. He nods his head toward the door, and we walk inside together wordlessly. We stay in comfortable silence until we reach my room.

"Goodnight, Sonnet," he says as he pecks both my cheeks. Right, this is Europe where friends greet each other with kisses on the cheek. It's only natural to see each other as friends given we'll be going to all the same cities and sights as a group. I have ten days to decide whether exchanging contact information with him at the end of this is a good idea or asking for heartache.

My room and bed are the perfect size for one person who's used to having her own space. If I were sharing this with a husband, we would be stepping on each other's toes. I grab my pajamas and toiletries from my suitcase and take my first shower since arriving in Italy. I can barely keep my eyes open as I crawl into bed and set my alarm for the morning. I crash into a deep, dreamless sleep.

FAINT SUNLIGHT PEEKS through the curtains when my alarm jolts me awake. My body is at war deciding between sleeping through the day and satiating my grumbling stomach. It only takes my mind a few seconds to remember where I am and what day it is. Today is the day that we explore Vatican City and Rome. Adrenaline alone fuels me as I wash my face and get dressed for the breakfast spread and full schedule that await.

Italians know how to do a breakfast bar. The various tables are covered with fresh fruits, meats and cheeses, pastries, and hot pans containing eggs and sausage. There's an automatic coffee machine that displays the usual Italian coffee options of americano, espresso, macchiato, and cappuccino. One sip of my cappuccino convinces me to buy all my coffee beans imported from Italy for the rest of my life. I need an espresso machine and milk frother to replicate this heavenly beverage. Alex sits down beside me looking like a man who hasn't had his coffee yet.

"You're not a morning person either?" I ask him as I take another sip of caffeine juice. My body is at a disadvantage compared to him given that I only made the transatlantic flight yesterday.

He hugs the small mug to his mouth as if it were his lifeboat. "I didn't wake up early enough to go for a run," he says after taking a drink. "That usually helps more than the coffee does." Of course, he's one of those guys who goes for a run every morning. But I'm one of those girls who works out six days a week in the morning, so I'm in no position to judge his healthy habits.

My coffee runs out too quickly, and I gaze longingly at the machine. "The coffee is all-you-can-drink, right? I could use another cappuccino."

He laughs at my question and holds out his hand for my cup. "You eat, and I'll get us both refills. I don't want to risk being around you if you don't get enough food or that second cup." He closes his statement with a wink that gives me butterflies. It's too early in the day for that nonsense. Once he walks away though, they calm down enough that I can refocus on the fruit and pastries I grabbed for myself.

Alex drops off the refills at our table before going to fill his plate. Or two. By the time he's walking back to our table, he's balancing three plates of food in his hands as if he were a waiter.

"You know that they aren't running out of food, right?" I say as a joke when he sets down all three plates in front of him.

"I got extra in case you didn't get enough." He shoves food into his face to hide whatever expression had accompanied those words. I steal one of the two croissants from his plate closest to me and tear off a piece to eat. I would live here forever if it meant I could eat these every day and walk enough to never gain weight. Clearly, that's the secret; they use better quality ingredients in their food and spend more time walking.

We eat until the plates are bare and run to our rooms to brush our teeth before boarding the tour bus waiting outside the hotel's front entrance. Marisol is standing at the bottom of the steps to take a head count. Most of our group is already on the bus sitting in their family and friend units. I choose a window seat a few rows behind the driver, and Alex fills the seat beside me. If he weren't someone I wanted to be around, I would find his actions annoying. So far though, all I want is to be around him and peel back the layers of who he is. I want to lose myself in those blue eyes until I find I'm a different person than the one I left behind in America.

"Do you mind if I sit next to you?" He waits a full minute after he takes the seat to make sure I'm not opposed to the company.

"As long as I get the window seat, I don't mind," I say, permitting him to sit next to me for all future coach rides on this tour. His presence isn't overwhelming or energy-draining as long as he isn't touching me. Or smiling at me or flexing his muscles. Or complimenting me. As long as our rides consist of sitting here in our own worlds with the occasional platonic conversation, I don't mind sharing space with him.

After Marisol completes her final headcount, we're on our way to Vatican City. My eyes are glued to the buildings outside the window just as they were yesterday. American cities don't look like this; the buildings back home are newer and shinier with a few historical buildings scattered among the towers. In cities with ancient roots like Rome, their focus is more on historical preservation than it is on tearing down and rebuilding. Here, I expect the buildings to be old.

Through the window, I take photos of apartment balconies with vines of vegetation blanketing the trellises. The faded paint on the facades gives the buildings character rather than making them appear run-down. Lines and lines of cars park along the streets wherever possible.

"I've heard that there are twice as many cars as there are parking spaces in Rome," Alex whispers before returning his attention to the book in his hands. I shift my position to read the title of the paperback he's holding. There's no hiding the mixed expression of surprise and horror that takes over my face.

"*The Fault in Our Stars?* That's what you're reading right now?" I don't attempt to mask the incredulity in my tone as I ask.

He shrugs as he says, "I was in the mood for a romance."

"Alex, that book is a tragedy," I say as if it should be obvious. Romance, sure, but also tragic.

"What do you mean?" He asks with such sincerity that I hate to be the one to burst his hopeful bubble.

"It's a love story between two teenagers who have cancer. It's one thing for a love story to have one protagonist with cancer because maybe they'll survive, but when both characters have cancer, the odds that they'll both survive..." I trail off because I don't want to give away the plot, even if he should have assumed it.

He sticks his bookmark in to save his spot before he closes the book. He shifts his body and attention toward me as he says, "Death isn't the worst thing to happen to a love story. Giving up and walking away is. The real tragedy is when someone doesn't choose you after promising they always will. I would rather lose someone to death than to lose them because they chose a life without me."

The seriousness in his statement has me wondering whether he meant it about his past or if it was his way of showing he understands me. I might have been the one to officially end my relationship, but Rich was the one who chose something —someone—else first. If he hadn't taken that step away from me, I would have gone through with all of it and stuck with my choice come hell or high water. Would, should, and could aren't what is though. "What is" sits in front of me reading a coming-of-age romance novel as if that's normal behavior for a man in his late twenties.

Before I can piece together a response to him, the bus pulls over to allow us to disembark. Marisol is joined by another tour guide who specializes in the Vatican Museums. Together, they hand out our headsets for the guided tour. Once all of them are working, the other tour guide Giorgia introduces herself to us.

88

When Giorgia spots me, she exclaims, "Mamma Mia! We have the same hair!" Though hers is a shade of light brown, our wild curls bear a close resemblance. A few years ago, I retired my straight iron and curling iron and began the process of recovering and reviving my natural curls. What she sees now is years of research and trial and error as I learned what my hair does and doesn't like. I'm still baffled by it sometimes.

Beside me, Alex chuckles at the exchange. When he knows we're out of earshot he says in my ear, "It really is great hair though."

Alex

I'm unsure what I expected the entrance to the Vatican Museums to look like, but the tall stone walls that grow nearer remind me more of a medieval fortress than that of the heartbeat of the Catholic Church. Lines of people stand outside, and we follow the yellow scarf Giorgia holds up on a pole. Other groups are in the area, each with various scarves on similar poles. My attention is divided between keeping up with Giorgia and making sure Sonnet is also keeping up. Anytime we're stopped for a few moments, I take photos on my phone. All of us take more photos than we possibly know to do with.

The museum that Giorgia takes us through—there are so many museums here that one could spend days in Vatican City going through them all—is filled with old things that are likenesses of dead people, as revered art typically is. Back in those days, the only way to preserve the likeness of something or someone beautiful was to paint or sculpt. If Sonnet and I were alive in that era, I would gladly spend years replicating her likeness into art. Unlike some of these sculptures, she would be clothed. Assuming I were her husband, I would leave certain things for my eyes only; I would take the details of her curves to the grave.

"Everything is so...detailed," Sonnet says quietly as she gazes up at the gold mingling with the marble in the ceilings. She's right though; even the tapestries have a texture and detail that put a few modern art styles to shame. In an age without the distractions of modern technology, people turned to art to express themselves. On occasion, art and technology mingled together.

Somehow, I manage to balance taking photos of the art to appease my mother and taking glances at Sonnet to appease my curiosity. Seeing her mesmerized by our surroundings makes me enjoy it more than I would on my own. While this doesn't bode well for my head or my heart, I'm almost beyond caring enough to stop. It's been over seven years since a woman has held my attention, and finding that again comes with the temptation to overindulge myself.

"Are you Catholic?" Sonnet asks me as our group transitions from the museum to Saint Peter's Basilica.

"No, why? Are you?" I both ask and answer her.

"No," she says. "I wanted to make sure you weren't before I say something that a devout Catholic might find offensive."

I stop her with my eye contact when I say, "Now you have to tell me what it is."

Ensuring that no one around us can overhear, she says, "We're in a crypt for dead men whom the Catholics consider saints. To them, it's a sacred graveyard, but to me, it's just creepy."

I give her my smile and a shake of my head. "They've been gone so long, there's nothing left but dust anyway." At least these buildings are beautiful, functional tombs. The paintings on the domes are just as magnificent as those in the museum. Multiple signs are posted outside the Sistine Chapel: no talking or photos. We're expected to admire one of Michelangelo's iconic works in silence and without our phones. It sounds like the perfect place to take a nap.

Without conversation or the ability to use my phone, my only remaining distraction is Sonnet. Since I can't stare at her for ten minutes straight without coming across as creepier than the dead bodies, I force myself to follow the lead of those around me and crane my neck toward the paintings. Some can only dream of visiting Vatican City to see these Biblical representations featuring naked characters. *The Creation of Adam* portion makes sense to display a naked Adam; the others seem over the top.

"They should have a rating system for museums as they do for movies," she says once we're no longer in the silent zone. "Today has not been rated G in the slightest."

Though I agree with her, I shrug and say, "Life isn't rated G."

Saint Peter's Square is filled with chairs for an upcoming event involving the pope and other leaders of the Roman Catholic Church. I will never understand a belief system that seems to put more emphasis on commemorating the dead than on celebrating the living. Still, the view of columns forming a semi-circle with the iconic stone pines in the background is breathtaking.

"Will you take a photo of me with the Basilica in the background?" she asks me before handing me her phone. I do as she requests, wishing I could send this photo to myself. Am I really this pathetic, or is the romantic air too much for my self-preservation? We swap phones as she returns the favor. My mom will appreciate that I took the time to include one of myself in the bunch of photos I plan to send her when we get back to the hotel's internet.

Giorgia and Marisol lead us to a small cafeteria off the square where our group takes up over half the seating. Sonnet and I both choose the lasagna. It's not my mom's lasagna, but I've never heard of gross lasagna in Italy. She pays for her meal before I can beat her to it, but it's probably for the best. We just met yesterday. Today is only the second day that I've known her. It's already more time than I spent around the last girl to capture my heart.

"I need to start buying souvenirs for all my friends and family back home," she says as we sit at a small table in the corner. Apart from my mother and Derek, I don't have anyone at home expecting me to bring them a gift. Being the sole heir of a valuable legacy is lonelier than I had assumed when I was younger.

Two clean plates and full stomachs later, I follow her into the gift shop next door where she walks away with nothing bought because most of it is Catholic-themed. I'm unsure what she expected from a gift shop in Vatican City. Marisol herds our group together again and leads us to where the coach is parked underground. One look at the itinerary puts the day into perspective; the best is still coming.

Over the intercom, Marisol points out famous sights on our way to the next stop, and Sonnet is accommodating in allowing me to lean into her space to take my photos. My nose picks up hints of coconut and peaches each time. The place where the Apostle Paul is thought to have been buried —lean. The pyramid of Cestius—lean. The bus stops and pulls over before I grow used to her scent.

We disembark into the heat and humidity of a Roman afternoon in the summer. We couldn't have asked for better weather with clear blue skies and a slight breeze. I examine the nearby aqueduct that's presumably no longer in use, apart from its symbol of history and old technology. Palatine Hill is one of the most recognizable sights in Rome. Our whole group is quickly preoccupied with taking photos of and with the Arch of Constantine and the Colosseum. Marisol points out the lines of people waiting to tour the inside of the ruins and explains that with the visitor cap, only three thousand guests are allowed inside at any given time. Given that what's inside is mostly ruins, the outside is the best part about coming to the Colosseum.

"We don't need to see the inside anyway," I say to Sonnet as she zooms out on her camera app to capture it in its entirety, "it's where people and animals fought and were often killed for entertainment to appease the masses."

"Bread and circuses," she says with a knowing smile. Her dark hair is more brown than black in the sunlight. The brightness lightens her eyes while deepening the chocolate hue. It's as if I'm seeing her for the first time again, leaving me speechless and defenseless.

"No more talk of death," I say to her once my brain has finished its reset. "We need dozens of photos of you with the Colosseum in the background. Dick is going to regret that he ever jeopardized his relationship with you."

She humors me, but I sense that there's something on her mind. I haven't known her long enough to accurately sense those things about her yet. Once I hand her back her phone, her smile fades.

"What's wrong?" I ask because my instincts are usually right.

With a wry smile, she says, "He might be more to blame, but he's not the only person responsible for how our relationship fell apart. The last time I talked to him, he said that he always felt as if he were trying to live up to an impossible standard and expectation that I had. He's probably right about that."

I stop walking and lightly grab her arm to keep her from walking away. I want to remove every possibility that she'll brush off what I have to say. "Sonnet, whether those things are true or not, that doesn't excuse his cheating. He could have communicated with you about how he felt. Instead, he chose to act out of his insecurities and to blame you for his mistakes. Marriage is a lifelong commitment to a partnership, and he didn't treat you like a partner."

She bites her lip and nods in understanding. Resisting the urge to touch her again, I gesture forward to continue our trek around the Colosseum. Though my speech doesn't bring back her smile, it's a step in the right direction in building trust with her.

Ahead of us, Lawrence and Jean are struggling with their smartphones as they try to find the right angle for their selfie. I offer to take the photo for them, and Jean visibly relaxes. In my peripheral vision, Sonnet is lingering behind waiting for me with a smile on her face.

"Sonnet, come take a photo with us," Jean says to her after I've taken a few with just her and Lawrence. Without argument, Sonnet joins them, her grin upstaging the sun with its brilliance. Members of our tour group reconvene, and we take a large group picture together. I make sure to stand next to Sonnet.

The drive back to the hotel includes more sights and whiffs of peaches and coconut. Marisol announces the meeting time for those of us doing the evening excursion. I signed up for all of them because I'm here to experience everything I can on this trip. What I don't know is if Sonnet did something similar or if she limited the optional excursions to save money. Part of me would feel guilty going and leaving her on her own for the evening.

"Should we meet up ten minutes before and walk down to the bus together? I think I need a short nap to recharge for round two." Her question and statement assume that I'm going, and I'm thankful I'm not the one who has to bring it up.

We part ways in the hallway to go to our separate rooms. I text a few photos to my mom including the group photo before I call her to check in. She answers on the third ring with, "I love you, but are you going to call me every day of your trip? Some of us have a life."

I match her teasing by saying, "I thought you wanted updates from me, but I can hold off until I come home."

"But then I wouldn't have as much fun interrogating you about this girl standing next to you in the group photo you sent," she says. My mother has never been one to beat around the bush, so I should have anticipated this from her. "Is she there by herself or with a friend? Is she single? She's very pretty."

I blush because my mom is the one person I can't hide anything from. Her instincts are sharp enough that she could probably sense the moment I met Sonnet. It's difficult to know what to tell her or what to keep to myself because I'm not sure what's going on. Meeting her or someone like her was the last thing I expected to happen on this trip. Or any trip. I had unconsciously resolved myself to a lifetime without finding this kind of chemistry again.

"Alex, are you still there?" Her voice echoes from my phone, snapping me out of my inner dialogue.

"Sorry, I was just thinking." That response will only feed her curiosity more.

My mother doesn't bombard me with more questions though. Instead, she says, "I can still remember how I felt when I met your father for the first time. Immediately, I knew something about him was different. It was as if I had been sitting in a dim room, and someone turned on the lights. It can take a few moments for your eyes to adjust, but once they do, you realize that everything is brighter and easier to see. Either way, I'm sure you'll tell me about her when you're ready. I'm just happy to see that you're not a complete robot."

I laugh at her last comment and give her a condensed walkthrough of my day so far. "This evening we're going to the Spanish Steps and Trevi Fountain before a nice dinner."

"Make sure you take a coin or three with you to make a wish in the fountain," she instructs as if I'm unaware of the legend. "And make sure you get photos. If you can, take one of Sonnet. Or with Sonnet." I picture her wink punctuating that request. Though I'll likely never bring it up to her, I suspect my mother is sad that my father passed away before I gave them any grandchildren. She doesn't go as far as to try to set me up with someone, but she's the first to ask me about any dating rumors involving me. My mother has always loved a good wedding.

"I'll call you in a few days?" I ask her, partially as a joke because I know she's eager for any updates now that she's sniffed out a single female in my group.

"I'll take anything you're willing to give me," she says in her trademark motherly way.

With another hour remaining before the time Sonnet suggested we meet, I pull out my book and return to the spot where I'd been before she interrupted me earlier. What I didn't disclose to her is that this is my second time reading this particular novel. For some morbid reason, my father's passing has given me the urge to read various romance novels involving bittersweet endings. It's not "happily ever after," but it is passionate love amid the unfairness of life. Sometimes, you take what you can get.

I'm lost in the pages when I hear a knock on the door. One glance at my watch confirms that an hour has flown by. I open my door and need a few seconds to reacclimatize myself to the effect she has on me. She's changed into a yellow sundress that makes her skin glow like sunshine. Did she bring many of these dresses with her? Is this magnificent view something I'll be privy to every night on this tour?

"You weren't in the lobby or the hallway, so I assumed you were busy reading about kids with cancer," she says with her teasing tone.

I pat my pockets to ensure that I have my room key, phone, and wallet before I step into the hallway. "How was your nap?"

"Not long enough, but I'll manage," she says and shrugs. "I certainly suffered worse during finals week in college. I don't miss those days of minimal sleep and assignments demanding high brain functionality. I blame college for my lingering caffeine addiction."

"Are you telling me that you would give up coffee if you could?" I ask her knowing full well that I wouldn't. I enjoy the taste of coffee and the peace of drinking it in the morning.

"Nope, never," she says insistently. "Cappuccinos are too delicious to give up. I drink coffee for more than just the caffeine now anyway. It's also about the warmth. It forces me to slow down and appreciate the moment."

As we walk toward the waiting bus, I notice details about her that hadn't caught my eye before. Her muscles—particularly her calves and shoulders—are strong and toned, presumably from consistent strength training. I add it to the mental list of things I find irresistible about her, a list that's longer than it should be after only twenty-four hours. Though there are fewer people on the bus for this optional excursion, I sit next to her. I could sit in one of the empty rows to test whether she would say something, but I'd rather not take the risk.

We are dropped off a short walk from the Spanish Steps. Every time I walk along these streets, I'm thankful for the anonymity. A few women might spare me a second glance but not out of recognition. Without the notoriety of my last name, I'm still what others consider to be objectively attractive. Fine, I'm blessed with the best features from both my parents who are—and were—above-average attractive. The guy in the billboard ads doesn't feel like me.

Beside me, Sonnet takes photos of random buildings simply because she thinks they're beautiful. To her, the ordinary bright orange apartment building is worth pausing to admire, even when famous sites await us. Marisol leads us to the top of the steps overlooking the Piazza di Spagna. There's constant movement on the stairs as people go up and down, but no one tries to sit on them like they used to. The fines seem to do enough to keep the groups from loitering on the monument.

As we slowly descend the steps, Sonnet's sandal slips, causing her to nearly lose her balance. Instinctively, my hand goes to her lower back to steady her. For the remaining stairs, I keep a close eye on her to ensure she doesn't fall and hurt herself. We make it to the end without incident, and she turns around to take photos from the bottom. She must have taken twenty different photos at various angles. Honestly, she's probably doing a better job documenting this than I am.

When she turns her attention to me, she wears a conniving expression.

"What is that look?" I ask her.

"Will you take a photo with me?" She asks. "A reenactment from the trailer of *Roman Holiday*."

I decide not to pretend I don't know what she's talking about. "Gregory Peck and Audrey Hepburn, right?" She beams at my knowledge of the 1953 film and asks someone else from our tour group to take the photo on both our phones. My mother will frame this picture because it's always been her favorite movie.

Another short walk, and we're face to face with the Trevi Fountain. Tourists from all over the world are gathered around it taking photos, talking, and throwing coins into the water. There are rails to help guide the lines trying to get to the lower level by the fountain's edge, but it's clear that no one is moving. Sonnet comes to the same realization a few seconds before me. Without thinking, I follow her lead as she crawls under railings and into empty pockets of space until we're in the perfect position for both the coin toss and photos.

"Did you bring money to throw in?" She asks me as she pulls three pennies from her crossbody bag. I note that she thought to bring an anti-theft purse.

I pull out the coin I had set aside for this very venture. If the legend is to be trusted, one coin means you'll return to Rome, two means you'll fall in love with an attractive Italian, and three means you'll marry the person you met. Since Sonnet isn't Italian that I know of, I stick to one coin. I, however, fit the category of an attractive Italian who could fulfill her three-coin wish. We both throw our coins over our left shoulders with our right hands. Then, we take turns with the obligatory photos featuring the fountain in the background. The sunlight hits just right to where there's a glow around her in the picture.

Satisfied with our documentation, we move out of the way to allow someone else to get their chance to make a wish. Near the fountain, there's a gelato shop with a line trailing out the door. Sonnet looks longingly at what little she can see around the crowd of waiting customers.

"We're about to go to dinner," I remind her, knowing she'll regret it if she eats anything right now. The only true way to prepare for an Italian dinner is to treat it like a buffet; never eat before you go.

Her expression shifts to one of resignation, but it doesn't stay long because Marisol is gathering our group again. I glance at my watch and note that it's still early for dinner. Sonnet is going to resent that I stopped her right up until she has food in her mouth. Fortunately, her infatuation with Roman architecture keeps her appeased until we're walking into the bustling restaurant. Marisol leads us upstairs to a private dining area for our group. Sonnet and I choose seats next to each other at the largest table and are joined by Lawrence and Jean as well as another couple and the two best friends who came here for a fortieth-birthday trip.

On the far end of the table adjacent to the window, there's a vase full of roses that will be handed out to all the ladies at the end of the meal. Sonnet stops to take a photo of the roses with the view outside the window in the background. I excuse myself to go to the restroom. The bathroom isn't the only thing I intend to find though. The waiter is easier to spot than I expected, easier than finding the bathrooms. I greet him in Italian, hand him twenty euros, and ask him to give Sonnet three roses at the end of the night. Because Italians are romantics, he obliges. I likely could have gotten him to agree to it for free.

Sonnet

⟋⟍

The waiter places two bottles of wine on each of our tables, a red and a white. I pour some of the white one to taste it. *Gross, no.* I force myself to empty the glass. I do the same with the red, not bothering to finish what remains. Maybe I'll finally find a wine I can tolerate by the end of this vacation, but not likely. Alex returns to his seat next to me, and I immediately notice the difference between his presence and absence.

Leo and his wife Carlotta have been telling the rest of the table the story of how he and his wife left Sicily and ended up in Vancouver. Every year, they return to Italy to spend time on his family's land. The two fit the stereotype of loud, expressive Italians.

As Alex fills his glass with the first wine I tried, Leo asks him, "Are you single, married, divorced, or none of the above?"

"I'm single," Alex says to him, his voice full of hesitation.

"Let me give you some advice that I had to learn the hard way," Leo says, not at all discouraged by Alex's lack of enthusiasm. Leo gulps red wine before spilling his wisdom. "A relationship with a woman, especially a long-term one like marriage, is like an orchid. Have you ever owned and taken care of an orchid? They can be temperamental if you don't know what you're doing. If you water them too much, they die. If you go too long without watering them, they die. Sometimes, they catch a disease and die even if you did everything right. To top that all off, many don't realize that orchids will shed all their flowers and stay dormant for six to nine months. Half a year of nothing, and the only way it'll bloom again is if you keep watering it just right. The only way to know if they're still alive is to look at the roots."

"Are you saying you stayed married to Carlotta this long because you found the right balance of patience and persistence?" Alex asks Leo, just as perplexed as he was before the comparison.

Leo laughs so hard that his face turns as red as his wine. "Goodness, no! I'm saying I gave my wife an orchid!"

Alex turns to me, and I barely hold in my laugh at his bewilderment. "Leo, I think you broke him," I lean forward and say.

The room is full of exuberance and life as the waiter makes his rounds refilling the wine glasses while we wait for the first course to be served. Alex tips his head to my wineglass and asks, "Did you not like it?"

"I don't think I'm a wine person," I say to him with a shrug. "Truthfully, I don't like the taste of most alcohol. I also don't like feeling out of control, so the idea of being tipsy is unappealing."

"More for Leo, I guess," Alex says as he sips his glass of wine.

When the waiter offers to pour me more, I politely refuse. "You must not be old enough to drink," he says.

"I'm ten years past the legal drinking age in Italy," I say, unsure whether his comment was meant as a joke. He pretends not to believe me, and Alex smiles at the exchange though he's pretending not to pay attention. Occasionally, I've been mistaken for a few years younger than I am, but at twenty-eight, it's shocking to be asked if I'm even eighteen.

With every course, I'm more and more thankful that Alex stopped my earlier mission for gelato. During the main course, two men with their classical guitars play and sing songs in Italian while we eat. The only one I recognize is "Volare." Just when I'm certain that I can't eat another bite, the waiters pass around tiramisu and espresso. *Must make room.* A few quiet burps later, I enjoy my dessert without worrying about it stacking up in my esophagus. I eat every bite, savoring the cream and coffee. This tiramisu is worth the jet lag.

In the final act, the waiter picks up the vase of roses I admired earlier. He goes around to each lady in the room and gives her one rose and a kiss on the cheek. Because of where I sit, I'm the last one he approaches. The waiter hands me three roses before kissing my cheek. Though I don't know why I was favored, I'm flattered by the gesture. I smile at the flowers, one red, one yellow, and one pink. The last time someone thought to give me flowers was when Rich proposed. A teeny, tiny part of me—the part I won't allow to have any say in my decisions—hopes Alex has something to do with this.

The sky finally allows the night to take over for its rightful turn during the drive back to the hotel. It's just dark enough that buildings have turned on their lights while still bright enough that I can take decent photos. This segment of the tour in Rome doesn't seem long enough for the significance it's had throughout the history of the world. It wasn't built in a day, and it can't be explored in one either.

It's not until my phone reconnects to the hotel's Wi-Fi that all the notifications pour in nonstop. Several missed calls and texts from Taylor appear in succession. She must have finally looked at the photos I sent her before I took my nap earlier this afternoon. I look at the most recent message from her.

TAYLOR
Call me! As soon as you can! It's urgent!

"I'm going to turn in for the night," I tell Alex as we walk through the front doors together. "My best friend left me a bunch of texts and voicemails. She's in the third trimester of her pregnancy so it could be important."

"Of course," he says with an alluring smile that makes me want to stay and hang out with him. It's a smile that encourages bad decisions. "Goodnight, Sonnet."

"Goodnight," I say before tearing my gaze from him. If I can walk away without looking at him again, I'll follow through on my intentions. Must keep moving toward my room. Do not look back at his beautiful face. Look at him tomorrow.

Knowing how long-winded Taylor can be when something excites her, whether negatively or positively, I rush through my bedtime routine of showering and brushing my teeth before I sit on my bed and call her. It's better to be in pajamas now than to try to hang up before she's finished. She answers on the second ring.

"I've been waiting hours for you to call me!" She yells. I pull my phone back from my ear in reaction to the sudden loud noise.

"What is it? Is everything alright with the baby?" I ask, masking the slight panic that's trying to climb its way into this moment.

"Of course, the baby is fine," Taylor says as if my worried questions were no big deal.

I take a deep breath to calm myself. "Then why did you leave so many voicemails and text messages? I thought it was an emergency."

"Sonnet, this is an emergency. Do you have any idea who that guy is standing next to you in the photo you sent me?" My silence is enough to encourage her to continue. "Alessandro—or Alex—De Luca, the only son of Vincent De Luca, the recently deceased CEO of De Luca Enterprises. He's about to step into his father's seat as the head of a billion-dollar company. He's been voted the 'Sexiest Man' and 'Most Eligible Bachelor' at least twice, and he's only thirty. All his red carpet appearances have been with models, but never the same one twice."

The logical part of my brain takes over as I say, "Maybe this guy just looks a lot like Alex De Luca." And has the same first name. The Alex I know is wealthy and dresses in high-quality fashion, but he's not billion-dollar-empire flashy. He just rode on a coach all day while taking photos through the window like an average tourist.

"Even if that were true, I would still say marry him and have his beautiful babies," Taylor says, interrupting my logical train of thought. "Sonnet, I'm almost certain that's him. The article I read about his father's death mentions that he would be traveling with his mom to his family's land in Italy for the funeral. What are the chances that there would be two men who look like that in Italy while you're there? I just sent you a photo of him so you can see for yourself."

I switch my phone to speaker and navigate to my texts from Taylor. The man in the online Dior advertisement is undoubtedly the same as the man I just said goodnight to an hour ago. In the photo, he's serious, all shadows and sharp edges. Alex in real life is bright with smiles that have a dozen meanings behind them. Both versions make my heart race for different reasons.

"So, now that you know who he is, what are you doing about it?" Taylor says, her voice softer because, despite the ocean and time zones between us, she can sense what I need from her.

"Taylor, guys like that don't end up with girls like me. I'm the only single girl his age in our tour group; I'm pretty and convenient. As soon as he's back to his normal life, I'll be a memory whose name he can't remember. And I don't blame him for any of that. I'm not exactly in a place for some great Cinderella romance. Experience has already taught me that lesson once. The last time the clock struck midnight, I was left with unrealistic expectations and memories of a guy who seemed disinterested in a long-distance relationship."

"It's not unrealistic to want chemistry with someone. I wouldn't be pregnant right now if Gabe didn't make me feel all those things you want with someone. I know there are a lot of reasons to put your guard up and distance yourself, but you might miss out on something incredible because you didn't open your heart. I'm not saying make out with the dude—actually, I will buy you cheesecake for the next year if you let him kiss you when he tries. Yes, I said when not if."

"Taylor, what was your point?" I ask to steer the conversation away from the topic of Alex's lips.

She's silent for a moment, and I can imagine the expression on her face. "My point is, don't let fear decide for you."

Her words hit the bull's-eye of where my life took a detour. Looking back on the pivotal moments in my and Rich's relationship, I made decisions because I was afraid he was the best that would come along. I said yes to a first date because I was tired of saying no. I said yes to a proposal because saying no would mean going back to square one when I felt as if I were running out of time. I said yes for all the wrong reasons.

Ordinarily, my brain would keep me up for hours after a conversation like that, but the lingering jet lag proves to be useful for one thing: knocking me out so I don't overthink.

I pack my things as I get ready in the morning, checking and double-checking that I've picked up everything I own. The downside of being on a tour that requires moving hotels every night or two will be the nagging thought that I've forgotten something at one of the previous stops. Living out of a suitcase is bound to get old fairly quickly. I'm zipping up my suitcase when there's a knock on my door.

"Sonnet, are you ready to go down to breakfast?" Alex's deep voice echoes through the hotel door and to the chambers of my heart. The last thing I want to do is push that man away when all he's done so far is help me out when I didn't know I needed it. I open the door and am bombarded by all the reasons I want to see where things could go. This vacation is a longer period before midnight than the masquerade ball was. There's so much more time left to get to know Alessandro De Luca.

He helps me pull my suitcase out to the hallway where others from our group have left theirs for the luggage service. As much as I want to ask him all the questions swirling in my mind, they will be received better if I wait until we have both food and coffee in front of us. The restaurant is buzzing with life as guests fill their plates from the breakfast bars. We join the frenzy and are rewarded with fruit and pastries.

I don't even have to be the one to bring it up since he says to me, "You'd better tell me what's on your mind." The lack of caffeine must have interfered with my ability to hide these things from him.

"Why didn't you tell me your last name or that your father recently passed away?" Fortunately, my tone is soft rather than accusatory. He still freezes, unable to hide his shock.

Alex

I don't know how she figured it out, but she knows. She knows my last name, and she knows about my father, which means she's put all the pieces of my identity together. Anonymity was good while it lasted.

"I don't know your last name either," I finally say in a weak argument. I lose all leverage when my mind decides to recall that Marisol used her full name while taking roll-call that first day when we met.

"My last name isn't tied to anything significant," she says.

I brace myself for the worst possible reaction from her. She has a right to be upset. In this small window of time, she's shared things with me about her life and her past, but I haven't reciprocated in the same way. I've given her crumbs of myself while she's been giving me slices of bread. Despite that, she's patient in waiting for my rebuttal.

"It's rare that I get to go anywhere that I'm not immediately recognized," I say. "All my life, I've been the only son and heir to Vincent De Luca. While the perks are nice, the drawbacks can be taxing after a while. My father's passing was unexpected and unplanned. I thought I had years before I would have to step into his role—years that I could have spent traveling, getting married, and starting my own family. Instead, my life as I've known it is a ticking time bomb. My father rarely took vacations that weren't also business trips, so I booked my spot on this tour as a last chance to be unknown."

Under the table, my leg shakes, a nervous tick from junior high I've never been able to stop. "Your secret is safe with me," she says after taking a long sip of her cappuccino. Part of her is enjoying making me sweat. "I'm not even mad. I just wish I had found out from you because you felt like you could tell me rather than finding out from my dramatic best friend. I felt blindsided by the truth."

I lightly touch her hand to prompt her to look at me. "I'm still the same guy I was yesterday and the day before. You just know about my nearly bottomless bank account now."

"I knew you were rich from the first day," she admits, and I can visibly see her guard come down. "I also knew you looked familiar, so at least I can stop wondering about that too. I've seen your photo a few times online and on magazine covers."

I tease, "I'm not sure if I should be relieved or offended that you didn't immediately recognize last year's 'Sexiest Man' when meeting him in person."

"I mean, you're okay, I guess," she teases. The fact that she downplays it rather than fawning over me like most women only makes her more attractive. I'm beginning to wonder if she's the embodiment of my perfect woman. That, and I'm still the hopeless romantic kid I was over seven years ago.

Time passes at an unfair velocity when I'm with her, and we find ourselves rushing to finish our food and brush our teeth before joining the others on the bus. By this afternoon, we'll be in the region of Tuscany. We sit in our usual arrangement of her on the left window seat and me beside her. This time, she has her own book to read during the hours we'll be riding through the Italian countryside.

As payback for yesterday, I say, "Let me guess, it's a book about people who write books but have writer's block, and they somehow help each other break through that while simultaneously falling in love." She looks at me but doesn't comment. I continue, "Oh, and the sex is mind-blowing because it's always incredible between the characters in open-door romance novels. The only time it's ever awkward is when it's teenagers with no previous experience. While I agree that chemistry is an important element to a relationship, that can set people up for unrealistic expectations." I went further with it than I had intended.

"I wouldn't know either way," Sonnet says, the slight blush on her face contrasting with her bluntness. She's not embarrassed by it as much as she seems uncomfortable talking to me about it.

"I'm going to assume that you're abstinent by choice," I say because based on what I know about Richard Morrison, I don't see him being the one wanting to wait.

She nods and says, "Part of it is due to my beliefs, but the older I've gotten, the more it seems logical to wait until marriage. I don't know. When Dick's friends heard about the wedding being called off and how I found out about the cheating, one of them said the whole thing could have been avoided if I hadn't insisted we wait. Maybe he's right, but Rich waited the two years we dated before we were engaged. He could have waited six more months until the wedding. Unless the cheating had been going on for years."

"Sonnet, no," I say more forcefully than I intend. "Dick and his friends are not right. You could have made him wait for five years, and it still would never justify how he treated you. That was your boundary, and you deserve a guy who's willing to respect that and respect you."

"Coming from a guy who has probably slept with how many models?" She asks in a way that's meant to be subtle. She's curious yet also doesn't want to know. The question gives me déjà vu.

"Zero." My answer, the truth, is the one response she doesn't anticipate. I can already interpret her expressions. "Every one of those red carpet appearances was only for the event. I've been on a few dates here and there, but I'm not that guy. I couldn't even tell you the last time I kissed someone."

The last part is a lie. My last kiss is branded into my soul so permanently that I haven't been tempted by any woman since. Until a few days ago, that is. The few times we've been alone, Sonnet's lips have tried to beckon me like a siren's call. I'm afraid that if I give in, it will be just as good or better than the one I relive in my imagination. This woman could completely turn my world on its axis when my timeline and plans have already been disrupted. Life is simpler when I'm surrounded by women I have no interest in.

"The best kiss of my life certainly wasn't with Dick," she murmurs to herself.

"Coming from a girl who has kissed how many men?" I say, turning her question back on her.

I'm ignoring the warning bells in my head telling me to change the topic or let her go back to reading her romance novel. Something? Anything?

Her sly smile is only making this worse. "Two. Only two."

I mean, I understand that she's likely more cautious given her standards, but two is a low number for an astounding woman of twenty-eight. And one of those men had to be Richard. "What's the story with the other guy? A rebound?"

"A fling before I met Rich," she says without explanation. Though I wait to see if she'll share more about this mysterious—and apparently amazing—first kiss, her body language communicates more than her words could. *Fling* is not indicative of his residual effect on her but of the length and seriousness of their relationship. I guess that he's her first love, the one that Dick thought or knew he was trying to live up to. My assumptions are based on my own experience, though my first love came years after my first kiss.

I decide to draw a line in our relationship out of protection for her. I block out the sound of the little devil on my shoulder calling me an idiot. "Sonnet, I'm not going to kiss you."

"Because it wouldn't mean anything?" Nothing is joking or teasing in her question. Does she not see how wholly she enchants me?

"Because it would mean everything."

We read our books in silence until the bus pulls up to a rest stop. After a quick restroom break, Marisol leads our group to the funicular station. Every ten minutes, the cable car transports a group up the incline to the city center of Orvieto. Before she hands out the tickets, she gives us detailed instructions about departure times given the ten-minute gaps between the funicular trips. It's overkill, but it's because she's done this before and has likely had people who didn't think through the logistics.

The hill did not deter whoever built the Duomo di Orvieto. The looming, gothic-style cathedral displays the same intricate details that one expects to see in the major European cities. Marisol relays the cathedral's history to the group, but we're only half listening as we take photos of the dominating monument.

"Did she just say that Orvieto is built on a volcanic plug?" Sonnet whispers to me.

"I'm sure it's extinct," I reassure her. If the cathedral's flagstone has been here since 1290, we don't have anything to worry about. I see an advertisement for tours of the city underground consisting of caves and tunnels built into the volcanic rock. It has to be extinct, right?

We only spend fifteen to twenty minutes inside the cathedral before Sonnet is ready to meander through the streets of this quaint Umbrian town. Once again, I follow her lead without discussion.

"There's something heartwarming about small towns like this where most people can and do walk to wherever they need to go," she says as she admires the cobblestones beneath our feet. It's like a small village out of a fairytale.

"It's romantic," I say without thinking first. Me and my hopelessly romantic brain and the beautiful woman.

"It is," she agrees wistfully. She stops to admire and take photos of flowers for sale in the middle of the square. I would buy all of them for her if it didn't contradict my promise to her on the coach. And if we weren't sharing a coach with twenty-plus others.

Occasionally, a car drives through, honking to scare pedestrians out of the way. We keep going, pausing to document the scenes with our phones. We reach an overlook with an unobstructed view of the surrounding region. If I were trying to get a girl to kiss me, this is where I would make my move. But since I'm not, I continue in my role as a tourist.

We walk back through the winding streets until the Duomo is again a major part of the landscape. There's a restaurant on one of the corners of the city center. Both our stomachs growl as if on cue.

"Is it a bad idea to eat gelato for lunch?" She asks as she spots a group eating from cones.

"If it helps, I had the same idea," I say as I nudge her toward the front entrance. "Dinner is so late here in Italy that I almost need two lunches to survive the wait. We'll eat real food in Siena."

Inside, there are two people in line, Lawrence and Jean. When Jean notices us, she tells the man behind the gelato display, "Oh, and add whatever they want, my treat."

"Jean, you don't have to pay for ours," Sonnet says.

"I insist," Jean says in a way that shuts down any further argument. The man behind the counter loses track of the exchange in English, so I relay the information to him in Italian. I order a medium chocolate cone and then wait for Sonnet to decide what she wants while he scoops the previous orders. Her stracciatella is the last to be served as Jean hands the man money for our desserts. I'll find a way to repay them before this tour is over.

We walk outside with gelatos in hand as the restaurant fills with a lunch crowd. One of the families from our group is sitting at one of the outdoor tables eating sandwiches. The everyday grind of phone calls and meetings is a distant memory compared to the sweet taste of cold cream on my tongue and the warmth of the Italian sun. If I stick to towns and villages like this one, maybe a vacation in the future isn't impossible.

Marisol's earlier insistence works in our favor because everyone is on the bus by the time we planned to depart. Sonnet and I return to the comfortable silence of words on paper as we cross the regional borders into Tuscany. Though tonight is our only night in Siena, the next two will be in a different Tuscan city.

After a few hours on the bus, the walking and fresh air relieves my limbs. First, we see the city center from a distance, a view worth several photos. I take a few of Lawrence and Jean as they smile with their arms around one another. Our culture might be obsessed with youth, but there's nothing quite like seeing an older couple infatuated with each other after years of life together. My heart aches with the hope that I can be like them one day. To my surprise, Jean asks Marisol to take some photos of the four of us—her, Lawrence, Sonnet, and me.

As Marisol leads us to the famous city center, I notice the groups of locals laughing and enjoying life together. If there's anything I'm learning on this vacation, it's that I need a community around me all the time. I need people who are like family whom I can share meals with and who aren't afraid to call me out when I'm being a stubborn fool. I also note that Siena would be a great city for running. The arch in front of us opens up to the expansive Piazza del Campo, a shell-shaped public space known for horse races.

Marisol barely announces the rendezvous time before the group scatters to do various activities. Some head toward the Torre del Mangia in the Palazzo Pubblico while others walk in the direction of the Duomo. The wider edge of the piazza's shell is lined with restaurants. I turn to Sonnet to let her decide our next steps.

"Do you want to go in the tower?" I ask her. It's not my first choice, but I'm stuck to her like glue. I'm sure she would be fine if I left her alone, though I don't doubt she would attract a line of Italian men if I weren't near. I owe it to her as a friend to keep away unwanted attention.

"No, let's walk to the Duomo and then see if any of the restaurants in the piazza serve pizza," she says. It's exactly the plan I would have formed had she insisted I take charge. The fact that she didn't feel the need to ask for my opinion goes on the list of the many things I like about her.

Sonnet

I t's been hours, and my emotions are mixed. Every time I replay his words in my head, I get butterflies, goosebumps, and a faint stab of disappointment. The improbable connection I feel around him is two-sided, but he has no intentions of acting on it. It's better if he doesn't because a long-distance relationship between people who have very different lives isn't a likely future. An incredible kiss doesn't translate to a future in the real world.

For someone who must be used to getting what he wants, he's not at all pushy. Some things—some wants—can't be bought, which would explain his patience and deference to my preferences. I may even have to force him to choose next time we're left with multiple options to fill our time. What could a man like him truly desire?

Naturally, I walk faster than the average adult, specifically in the grocery store. Alex's stride is long enough that I can tell he's walking slower than his usual pace to keep in step with me. I subtly admire how strong and agile the muscles of his legs are, struggling not to trip over my own in the process. The man beside me has been a model in high fashion ads. We walk past some of the luxury brands that have likely photographed him. He belongs on the front pages of magazines and splashed across billboards.

"Sonnet, I would hate for you to trip and hurt yourself because you were too distracted staring at me," he says with his eyes still facing the street ahead of us. My face flushes with embarrassment at being called out like that. "There's a lot of walking on this tour, and I need you in one piece to keep me company."

While his method is unorthodox, my mortification makes me so self-conscious about making eye contact with him that I force myself to look only at our surroundings. There are so many people out eating and shopping at every place we pass. It gives similar vibes to when my friends and I were teenagers and would hang out at the mall and food court together. If Taylor were here, we would spend the whole afternoon perusing every store until either the bus was getting ready to leave or she got too hungry to continue. I'm going to need that pizza when we get back to Piazza Del Campo.

After what appeared to be an endless line of buildings in various shades of brown, the Duomo is impossible to miss. The architecture is similar to that of the Duomo in Orvieto, including the alternating black and white marble stripes. Buildings of this size took so long to construct that the various architectural styles would evolve and mesh before completion. Neither of us moves to go inside, satisfied with the façade and ready to walk back.

The Italian sun is ruthless once we're out of the shade. The square is exposed to the sunlight. The Fountain of Joy attracts birds trying to cool off from the heat, and some restaurants have fans blowing mist on their customers.

"I don't care where we eat as long as it's one of the places that has those," I say as I point to one of the fans. Using the back of my hand, I wipe sweat from my forehead before it can drip into my eyes. It's too hot to be concerned about how unattractive I must look now; my only concern is water and the artificial breeze.

Alex scopes out the options and leads me across the piazza to a restaurant with an open table next to a misting fan. In Italian, he asks the hostess if we can have that table. It's not as if any heterosexual female younger than forty is going to say no to that smile and those eyes. My presence doesn't seem to be a factor as she openly gawks at him. Is this his normal? I witnessed the entire conversation; there was nothing close to flirting on his end.

Across the piazza at the Palazzo Pubblico, a group wearing formalwear is gathered around a classic sports car. When the doors to the building open, a bride and groom walk out holding hands, and the crowd erupts with applause.

"Now, that is romantic," Alex says as he watches them hug their guests.

Our waiter pours the water Alex ordered for us into the glasses on the table. We quickly place our orders, one pizza each, and return our attention to the newlyweds. "I would hope that a wedding is romantic," I say as I remember all the planning I had put into mine before canceling it all.

"If you had gotten married to a man who was cheating on you, I would argue that the wedding is more tragic than romantic," he says before he opens the bottle of water on the table to refill my glass. "Rather than sitting here with me observing an Italian wedding, you would probably be up in the tower with him."

I laugh because Dick really would have insisted that we climb the tower while we're here. "Towers only seem romantic until you're stuck in them. They're basically high-altitude prisons if you're a Disney princess."

"Sonnet Kincaid, are you a Disney princess?" He asks with mock seriousness. "Is that why your curly hair always seems to look flawless? I won't tell anyone if you are, but I should warn you that I'm no Prince Charming."

I shake my head at his ridiculous words as I say, "Flynn Rider wasn't a prince. He was a thief."

"Right, I forgot about that. She's the one who was of royal birthright."

"Last year's 'Sexiest Man' is a huge hopeless romantic," I tease with a grin I couldn't suppress if I wanted to.

His smile matches mine, and my heart squeezes. "It's my character flaw. I'm sure you bring out that side of me because it's normally hidden under lock and key. Some people are the type who don't know that their best fit is right in front of them, but I'm the type who knows right away when I'm talking to an incredible woman. I like you, Sonnet, and women like you are rare."

"But you're not going to kiss me," I repeat his earlier phrase, the words making more sense to me now than they had before. I tuck away the "rare" compliment to obsess over when I'm alone in my room tonight.

"If we kiss and it's the most amazing kiss either of us has ever had, it's going to be very hard to move on from each other when reality hits," he says, and I can tell he's struggling to swallow the pill as much as I am. Self-preservation screams at me that Alex is correct. I've had unrealistic expectations for years after a perfect night with a masked stranger I only spent five hours with. By now, Alex and I have known each other for around forty-eight hours, and I have yet to find a concrete flaw about him. Wait, forty-eight hours? How is that possible?

The waiter brings over our pizzas, and my focus is automatically carb-focused. We're pigs because the only thing either of us has eaten since breakfast in Rome was the gelato cones hours ago. I do not care. This is how pizza should be—authentic. I may as well be participating in an eating contest because I'm chewing on my last slice as Alex takes the first bite of his final piece. I win.

The men in suits from the wedding celebration sit a few tables from us. In my peripheral, I see Alex reposition himself to be slightly closer to me. I look at Alex with my eyebrow raised in question.

"I'm going to go to the restroom," he says as if that were an explanation for my unspoken inquiry.

While he's gone, the waiter asks if we want anything else. Because his interactions at our table have primarily been with Alex, he uses Italian rather than English. When he realizes and tries to ask in English, I hold up my hand to stop him and ask for the check in Italian. It's the first time I've had to use my knowledge of the language in conversation since arriving in Italy, but the waiter brightens the same way I've seen others do when Alex speaks Italian.

"Why do you pretend not to know Italian around the tour group?" Alex asks as he sits down, his sudden reappearance making me jump. I didn't know he was watching.

"It's not intentional," I say to explain myself. "I haven't needed to use it, and it's much more entertaining when the locals have no idea that I can eavesdrop on their conversations. No one expects an American tourist like me to know the language."

He shakes his head as he mutters, "Bella donna pazza." Beautiful, crazy woman. It's the words of a man in danger of falling in love if the movies are to be believed. First, he says it in exasperation, but by the end, he says it to her with all the love and adoration a woman can only hope to find one day. Beautiful, crazy woman. By the end of this tour, he won't need to kiss me to make it hard to move on.

The waiter hands us our checks, and Alex immediately swipes mine away from me. He has the same look in his eyes that Jean had earlier when she insisted on treating us. I'm not confrontational enough to argue with him on this.

"Just this once," I say to him. "For the same reason that you won't kiss me, I can't let you spoil me."

"Sonnet, it's a € 10 pizza; I would hardly call that spoiling you." Ten euros must seem like dust compared to his bank account balance.

"But pizzas for lunch every day add up, and then it'll be other gifts that I can't accept from you.

I didn't ask you about your last name or your father because I expected anything from you. I don't want your money." He nods in understanding.

Once the waiter returns with Alex's credit card, we only linger for another five minutes before we leave the table for the next set of hot and sweaty customers. I had always assumed that Italy's climate wouldn't include this unforgiving heat, but I was mistaken. We're close enough to the departure time that we choose to spend the remainder of our afternoon in Siena at the meeting point. The bride and groom from earlier are long gone, likely somewhere with air conditioning.

Lawrence and Jean are carrying shopping bags as they walk up to our growing group, reminding me to keep an eye out for souvenirs. I bought a few trinkets at the hotel gift shop in Rome, but not nearly enough to cover the mental list in my head. As far as I can tell, Alex hasn't bought anything either, though men are less likely to expect their friends to bring them back something from their vacations.

The walking in the heat must have exhausted me more than I thought. I wake up as our coach pulls into the parking lot of our hotel for the night. It takes my brain a few seconds to process where I am which is why I didn't immediately notice I had fallen asleep leaning on Alex. When I peek over, he's also waking up from a nap. Maybe he doesn't know I used him as a makeshift pillow. He yawns, which makes me feel like yawning. The sleepy expression on his face decimates my ability to emotionally keep him in the friend zone. Waking up to that face every morning would be heaven on earth.

"Did we sleep the whole drive here?" He asks me as if I'm any more alert than he is. I don't miss how he said "we" either.

"I don't remember anything after we climbed onto the bus, so my guess is yes," I say to him as I blink to encourage my contact lenses to behave. "It couldn't have been that long of a nap since we're still in Siena. It's not like we're driving through Texas."

He rolls his neck and shoulders to loosen his muscles. I might need to blindfold myself if everything he does is going to give me shivers. Wearing a jacket is too conspicuous for late May unless it's raining. The only day with a chance of rain is the morning of the day after tomorrow, and it's predicted to clear up before noon.

When I researched the hotels last week, this one had inviting pictures of their fitness room. While walking provides sufficient exercise to counteract the gelato and carbs, my legs are itching for the challenge of a cycling workout. After dinner tonight might be my best chance. We walk into the opulent lobby, claiming our suitcases and room keys. I open the door to my suite, and I never want to leave. The room is spacious compared to that in Rome, complete with a large shower. I add washing my hair to the list of after-dinner tasks.

The Wi-Fi also seems more stable here once I log into the guest internet. This time, there's only one text from Taylor asking for an update on how my conversation with Alex went. For someone who is married, pregnant, and working full-time, she seems to have too much free time to check up on me. Rather than call her and risk her hijacking all my rest time until dinner, I text her a thumbs-up emoji. I haven't yet unpacked my toiletries when my phone rings with her assigned ringtone.

As soon as I accept the call, she says, "Did you think I would let you get away with an emoji response to a question like that? I want details."

"I was hoping you would be too busy finishing up your baby registry to pry into my vacation," I say. I've been badgering her about her wishlist since she learned the gender. Her baby shower is two weeks after I get home, and guests have been asking about gifts since I sent out the invites.

"I finished and shared the link with the guest list last night," she says before circling back, "so all I have to keep my mind occupied is you and the eye candy. How did things go when you asked him about his secret identity?"

I sigh knowing the only escape is to hang up. She would only call back incessantly until I answered again. "He's here on vacation because he needs a break from his normal life. He wasn't trying to lie or hide anything from me. The guy lost his father a month ago, and not only is he grieving that loss, but he's also expected to take over for his father sooner than he thought. I can't blame him for not wanting to spill all that to a woman he's only known for two days."

"That sounds a lot more stressful than growing a human being that likes to kick my bladder," Taylor says. I can hear the sound of car engines in the background. Our call must be going through the hands-free Bluetooth in her car.

"It all sounds about as stressful as planning and canceling a wedding in less than six months," I say to get my point across. Though I'm hesitant to repeat his words, I know she'll ask if I don't tell her now. "He promised that he's not going to kiss me."

"He said that? I hope there's an explanation here that doesn't make him sound like a huge jerk. I was starting to like him for you." Considering she was never a fan of Rich or most of the guys I showed mild interest in, it's jarring that she would approve of someone she's never met.

I close my eyes to focus on the full context of the conversation so I can better convey it to my best friend. "He's not going to kiss me because he thinks it'll make it harder on both of us when we have to part ways at the end of this vacation. Which is probably a correct assumption. It's only been two days, and I already feel more intensely for him than I did for a man I was going to marry. I'm unsure if that says more about my poor taste in boyfriends or more about whatever this connection is with Alex."

"It says a lot about both. Dick looked good on paper, but something about it never quite fit right. If I had to describe it, I would say that you enjoyed how much he initially adored you more than you adored him in return. Over time, he picked up on it. Rather than talking to you about it, he grew to resent you and used that to justify his unfaithfulness."

"Why didn't you say anything?" In most situations, Taylor is the one I can count on to call me out on things like that. Even though she didn't hide her misgivings about Rich, this is the first I've heard the full extent of her doubts.

I hear ruffling on the other end, likely Taylor transferring the audio from her car speakers to the handheld. "You hadn't given anyone a chance in so long. And you were happy at the beginning. I was waiting to see if you had that moment when you were so in love with someone that you couldn't imagine a future without him, but you never seemed to get to that point. As complicated as the Alex situation is, that's what you deserve. You deserve to feel 'in over your head' and 'out of control.' If you get to the end of this vacation and you two still haven't found a way to continue whatever it is you're doing, I'll be the one picking you up from the airport and helping you heal your broken heart. Because it was more bruised than broken when you had to break off your engagement."

"Is there any way to abort now and come out unscathed?" I ask with a humorless laugh.

"I think it's too late for that," Taylor says. "Now that I have a better look at the whole situation, I respect him for making that boundary. Does he know that you're a virgin?"

"Yes," I say with a groan. "Don't ask how that came up in conversation. It's what led to his brilliant promise. Speaking of, he's never had any relationships with those models he takes to events. I guess they're just his dates for publicity. I want to take his word on it, but it's hard because they're models."

Taylor takes a few seconds to respond. "Sorry, I'm going to have to go. But first, you need to stop comparing yourself to girls he did or didn't date. I know Dick's actions did a number on your confidence, but you're gorgeous enough to be a model. The only reason you don't have Italian guys lining up out the door is that you've been spending most of your time with Alex. Don't try to tell me you haven't because I know you, and any girl would be in your shoes.

Okay, I love you, bestie!" She hangs up before I can return the farewell.

I finish unpacking my workout clothes for later and the toiletries I'll need for washing my hair. Washing and detangling my curls is an event in itself, magnified by the fact that I'm not in my shower at home. I still have thirty minutes until dinner to explore the hotel grounds and locate the fitness room. Once on the ground floor, I follow the signs until I reach my target. I take inventory of the machines and rules posted on the door, praying it will still be empty after dinner.

Alex

I use my spare half hour before dinner to walk to the outdoor pool. The area is vacant, likely due to the time of day. I slip off my socks and shoes and stick my feet in the cool water. It's refreshing and peaceful, allowing my thoughts to untangle and compartmentalize.

At this point, if I'm not already a complete goner, I will be by tomorrow or the day after. I had rationalized what happened seven years ago as youthful folly—feelings that only existed because I was young with underdeveloped frontal lobes. This is worse. Self-control and self-preservation have been the only things keeping me from doing something insane and stupid. Is there a way that we can make this work once we're both back in the States? The last thing I want is to upend her life while dragging her into mine. The hard part is that I can see her in my world, but it's not a decision I could ever make for her. It might be time to talk to my mother and get her perspective.

I have enough connection to the Wi-Fi to make a video call to my mom. When she answers, her living room curtains fill my screen.

"Mamma, you need to tap the icon in the corner to switch your camera to the front-facing one so I can see your face," I say to her. This happens about a fourth of the time we have video calls. A few seconds later, her beautiful face appears. She looks better rested than she did a few days ago.

"Alex, you've been getting some sun," she says with a smile that will always comfort me. "Your tan reminds me of how dark you were that year you lived in Treviso. You practically lived in the sun."

I hadn't stopped long enough to inspect my tan lines in the mirror, but her comment makes me thankful for my Italian blood. If I were Irish, I would likely be as red as a lobster. "You remember what life is like in Italy. A lot of walking in the sun. Today was a bit on the warmer side."

"Any other updates that you would like to share?" She asks trying to be subtle.

"Is it too soon to be entertaining the logistics of a future with her?" I won't say her name because I know I don't need to. My mom already knows whom I'm talking about.

I anticipate the knowing expression on her face. "Absolutely not. You're not a teenager or in your early twenties anymore. At this stage of your life, you should be thinking about whether the person you're interested in is someone you can have a future with. This isn't what you want to hear, but whoever chooses a life with you will be giving up the benefits of a normal life. Your father valued our privacy, but even that comes with the cons of constant security to protect that. Relationships are give and take. You can't predict what she may decide; all you can do is inform her of all aspects of the situation and let her choose."

Letting her make the choice is opening myself up to rejection, the thing I try to avoid. "Mamma, I gotta go. Dinner is starting soon, and I'm outside by the hotel pool. I'll call you in a few days."

Her advice doesn't lessen my conflicting emotions. If anything, it pulls my head down from the clouds and back to earth. Sonnet makes me wish I were just Alex instead of Alessandro De Luca. On my way to the dining room, I notice the sign pointing in the direction of the hotel fitness room. A good run or strength workout is exactly what I need after dinner to exhaust myself. When I walk into the dining room, Sonnet sits at a table with Marisol, Lawrence, and Jean. I take the open seat to her right.

"There he is," Jean says as I sit down. "I was about to send Sonnet out to look for you." Knowing that they were waiting for me warms my heart. Lawrence and Jean feel like family with how welcoming they have been since we met.

"Excuse me a moment," Marisol says as she stands and walks to the entrance to greet a man I don't recognize. He's tall, likely only an inch or two shorter than me, with a full-trimmed beard and a shiny bald head. She leads him to our table. "Everyone, this is my fiancé Andrea. He's in Siena for some work things, so I invited him to join us for dinner tonight."

"Oh, I love bald guys!" Jean exclaims as she lovingly rubs Lawrence's mostly bald scalp. "They're the best because they try harder." None of us know what to say in response to her comment, so we introduce ourselves to Andrea.

Seeing Marisol and Andrea together sparks questions, but I don't know them well enough to ask most of my inquiries. Plus, I can't hijack the conversation to ask them all. Sonnet must be on the same wavelength because she starts with the least intrusive topic.

"How long have you two been together?" I nudge Sonnet with my elbow as a gesture of thanks.

"We've been engaged for almost three months," Andrea says as he looks at Marisol with doe eyes. "We dated for a year before I proposed." I don't know how much time Marisol spends working as a tour guide compared to her breaks at home, but their relationship must be long-distance during her travel stints. Planning a wedding on that schedule can't be easy either.

Jean is the next to ask the couple one of the many matters coursing through my head. "Do you have a wedding date set yet, or is it tricky planning a wedding while herding around groups of tourists?"

Marisol laughs and returns the same doe-eyed expression to Andrea. "We're getting married during the tourism off-season. We both prefer to do it in the cooler months anyway. As for your second question, you'd be surprised how much I can get done during downtimes at the hotel or on the longer bus rides."

At this rate, the women will ask everything for me while I sit back and listen. Perhaps, this is why females tend to talk more than males on average.

"I've been trying to convince her that we should just elope," Andrea says with a glint in his eyes that convinces me he's only slightly joking. Marisol shakes her head at him in amusement. They seem like a good fit for each other.

Before anyone else bombards them with another question, the staff passes around the first course. Jean takes over the conversation as she retells how she and Lawrence met when they were younger. Although she told the story to me and Sonnet at dinner a few nights ago, she includes details this time that she didn't the first time. In this rendition, she mentions how she flew out to meet him for a weekend in Japan. Because he was in the military, he moved around frequently. In a way, it bears some similarities to Marisol and Andrea. It's not until I'm comparing the two couples that I realize Sonnet and I are the only ones at this table who aren't a couple.

Conversation flows naturally during the other courses as Andrea and Marisol share how they met on a bike tour of Florence. Just about any meet-cute in Italy, France, or Spain will seem extraordinarily romantic. Romance is infused in the air. We breathe it in until it's ingrained in our DNA like a new blood type. Maybe that's what can explain the anomalous connection I feel with Sonnet. It could be an influence of our environment. Would I feel this intensely if I crossed paths with her on the street in my everyday life? Yes, because I've done so before in a younger life.

I'm in a haze as I walk back to my room to change into a T-shirt and basketball shorts. I know I said goodnight to everyone else at the table. Sonnet was the first to dismiss herself from our table. I wander down to the lobby where I saw the fitness room signs earlier. I take a right down the hallway of various hotel amenities until I see the correct door. Someone else is already in there, but as long as they're not using the same equipment I need, I don't mind sharing. When I walk in, my eyes immediately make eye contact with the breathtaking woman on the cycling machine.

Sonnet is in a neon orange workout tank and black patterned yoga pants that reveal her every curve. Despite my sudden appearance, she focuses on the high resistance interval. I could stand here and watch her all night if that weren't crossing the boundaries we're trying to keep. Tearing my attention away from her, I scan the machines and equipment in the room, settling on the weight machines. I feel her gaze on me as I warm up my muscles. The only way I'll keep myself from ogling her is if I work hard enough to be sore tomorrow. It's a small price to pay to preserve my sanity.

When I glance at her between reps, her eyes dart away from me and back to the screen. We might as well be two middle-schoolers who like each other and won't admit it. Neither of us is willing to make eye contact as we do our separate workouts, but the tension in the air is thick with electric charge. She finishes before me and takes the time to wipe down the machine and stretch. I close my eyes to give her privacy and spare myself the images later. The last thing I need is to let my imagination take things too far in my mind.

Rather than leave when she's done, she sits on the bench against the large mirror to wait for me. Or to check me out.

She's a master multitasker from what I can surmise. I finish my current set of reps and decide I've accomplished enough for this endeavor.

"I wish all the hotels had a setup like this," I say to her as I stretch the muscles I worked. Hours of walking and sitting on a bus tomorrow don't mix well with stiff and sore muscles.

"Me too," she says as she twists to stretch her back. "I have a spin bike at home that I use twice a week. The uphill walking certainly isn't easy, but it's not the same as the workouts I get on my bike."

I picture us together on a Saturday morning going to spin classes together. It wouldn't bother me if I were the only male there because I'd be there with her. It's hard to keep myself from wanting all her mornings, afternoons, and evenings. Tonight, I've proven that I can work out with her and keep my hands off her.

When we walk into the elevator, there's a girl a few years younger than us. "Quale piano?" The girl asks us as she hits the button for her floor.

"Quattro," Sonnet says without the usual hesitation of someone whose first language is English. The girl doesn't ask if mine is different; she assumes we're together. Our rooms are on the same floor, so I don't correct her presumption. Instead, I do the most senseless thing I can and intertwine my fingers with Sonnet's. Holding her hand is comparable to touching a live wire—the sparks are overwhelmingly powerful. The small display of affection shocks my system even though I initiated it. Somehow, the euphoria is both foreign and familiar, contradicting and making my head spin.

"Buonanotte," the girl says with a smile as she exits the elevator onto the third floor.

Sonnet returns the sentiment, "Buonanotte."

I'm frozen for the seconds it takes the doors to close again. Time slows and stops as Sonnet's thumb caresses my hand. I broke the physical barrier, and now she's breaking me. She's fracturing the walls I erected seven years ago when I decided that love wasn't something I could afford to run after again; I could live the rest of my days feeding off the memory of one perfect night. One handhold makes the philosophy I've lived by for seven years suddenly sound unconvincing.

When the elevator dings upon arrival on the fourth floor, Sonnet tugs on my hand to bring me back to the present. We're at a hotel in Siena returning to our rooms after a post-dinner workout because, in instances like this, she and I are the same person. I follow her because my hand is still holding hers. Her door appears first, and I gently let go. My hand feels naked without hers.

"Goodnight, Alex," she says with a small smile. Her dark chocolate eyes sparkle as she looks at me the way my first love once looked at me.

"Goodnight, Sonnet," I say, stepping back to distance myself from the temptation to break my promise. I keep stepping back toward my room as I watch her unlock her door and disappear into her room.

She's not trying to seduce me the way other women have attempted, but she's more enticing than they were because she isn't like any of them. She's like the girl I had to leave, the one I wish I could have stayed for. Her existence proves that a person can have more than one soulmate and more than one "best fit." It also means I might need to make a special call to my therapist about my penchant for love at first sight if twice can be considered a concerning habit.

I fall asleep while sorting through my photos from the day and wake up the next morning to the group photo I took with Sonnet, Lawrence, and Jean.

Sonnet

As usual, my hair is still damp when I wake up the next morning. A disadvantage to having a lot of thick, curly hair is that it often takes a full twenty-four hours for it to completely air dry. On the bright side, this is the first morning since arriving in Italy that I haven't felt the jet lag. As I get dressed and pack my suitcase again, I mourn that this was only my room for one night. It's the most upscale place I've stayed in since reaching adulthood due to my limited, yet growing, budget.

When I open the door to pull my suitcase into the hallway, Alex is standing with his fist in midair to knock. His cerulean shirt brings out the blue in his eyes in a way that will be unfairly distracting. My green flowery midi dress is flattering for a $12 sales find. His shirt costs close to the same as the entirety of my suitcase. Armani and Old Navy are two different price points and qualities. Despite the disparities, his eyes roam over how the dress accentuates my smaller waist. A blush creeps up my face as I momentarily forget how much I need both food and caffeine.

"Buongiorno," he says with a low rumble that sends shivers all over my body. Yep, we need to be around other people as soon as possible. Being away from each other all night has done nothing to lessen the tension that started in the fitness room last night.

"Come on, let's go before all the good pastries are gone," I say as I grab his hand and pull him toward the elevators. The hallway is filled with suitcases from others in our group, a sign that we're late compared to the rest. We hold hands until we reach the dining area and separate before we walk into the madhouse of hungry guests. This breakfast layout is less organized than the hotel in Rome, but we still manage to find fruit, croissants, and coffee.

It's not until we're on the bus that Alex says, "Wait, your dress has pockets," as if it were an earth-shattering revelation. I want to marry this man for his reaction because it's the same excitement I felt when I discovered the dress I bought has pockets. I'm still waiting for a red flag or deal breaker that will make the fluttering in my stomach go away. Maybe if he has a secret wife and kid at home. His being a serial killer would also be a big enough warning bell to warrant permanent distance. Sociopaths are typically charming.

"Do I want to know what's going on in that head of yours?" He asks without looking up from his book. This book is new, with the bookmark poking out within the first few chapters. He turns the cover toward me to spare me the effort. *Twilight.* Just when I thought his taste couldn't get any worse.

I laugh harder than I've laughed in years. If others on the bus look at us curiously, I'm too blinded by my tears to notice. By the time I collect myself, he's put his book away and is watching me with a goofy smile.

"I'm sorry, but you're actually reading that?" I ask him between taking deep breaths.

He stares at me with complete seriousness for a solid thirty seconds before he laughs and slips the dust jacket off to reveal a different book underneath—*The Hunger Games*. Still, the dust jacket came from somewhere.

"I like romance, but I draw the line at vampires and werewolves," he says, still laughing. "I watched the first movie to impress a girl in high school and immediately regretted it. I'm pretty sure she broke up with me because I couldn't stop laughing at the terrible acting."

Occasionally, I'm in the mood to watch the movie series *because* of the terrible acting. But I refrain from sharing that tidbit with him. "In her defense, the books aren't nearly as bad as the movie. My teenage self cried when Edward left her in the second book."

Alex looks taken aback at that. "You mean, after all that drama, the vampire leaves the accident-prone human. The least he could do was stick around after almost getting her killed. See, this is why I refuse to get into the whole supernatural romance sphere. At least the dystopian love triangles make sense."

We allow the comfortable silence to settle as we read. I periodically take breaks to admire the expanse of the Tuscan landscape. From the coach, I can see villas with driveways lined with Italian cypress trees, an image straight from a postcard. At dinner last night, Jean told me that she and

Lawrence are staying in a rented villa for a week once the tour is finished. The prospect makes me wish I had the money and the companion to do the same.

"My extended family has land near Treviso, and it takes my breath away every time," Alex says. "Tuscany is just as beautiful in a different way. I have yet to see a part of Italy that isn't captivating." I have yet to see a part of him that isn't captivating, and it's maddening.

Because our next destination is at the top of an incline, the bus drops us off at a parking lot near a grocery store. As we approach the beginning of the street leading to the city center, there's a large stone wall with an archway around the path. Right away, I know we're entering a town with medieval architecture. Yesterday's route is nothing compared to this climb, passing various shops and restaurants along the way.

San Gimignano is famous for its tower houses and medieval walls that stand preserved around the town. Somehow, this place gives me more fairytale vibes than any of the previous cities we've been to so far. Here, they embrace their historical roots by displaying colored flags brandished with a coat of arms. While perusing the fresh food at the farmer's market, we see a man dressed in a coat of mail with a sword strapped to his side. Everything about this place is charming. Photos don't quite capture the essence, but it's the only way to take this back with me.

"Let's go find that view Marisol mentioned earlier," Alex says with a gentle tug on my arm. "Then we can get some gelato and check out the shops." I don't argue with him; I'm glad he took the initiative to tell me what he wants to do rather than defaulting to my will again. Plus, I like his plan. He should make the plan more often. I'm willing to follow him to whatever adventure he chooses.

Together, we find the path that winds around the outside of the buildings, giving us a clear view of the Tuscan lands around. Rolling hills of green with rows of grape vines, olive trees, and Italian cypresses cover the expanse. From here, we can see the rooftops of the buildings that line the path up the hill.

"Tuscany would be a great place to buy land after retirement," I say as I take photos of the landscape.

"We're a little young to be thinking about retirement, don't you think?" Alex says as he bumps into me playfully. All joking aside, the contact makes me shiver despite the warming morning air around us. His eyes catch my reaction, and rather than asking, he takes my hand and weaves his fingers through mine like last night. Maybe if he does this every day, I'll grow accustomed to the buzzing feeling. I'll take it over the abdominal cramps I've felt on and off since breakfast.

I don't look at Alex as I say, "I'm going to need to find a restroom before we eat gelato." I'm afraid that if I look at him, the truth will come out. I'm not ready to tell him everything; I may never be ready to tell him everything. Once he knows, it could ruin the fantasy of any happily ever after the way it tainted my relationship with Rich. For weeks, I've been able to forget it and ignore it, but this morning has given me a bleak reminder of my reality.

"Sure, let's go find one now," he says without asking further. I know he can sense the shift in my mood, but he respects my privacy for the moment. We walk back toward the piazza and find a restroom inside the gelato shop.

The situation isn't as bad as I felt it could be. My level of discomfort is rarely proportionate to the level of bleeding. If my menstrual cycles were still normal like they were for most of my twenties, I wouldn't have even had to give it a second thought in regards to the wedding and honeymoon. The timing would have been perfect with it ending a day or two before walking down the aisle. But that hasn't been my normal for the past year. At this moment, all I can do is breathe a sigh of relief that it isn't unbearable or heavy. Just annoying.

When I emerge, Alex waits near the gelato counter for me before placing his order. Knowing him, he's already had a lengthy conversation with the shop owner about how he's paying for my ice cream and not to let me pay for my own under any circumstances. Given the emotional turmoil I've gone through in the last ten minutes, I'm not up to arguing with him about it. He smiles at me and nods toward the display of flavors. We both order a stracciatella medium cone and walk back into the fresh air and Italian sun.

"Gelateria Dondoli is world famous for its gelato," Alex says as we walk away from the shop. "They've won awards and have been featured on television. One of their claims to fame is their experimentation with new flavors. And yet, we both opted for a classic flavor of chocolate chip."

"I know what I like," I say with a shrug and a small smile.

In one corner, we see a group of children coming from the direction of the Piazza del Duomo. All the girls are wearing white dresses as if they had been participating in a

Catholic ceremony. The boys around them are all in identical suits.

"Do you have any siblings?" Alex asks me as we watch the kids run around the piazza.

"I have a brother. He's three years younger than me," I say, praying that he doesn't creep closer to the issue—my current issue.

He's quiet for a minute or two as the sounds of Italian town life fill the space. "Sometimes I wish I weren't an only child. Both of my parents have several siblings, but for some reason, one was enough for them."

"Maybe they struggled to have more children after you," I blurt without realizing it. Looks like I'll be the one digging my own grave.

Alex's eyes scan my face, possibly peering straight into my soul. It's impossible to hide my unease regarding the topic of children. Unless Alex was a difficult and ugly baby who somehow transformed with age, I find it impossible to believe that his mother wouldn't have wanted more children. Culturally, Italians value family and community. It's how the mafia survives, after all.

"Sonnet, look at me," he says pleading. I turn to meet his eyes that hold so much longing. "I can't force you to talk about it if you're not ready or willing, but whatever is wrong, I want to know. Your mood changed so drastically that I'm worried about you. I just want to be here for you however I can, even if it's just a listening ear."

I can count on one hand how many people I've had this conversation with, including my doctor, Taylor, my mom, and Dick. The only male on that list, my ex-fiancé, used it as a weapon against me in the last argument we had. Right before I handed him the diamond ring and told him never to contact me again. Ever since, it's been a discussion I've dreaded having with someone again even though it's inevitable. Alex isn't Dick, but Alex is less of a guarantee than Dick had seemed. Alex isn't Dick.

With only a few bites remaining of my gelato, I finish the mid-morning snack before delving into the mess. He finishes his as if sensing my need for his undivided attention. We find an unclaimed ledge to sit on side by side. Alex takes both of my hands in his to calm me, but all it does is make my heart race even more. As much as I wish I were brave enough to look at him, I shift to face the piazza of residents and tourists.

"About a year ago, I noticed some abnormalities in my menstrual cycle," I say. "Rather than lasting the usual six or seven days, it turned into twelve to fourteen days with the last week fairly light. At first, I just kept an eye on it and tracked it in case it was merely stress-induced. Every month, I would hope for six or seven days only to be disappointed again. Then, Rich proposed, so I had another reason to finally make the much-needed gynecology appointment, which had a six-week wait. The first month or two of our engagement, the cycles got worse. They were so heavy that I started experiencing symptoms of iron deficiency. I took iron supplements because I couldn't go through an entire month feeling like that. The first time it happened, I had to get iron infusions due to severely low hemoglobin levels."

When I pause and take a few deep breaths, he squeezes my hand in encouragement. He nods for me to continue. "After a blood test and an ultrasound, my doctor told me that there was what appeared to be an endometrial polyp in the lining of my uterus, which is usually benign for people my age. Sometimes polyps can interfere with getting pregnant, but the biggest thing is the heavy bleeding every month. She prescribed me birth control pills to temporarily help with the bleeding until I could get scheduled for a hysteroscopy to remove the polyp. Normally, it wouldn't be a big deal, but the copay for outpatient surgery is a lot while planning and paying for a wedding. When I told Dick, he brushed it off and said that it wasn't a big deal and could wait until after the wedding since the birth control would help. It was one of the last things he threw in my face when we ended the engagement. He's always wanted a big family, and I couldn't promise him that it would happen for us since he thinks there's always a chance the polyp isn't benign or that it could grow back after removal."

By the time I've finished spilling my biggest insecurity regarding my future, Alex has wrapped one arm around me while holding my hands with his other one. My head is leaning on his shoulder, letting him comfort me while sitting down.

He waits until he's certain I shared all I intended to before he asks, "So, you're telling me that Dick blames you for a medical condition that you have no control over? Even though neither of you know whether or not it'll affect your ability to have children?"

"Alex, before I had a confirmed diagnosis from the doctor, my mind and Google searches went through all the worst-case scenarios," I say as I remember the worst parts of not knowing anything. "Planning a wedding is hard enough, but doing so while fighting off the anxiety that I might already be barren made it ten times worse. At times, it felt like it was my fault for waiting so long to get married and try for kids; if I hadn't been so picky, I could have gotten married and had children before any of these symptoms appeared. I've always assumed that being young meant I had time to delay those things."

He kisses my hair and rubs comforting circles on my back. This man whom I've known for less than a week is doing more to soothe me than my fiancé had. My eyes and throat burn with the unshed tears I'm holding back. If we weren't in a public square, I would have let them fall for him to wipe away.

"I know I've said this before, but you're better off without Dick," he says. "I understand the desire to have children, but if I had to choose between the love of my life and having kids, I would choose her. Though I can't speak for him, it seems he loved the idea of a family more than he claimed to love you. Anyway, enough about the past. Is there anything that I can do to help you for the remainder of this tour?"

"When I went to the restroom earlier, it's because I was slightly paranoid that I was having a sudden heavy flow," I admit to him, finally looking into his sincere blue irises. "At its worst, I couldn't go two hours without needing the restroom. It was often unpredictable when it did happen. Birth control has helped with that, but it still concerns me sometimes. The only way I know I'm good is to go to the restroom and check."

When we both stand, he pulls me into a tight hug. I inhale his scent, my brain neurons making associations between his smell and the sense of safety. He's the first to let go as he says, "Are you ready to do some souvenir shopping?"

We walk downhill toward the city gates, stopping whenever something catches my eye. By the time we're at the grocery store near where the bus is parked, I have five souvenirs in a gift bag. Alex bought a magnet for his mother in the same store.

"Should we restock on any snacks or water while we're here?" He asks me. I check my watch and see we still have a half hour before departure.

"It's a closer walk to carry water than our last grocery stop," I say as I walk toward the entrance. Inside, he finds his favorite crackers, and I find chocolate-covered digestive cookies. I carry the snacks while he carries the water. When he pulls out his credit card to pay, I don't stop him for fear of angering the lengthening checkout line behind us. I may need to sneak a € 20 bill into his backpack later to even the score.

Lawrence and Jean are among the few on the bus when we climb on. "Wasn't that such a neat little town!" Jean says to us as she stands in her seat. "I love seeing all the families, kids, and couples going about their lives as if tourists are as common as the birds. Having world-famous gelato must bring in a lot of people. I would come back just to try that place again."

I look up at Alex, seeing him clearer than I had this morning. He doesn't use my vulnerability or weaknesses against me. If I were a city on a hill, he would be the wall and gates around my heart. Now that I've let him in more than I thought I could, I can see how much he keeps his guard up.

Alex

Richard Morrison is scum. All I can picture is a scared and exhausted Sonnet trying to make sense of the uncontrollable symptoms happening in her body. In the few days and meals we've shared, I know she's conscientious of what she eats and regularly exercises. Her toned muscles and curves suggest years of discipline, not just a temporary lifestyle change due to the wedding or medical diagnosis. In her shoes, I would feel betrayed by my own body. It's a relief that she's abstinent because at least she hasn't had to go through the potential devastation of trying to have a child with that man.

As we drive through the vineyards to the main buildings of Castello Vicchiomaggio, I regret not eating more than gelato in San Gimignano. My snacks may come in handy sooner rather than later. The estate reminds me of the location where my cousin Matteo got married two years ago. When his then-fiancé/now-wife ran the idea of a vineyard wedding by him, he quickly agreed. Matteo loves wine almost as much as he loves her.

Once we all gather in a crowd outside, Brandy introduces herself as the winery tour guide. She leads us into the maturing cellar filled with French oak barriques and large barrels. I listen to Brandy's explanation of the process used to create the wines, but when Sonnet slips her fingers through mine, I'm a lost cause. If Brandy gives us a quiz at the end requiring us to know the difference between Chianti and Chianti Classico wines, I'll only know the answer because my father taught me about Italian wines. He ensured I was a wine expert before I was old enough to order wine in the States.

I glance at Sonnet and smile at the slight confusion on her face. She's just as lost as I am, but she doesn't possess the same background knowledge I have. We've been privy to wine at every dinner, and she has yet to taste more than a sip of any of them. Part of me wants to take on the challenge of finding a wine that she likes.

We walk into the tasting room, and I subtly nod toward the restrooms to ask her if she needs to go. She smiles at me gratefully and lets go of my hand before slipping away toward the women's restroom. I save her a spot next to me across from Lawrence and Jean.

"Watching you two is like watching one of my favorite Hallmark movies," Jean whispers across the table to me. "Have you two talked about how you'll handle things once you're no longer in Italy?"

Jean's question takes me by surprise because it's coming from Jean. My feelings for Sonnet aren't a secret, but I've been so caught up in trying to understand and analyze them that I hadn't made a plan for how to explain them to others on this tour.

Lawrence comes to my rescue and says to his wife, "Maybe we should mind our business concerning their relationship. Real life isn't a Hallmark movie." Oh, how I wish it were.

Sonnet emerges from the restroom and gives me a thumbs up outside Lawrence and Jean's view. In my imagination, I pick her up and spin her in my arms to congratulate her on...not bleeding heavily. My romantic gestures need some work before I execute them. She slips into the booth next to me as Brandy and the other workers pass around trays of bruschetta for each table. Next, they pour wine into our glasses as Brandy explains which one we're tasting and the nuances we should notice in this particular type. Despite her dislike for the wine, Sonnet drinks it all to empty her glass. She seems more interested in the bruschetta but is too polite to decline wine at a wine tasting.

After a few rounds, the others in our group order and inquire about the olive oil. Sonnet stands unsteadily, and my hand instinctively holds her lower back like it had on the Spanish Steps. My alcohol tolerance isn't a problem with the wine and lack of food to absorb it, but Sonnet seems like a lightweight. Whether she knows it or not, she's tipsy from the imbalance of bread and wine on an empty stomach. Her expression is irritated, as if she's upset at the sensation of being tipsy. It's the complete opposite of most people's reactions to the fuzzy numbness that encourages alcoholism.

I lead her outside toward the coach, and she's slightly wobbly. She drank the equivalent of maybe two glasses of wine, but somehow she's mildly inebriated. After helping her up the stairs to the cabin and into her seat, I hand her a bottle of water and the snacks we picked up this morning.

"Eat and drink," I instruct her as I sit next to her and help her open the box of crackers. If she weren't so quick to follow my instructions, I would be force-feeding her. After she's eaten enough to help combat the alcohol in her stomach, she rests her head on my shoulder like she did when she fell asleep yesterday. Within five minutes of the bus leaving the winery, she's asleep. My gaze shifts from her to the landscape out the window and back to her until I also succumb to the drowsiness.

The shops and restaurants of Montecatini-Terme whiz past as I blink my eyes awake. Sonnet stirs next to me before her head lifts and turns toward me, her dark chocolate eyes seizing my attention.

"How are you feeling?" I ask her. If I need to track down a sandwich or a pizza for her, I will.

"Better," she says with a sleepy smile. My promise is the only thing keeping me from kissing that smile. She turns to look out the window at the shops displaying formal dresses and other attire. Historically, the area was founded as a spa town with many mineral springs nearby. For the purposes of our tour, it offers many hotels while being in a central location to many of our upcoming stops.

Our hotel has an outdoor terrace dining area on either side of the walkway to the front entrance. Marisol reads our names and room assignments as we claim our keys and luggage. Sonnet's balance and strength are back to normal, though I follow her to ensure she doesn't need help carrying anything up the stairs. Besides, I have her extra water bottles stashed in my backpack. Her room is a few doors closer to the stairs than mine, making my actions explainable and not overbearing.

"Hey, do you have my waters?" She asks as she unlocks her door. I hold up my finger to indicate I need a moment. To avoid blocking the hallway with my suitcase, I roll it to my room, unlock the door, and stick it inside before turning around to walk back to Sonnet's room. I unzip my backpack and hand her the bottled water.

"I overheard some people talking about going to the pool this afternoon," I say. What I want to say is something along the lines of, *Meet me in twenty minutes so I can spend my afternoon admiring your incomparable beauty under the unfiltered brightness of the Tuscan sun.* But in the wrong context, that is more like a borderline serial stalker than a suave bachelor.

She's contemplative as she mulls over the proposition. "I won't go swimming because my hair takes forever to wash, but sitting by the pool sounds relaxing. Meet me here in fifteen minutes?" The question in her voice is laughable. Not only did I bring it up first, but I won't refuse an offer that means more time with her.

I give her a smile and a nod before rushing to my room to dig through my suitcase. Ten minutes later, I'm in a t-shirt and swimming trunks and pace the hallway outside her room. Because I'm pathetic and too nice to keep her waiting. I'm punctual when I meet up with women that I'm not interested in. When she emerges from her room, she's in a swimsuit coverup and flip-flops. She's holding a beach bag with a towel, water bottle, and book inside. The only thing in my hands is my towel because I will be swimming.

We claim two lounge chairs next to each other, and I empty my pockets of my phone, wallet, and room key.

"Watch my things?" I ask her as I set my towel beside my personal belongings.

"Of course, you don't even need to ask," she says as she slips on her sunglasses and unties the knot that held her cover-up in place. I freeze and keep my eyes down as she shrugs off the thin material. When I know she's lying in the chair, I utilize my self-control and jump in the water rather than allow myself to look at her. The cool water is a soothing balm to the heat of the sun and the warming effect her presence has on me. From the water, I can't see her swimsuit or her toned light-brown legs.

For the moment, I have the pool to myself. I get in a couple of laps before I reanalyze my surroundings. Monet and Maggie, the best friends celebrating their fortieth birthdays in Italy, are setting their towels down on the two empty chairs to the other side of Sonnet. Neither seem eager to join me in the water, so I continue with a few more laps, switching up my stroke to work different muscles. No matter how many times I've offered to pay my family to install a pool at their estate in Treviso, they refuse my request. My nonna claims I don't get any voting power since I don't live in the country.

After ten laps, I swim back to the pool edge where Sonnet reads her book. She's too lost in the story on the pages to notice my proximity.

"Sonnet, I think you have a visitor, and he's very nice to look at," Monet says to break her out of the book world. Monet gives me a wink before returning her attention to her book.

Sonnet sets her book down and sits up to look at me. Realizing it's not close enough, she scoots forward until she's only a foot away from me. Perfectly painted light blue toenails rest inches away as I admire her feet. I've never paid attention to feet, but she has the kind of cute feet that I would massage every night.

"The water feels great if you want to stick your feet in," I say to encourage her closer. "I promise I won't splash you or try to pull you in. I respect you and your curls too much to do that."

I must have said the magic words because she stands and takes a few steps before sitting again with her legs dangling into the water beside me. Her high-waisted bikini is modest compared to what's commonly seen on Italian beaches, but it still shows her smooth, glowing skin. Moles and freckles sprinkle across the light brown of her stomach. Richard Morrison is an idiot. Richard Morrison's mistakes are my gain.

Sonnet

◠◡◠

I feel the flush that overtakes my face at his stare. He's careful not to linger on any body part for longer than appropriate, but I notice how he's trying to count the moles and freckles that decorate my midsection. The water blurs part of his body under the water, but his defined chest is visible. I will forever picture his sculpted muscles anytime I feel them in his hugs.

"Are you done checking me out yet?" I say, shocked by my bluntness.

The sky and the blue water of the pool make the blue of Alex's eyes vibrant as they return to my face. His Adam's apple bobs as his expression morphs into a smirk. "I don't think I could ever be done looking at you, but I should probably stop now for both our sakes."

"I know you're used to hanging out with models, but this is what a normal woman looks like," I tease. "I have a birthmark on my right thigh and a few stretch marks from gaining weight and then losing it again. I also have scars on both my knees from skinning them in middle school—"

"Sonnet, you're the closest thing to perfection I've ever seen," he interrupts before he uses the side of the pool to pull himself up out of the water. There's just enough distance from me that he doesn't accidentally splash me in the effort. If this is his way to get my attention so he can have a serious heart-to-heart with me, it's the wrong move. With his torso out of the water, my entire focus has shifted to his olive-skinned upper body. He's a masterpiece of pectorals, abdominals, deltoids, obliques, and all the other core muscles I forgot after my college anatomy class. Alex takes his fitness as seriously as he's trying to take this conversation.

He snaps in my line of sight to break the spell. "I might need you to put on a shirt," I say, unashamed of my request. Given his stints with modeling, my reaction shouldn't be surprising. Alex has posed shirtless for magazine covers, after all. Rather than putting on his shirt, he pulls his towel off his chair to partially block my view of his body. It's sufficient.

"I'm going to let you in on a secret that isn't really a secret," he says as he bumps his foot against mine in the water. "So much of what you see is airbrushed. When someone looks flawless, they're either wearing a lot of make-up, or there's editing involved. The photo shoots for those shirtless spreads always involved someone specifically designed to oil down my body. It's completely invasive and uncomfortable and part of the job. As for you, I prefer a woman who is curvy over one who is tall and willowy any day of the week."

"You're wrong about one thing," I say as my eyes meet his again. "You look flawless now without make-up, editing, or body oil, and it's entirely unfair. You're not allowed to take off your shirt anymore."

His laugh unleashes the butterflies again, and I lay back and close my eyes to block the sun's brightness. A few seconds later, I sense the warmth of his body mere inches from mine. His fingers reach for mine until I meet him halfway to hold his hand. Holding hands is still new, but we've grown comfortable with physical contact. As comfortable as one can feel while her skin is humming with electricity.

"We should get ready for dinner tonight," his words say although his body makes no move to get up. Neither of us notices Monet and Maggie's absence.

"I hope there's time tomorrow to do this again." He gets up first and holds his hand out to help me up. I throw his shirt at his head to reiterate my former plea. This time, he obliges.

Everyone from our tour group is on the bus for this dinner excursion to an agriturismo. Neither Alex nor I bothered to bring our books for this ride since it'll be dark the entire drive back to the hotel afterward. Not knowing what to expect, I wear a royal blue midi dress with tennis shoes. Alex, per his usual, looks good enough to eat in a non-cannibalistic way. I am very hungry from not eating a proper lunch.

Despite its location in the countryside, our group is only part of the crowd gathered here for dinner. One of Fattoria il Poggio's workers shows us the vineyards and olive trees used to produce their wine and olive oil. In the distance, the sun begins its descent toward the horizon, promising only an hour or two more before dusk. At the end of the tour, our group is led to a long table set for a large party. We each take a seat, mine between Alex and Jean. Monet and Maggie are in the two chairs across from us.

"So, Sonnet, what do you do? Are you still in college, or are you working? I honestly can't quite tell how old you are," Maggie asks with her questions in rapid-fire, so I wait until she's finished.

"I graduated college six years ago," I say as my mind simultaneously tries to organize her remaining questions with the answers. "I work in the marketing division of an architecture firm. And I'm twenty-eight. Both my parents look younger than their ages, so I inherited good genetics."

Monet says, "I never would have guessed you were closer to thirty than twenty, but good for you. Whoever marries you will have a hot wife for many decades." I don't miss the raised eyebrows she directs at Alex with her statement. He takes the gesture in stride despite the uncalled-for remark.

"Sonnet just went through a broken engagement," Jean says to Monet and Maggie as if I weren't sitting beside her. "This was supposed to be her honeymoon, so she still came since any girl deserves to go on a vacation after going through planning and canceling a wedding. If you ask me, honeymoons are the girl's reward for pulling off the impossible." With Alex by my side and holding my hand whenever he can, I forget this was initially my honeymoon. Richard didn't often display jealousy, but there's no doubt he would feel threatened by Alex.

The various dishes of our meal are passed around. My hunger begins to subside with every bite of the delicious fresh food. After trying one sip of the wine that tastes as unappealing as the other wines so far, I stick to water. The server brings out tiramisu and espresso for dessert, following up with shot glasses of grappa. I may be completely sober, but Alex is relaxed from the alcohol. He's not drunk as far as I can discern, but he's talkative and lively with our travelmates around us.

From the open gravel space near our table, music drifts toward us. Others from all the groups trickle onto the rocks to dance. My eyes light up as I watch the dance floor forming.

"Dance with me?" Alex's hot breath tickles my ear with his request. Cue the stupid shivers.

I take his hand and let him lead me to the center of attention as I fight off the sensations of déjà vu. With the space filling up, the DJ plays the "Cupid Shuffle" to encourage the stragglers to join. I move the same I have at so many weddings since the song became popular. Every wedding but my own. Most of us know what to do without further help or instruction. Though some return to their tables or an observation point on the edge, Alex and I are just warming up. The Italian business heir is a practiced dancer as he takes the lead.

In another life, I would have dragged Rich out here with me, but Alex relishes the opportunity to hold me close before he spins me. His breath smells like a mix of espresso and alcohol from the shot of grappa. His hands never stray from my waist, careful not to cross the line. I'm convinced he's so careful with his boundaries that he never allows himself to lose control. The sky around us darkens from sunset to dusk as the lights illuminate and outline the dancing shadows.

Our communication consists of eye contact, body language, and the rhythm of the music.

Alex and I are thirsty and out of breath as he refuses to let go of my hand during our water break. It's as if one of us might disappear or float away if we let go for a second. He maneuvers his hand from mine back to my waist as I take another sip of water.

"Bella donna pazza," his lips graze my ear as he says those words with a new intensity. As if his words weren't enough to set my body on fire, he gently tucks my loose curls behind that same ear. Nothing on his face would suggest he's had a few glasses of wine and a shot; his eyes are hyper-focused on me. The unspoken tug-of-war ends when the song changes to one he recognizes and must like. Ten seconds later, we're back on the makeshift dance floor, engulfed by the magic of racing hearts and the Italian countryside.

THE BUS FILLS with singing and laughter as Marisol manages to herd us onto our ride back to the hotel. Sensing the mood, the bus driver turns up the speakers on the coach and plays classics like "Dancing Queen" by ABBA. It takes several songs before the majority start to quiet down, but there's a buzzing in the air.

"You two are so fun to watch, and so good at dancing," Maggie says to us over a Michael Jackson hit. "I studied dance professionally, and you both have a natural knack for it. Great chemistry, too." Maggie is sidetracked by the chorus before either of us can thank her for the kind words. The high energy tonight may result in a sluggish group tomorrow morning, but no one shows concern for the possible hangovers.

Alex is glued to my side until we reach the door to my hotel room. Moments like this are why he made his promise; without a boundary, we would easily fall into the trap of acting like hormonal teenagers caught up in fevered kisses. This way, we still salvage some semblance of logical thinking amid the tension. As I turn to tell him goodnight, I'm halted by the hunger I see in his eyes. Any doubts I still held about being a mere convenience melt away in the fire of his gaze. His hand reaches up to touch my soft curls before he kisses my forehead and hurries to his room. Alex never allows himself to lose control.

The hour it takes me to shower and go through my nighttime routine is necessary to allow my heart rate to recover. Mentally, I create a to-do list for myself toward a better future:

1. Stop comparing every guy to Richard/Dick/Rich. At this point, most guys will come out looking like a catch when compared to the worst parts of him. Instead, I should be eternally thankful that I saw his true colors before making a lifetime commitment.
2. Stop comparing every guy to my mystery masquerade man. The whole purpose of the experiment was to prove that as long as life didn't get in the way, love at first sight could remain perfect and untouched. He only seems perfect because I never saw the whole picture.

3. Start initiating deeper conversations with Alex. Strong chemistry doesn't always transfer into a strong foundation for a long-lasting relationship. I need to know if we want the same things out of life before this attraction gets in the way.

I send a few photos to my mom and Taylor to update them about my vacation. Less than a minute later, Taylor calls me.

"As happy as I am to hear your voice, the exhaustion from the day is starting to hit," I say to her in warning when I answer.

"Hello to you, too," Taylor says. "I thought about texting you, but I have both good news and bad news depending on how you look at it. Bad news is usually better in person; however, that won't be possible if I'm going to tell you before anyone else does—"

I interrupt, "Taylor, tell me the bad news."

She's eerily silent on the other side, and for a minute, I think we've been disconnected. "Richard is engaged."

The words don't compute. First of all, she called him Richard instead of Dick which is a sign of her own shock. Second, Richard proposed to me seven months ago after two years of dating. We've only been broken up for three months. How is it possible that he's met someone and is already making that commitment in such a short time?

I realize that I have yet to respond and ask, "Do we know who she is?"

"I did some social media snooping, and she matches the description of the girl you caught him with," Taylor says, hesitating. Of course, it's her. That would make sense because he presumably started seeing her while still going along with our wedding plans.

"Well, I'm glad it wasn't all a complete waste then," I say with some sarcasm, though part of me is glad for them. Dick's engagement means he's let go of us, which is exactly what I want. It means I'm free to move on without feeling guilty for doing so this soon. It means there's one less obstacle preventing me from falling for Alex.

Taylor says, "The good news is that my mom managed to get an amazing discount for catering from that brunch place we like. So you can cross food off the list of things needed for my baby shower."

"Dick getting engaged is good news, too," I say in case my reaction wasn't clear. "It's good for me, and I hope it's good for them. I don't even feel upset that it happened so fast. Shocked, yes, but not upset."

"It's hard to be upset about your lousy ex when you've got the sexiest bachelor hanging out with you in Italy," Taylor says, hitting the nail on the head.

I yawn before I can get a response in. It's time to sleep. "Speaking of Italy, there's a time difference that means it's my bedtime. Thank you for looking out for me."

As I close my eyes, my mind doesn't drift to thoughts of Richard's engagement or the baby shower I'm helping to plan. I'm reliving Alex's hands holding mine, on my waist, touching my hair. The last words I think as my mind surrenders to sleep are *Alessandro De Luca*.

Alex

I wake up to skies dark enough to threaten our morning in Florence. Light rain already falls on the balcony outside my room as I choose the navy shirt from my suitcase. The weather and my inability to get up when my first alarm sounded means a morning run is out of the question. At this rate, I need to hurry to walk down to breakfast with Sonnet. While I inspect my rushed shaving job, there's a knock at my hotel room door. Sonnet. This will have to be good enough.

"Give me a few seconds," I yell toward the door as I locate my wallet, keys, and phone. I should have enough time after breakfast to grab my water bottle, umbrella, and backpack before we need to be on the bus. When I open the door, she stands and bites her lower lip. It's a twenty-point deduction from my self-control power bar.

"Do you think the rain will ruin part of the tour today?" She asks as we pass a window in the hallway. So far, the rain hasn't let up since I dragged myself out of bed.

I pull out my phone and open the weather app to check the radar. "Most of it should be done about an hour from now," I say as I watch the clouds move away from our destination for the day. "With breakfast and the drive, it'll be clearing up around when we need it to."

She's satisfied with my answer, and I'm intrigued at how talking about the weather doesn't feel like meaningless small talk with her. The rain keeps us from being able to use the outdoor terrace, but the dining room is too nice to be a consolation prize. There's a consistent line at the automatic espresso machine, most of which are people from our group. My hangover from last night has more to do with the woman standing beside me than anything I drank at dinner. Unlike her, I'm not a lightweight.

Despite the busyness of the breakfast bar, Sonnet finds a secluded table for the two of us. My attempts at gauging her mood this morning are proving futile, so I wait for her to share her thoughts or whatever else women do to get something off their chests. Perhaps she needs a phone call with her best friend rather than a breakfast discussion with me.

"Taylor called last night with some unforeseen news," she says, and I sit silently while waiting for her to continue. "Richard is engaged."

I nearly choke on the sip of coffee I just swallowed. After clearing my throat, I say, "That's a bit soon, isn't it? Let me guess, his fiancée was the other woman in your relationship." Is Richard Morrison unusually attractive or something? How could he be on his second engagement in less than a year?

"Yes, which only adds to the proof that I dodged a bullet by ending our engagement," Sonnet says with a victorious smile. It's borderline scary.

"My other question is, did he propose to her with the same ring he gave you?" It's not a question she's asked herself yet. She pulls out her phone to do a little searching. If I had to guess, she probably blocked him on all social media sites, but he likely didn't block her. A two-year relationship also means they have mutual friends.

Sonnet's facial expression shifts from inquisitive to jaw-dropping to amusement in thirty seconds. "It's the same ring," she says while shaking her head and putting her phone away. "He didn't even have the decency to exchange the ring for a different one."

"Was it at least a nice ring?"

She contemplates her answer before she says, "Nice is a good word for it. It's pretty and a decent-sized diamond, but it wasn't my style. Maybe it was her style, and he gave it to the wrong girl to begin with."

Nothing about Sonnet gives off vibes of being hurt or upset over this news. She's here enjoying what would have been her honeymoon with the man, and she's entirely content with the news that he's marrying the other woman. "I'm beginning to wonder if you ever loved Richard."

My statement is met with a grim smile as she says, "I'm not sure if I ever did either."

"You would know if you had fallen in love with him," I state as my mind flashes to snippets of the one time I fell. It was so hard and fast that I didn't know the damage I had done to my heart until it was too late.

"I guess that's the difference between falling and settling."

The rain hasn't let up when we climb onto the bus. Sonnet watches the cloudy countryside while I hold her hand. Every time I touch her, my body better anticipates the sparks that come with it. I'm becoming acclimated to the effects of our tangible chemistry. She's restless as she fidgets with the zipper on her crossbody bag.

"Have you ever been in love?" She asks me out of nowhere. Or not out of nowhere. As much as we both reason away the growing bond between us, it's headed toward a destination faster than either of us knows how to stop. The only options are to hit the brakes and hope we don't crash or embrace it full-speed ahead.

"There was a girl years ago that I fell head over heels for," I say to her, choosing to open up rather than putting up walls again. "We never really dated, and what we had was very short, but it's taken me years to let go of the idea. Sometimes, the fantasy of someone is almost more heartbreaking than the real thing..."

"Because the fantasy in our heads is often perfect and unrealistic," she finishes as if she read my mind. "Reality will always be disappointing if we have unrealistic standards. That fling I had is so perfect in my head that everything else pales in comparison. I had to fight against that habit of comparing to give Richard a chance."

It's unnerving how accurately she describes my internal battle during most of my twenties. "Well, you're doing better than me, even if Dick was the one you gave a chance to."

Her smile is wry as she shrugs. She discounts how much courage it takes to be willing to give someone a chance. The risks of rejection, betrayal, and hurt are daunting enough, but all those things stacked up against an idealistic picture of romance make it nearly impossible. And yet, I want a partner to build a family with. I want a wife I can hold when she's had a bad day. Or a good day. I want the mess, the misunderstandings, and the making-up after a horrible fight. I want things that are normal in a life that will never be normal.

"Do you want kids?" She asks, moving on to another topic.

"Yes, of course," I say. Remembering yesterday's conversation, I add, "Having kids naturally would be great, but if that's not a viable option, I've always liked the idea of adopting. Even a combination of both biological and adopted children would be nice. My father made a big deal about legacy and how he's not just leaving me monetary assets. He emphasized instilling in me how to sustain and grow that for the generations beyond me. Although he never said it, I think he secretly hoped for a lot of grandchildren. It's hard not to miss him."

She squeezes my hand as a gesture of comfort. Behind her, Firenze comes into view as the sun breaks through the morning's cloud coverage. Perfect timing. Sonnet notices the deviation of my attention and turns to look out the window. She relaxes at the sight of the sky brightening as the rain loosens its grip on the day.

Without breaking her gaze out the window, she says, "When I was younger, I thought I wanted five kids. A short gig as a nanny lowered that number to three. Then, when I had all those concerning symptoms, I knew just one would be a blessing. The older I get, the less sure I am about that aspect of the future. There was no point imagining a future family when I hadn't found someone to start that family with. Even when I was engaged to Rich, I had a hard time seeing it."

But I can picture it. I can imagine Sonnet in a wedding dress walking down the aisle toward me. I can visualize her with a round, pregnant belly and swollen feet that I rub every night. I can see children with dark curly hair and her nose pulling on my pants leg when I come home from work. I'm terrified because I haven't known her long enough to be able to dream about these things so clearly. This vacation has been some strange time warp where each day feels like an entire month of being around her.

"What is your biggest dream?" I ask her because she's the one who started us on this flow of conversation topics.

"I want to write romance novels," she says without missing a beat. "I know it might sound silly—"

"Sonnet, that's not silly at all," I interrupt her. If Richard Morrison told her that her dream was silly, I might punch the man if I ever meet him. "It's not silly if it's your dream. Have you written anything?"

She blushes and says, "A few things, but none of them are ready yet. Something is missing in the stories."

"If you say it's a good sex scene where it's mind-blowing the first time, then I will say it's silly," I tease her. Her face flushes pink with the reaction I was going for.

"Uh, no, no sex scenes in my books," she says as she closes her eyes and tries to hide. "I wouldn't know how to write one of those. If the plot isn't good without one, then it wasn't a good plot. You don't need a sex scene to convey tension."

"Well said." As much as I would love to interrogate her further about her writing, the bus stops as Marisol stands to usher us off.

We follow Marisol through narrow streets and alleys until we round the corner of the Church of Santa Croce. She warns us about gypsies and pickpockets since we're in a bigger city again before delving into the church's history and the piazza. Every June, the piazza hosts the annual Calcio Fiorentino games, a sport that sounds like it could give rugby a run for its money. The game is played in sand and allows both boxing and wrestling. To me, it sounds like multiple concussions waiting to happen.

Once we've crossed to the other side of the piazza, Marisol gives another speech about the history of leather-making in Florence. Counterfeit leather goods are prevalent due to the popularity of genuine leather. She leads us into Peruzzi, a high-end leather store that she vouches as legitimate and quality. I can smell the leather as soon as we walk inside. My mother would go on a shopping spree in a place like this. When I glance at Sonnet, her eyes are alight the way my mother's would be. This is where I'll have to buy her a souvenir.

One of the store clerks greets Marisol and our group. We're standing among the display of leather jackets as the clerk describes the process of creating and dyeing leather. When he pulls a blue leather jacket off the rack, he gestures for Sonnet to be his model. She slips on the soft leather that may as well have been made for her. The group "ooos" and "aaahs" at the well-crafted jacket before the attention shifts to something else the clerk is pointing out. All except Sonnet, who is still admiring the piece. I watch her check the price tag before shrugging it off and hanging it back on the rack. Once I know she's preoccupied with something else, I check the price tag. A few hundred euros is a lot of money for most people, but I'm not most people.

Before following the group upstairs where the shoes are displayed, I arrange a tab with one of the checkout clerks, starting with a purse for my mother and the blue leather jacket. Sonnet will be angry with me for buying her something, but I don't intend to give it to her directly. On the second floor, people are spread out among the various shoe sections. I find Sonnet as she's eyeing a pair of gold accent oxfords on sale.

"You should try them on," I say to encourage her, but she jumps at the sound of my voice.

"There you are. You scared me," she says before contemplating the shoes again. "I don't know if these are in my size. I don't typically buy in European sizes and have no idea where to start."

"What's your US shoe size?" An employee walks up to us. His features are a unique mix of Japanese and something else, not a commonality in Italy. Then again, Sonnet also seems to be a mix of multiple nationalities and races. Some of the most attractive people I've ever met are mixed, the features of their parents combined in the best way possible. I wonder what her parents look like and who gave her those big chocolate eyes.

While my mind is elsewhere, Sonnet picks up the pair of shoes and sits on one of the benches while the employee disappears. He returns with insoles and slips them into the oxfords. When he hands them back to her, she tries on the shoes. It's then that I notice that the soles are wooden. The discounted price must be within her budget because she hangs onto the shoes once she has her own back on.

"Find something you like?" I ask her as I nod toward her bounty.

"I've been buying souvenirs for all my friends and family, but I hadn't thought about buying something to bring back for myself until I saw these. They're a great price for genuine leather," she says as she beams.

While I would be content with the things I already set aside, Sonnet refuses to return to the first floor until I've tried on a pair of shoes in my size. And she's right. My existing collection of Italian leather shoes could always use an addition. Every time I wear these in the future, I'll think about her. I hand the shoes to the same clerk holding my other items and pay while she pays for her shoes with another clerk. We arrange to pick up our bags later after we've finished our tour of the city.

Outside, Marisol introduces us to our local guide for the morning, Marco. Though the monuments and buildings in Florence aren't as easily recognizable as those in Rome, I pinpoint Palazzo Vecchio in the distance. On our way there, Marco leads us past the Baroque-style Complesso di San Firenze, the Museo Casa di Dante, and the unmistakable medieval red domes of the Cattedrale di Santa Maria del Fiore. Standing in the Piazza Del Duomo, the cathedral stretches to the sky with its colossal presence. Scaffolding is a sign of current preservation efforts on the facade of one of the domes.

Though not nearly as massive, the Baptistry of Saint John sits nearby as one of the oldest buildings in the city. The east doors are a copy of the internationally renowned *Gates of Paradise*. Several locations also hold copies of the original, many of which I've seen. Although not the original, seeing the doors on the building for which they were crafted gives the art its full context. Each of the ten panels depicts a different scene from the Bible. I may not be Catholic, but the majority of art and iconic architecture in Italy is a constant reminder that I need to go back to church.

We walk the Florentine streets until the Piazza Della Signoria opens and engulfs us in its history and art. Art that makes me glad I'm not here with my mother. Art that I would rather not inadvertently be compared to.

"Mmm, famous naked statues, just what we needed to add spice to this tour," Sonnet says quietly enough that I'm the only one who can hear her. She quells my annoyance by grabbing my hand to link our fingers together.

The Fountain of Neptune is the first sculpture on the list. It was created by one man and designed by another as a wedding gift for a Medici. The second statue is a copy of *Michelangelo's David*, a marble masterpiece created by a man as the name suggests. Before the original was displayed in the Palazzo Vecchio, it had been intended for a roofline of the Florence Cathedral. In Italy, no one questions naked art in churches.

"It's impressive that Michelangelo could sculpt a larger-than-life statue with parts of the body fairly proportionate," I say, careful not to make an inappropriate joke.

Sonnet's lips are tight as if she's doing so to keep herself from responding with something inappropriate. But now I want to know what she's thinking, even if it makes things awkward. I raise my eyebrows at her in question. She shakes her head and squeezes her eyes to block out my nonverbal inquiry.

I take advantage of her inability to see and touch my lips to her ear as I say, "Please tell me what you're thinking." She shivers involuntarily at the contact, and I back away to give both of us much-needed space.

She opens her eyes, refusing to make eye contact with me. "I was thinking that your chest and abs are just as sculpted as David's."

A grimace overtakes her face as a flush takes over mine. Then, I laugh because I don't know how else to react to her words. Over the years, I've received a lot of comments and compliments due to the shirtless magazine spreads, but hearing it from a woman who just saw me shirtless at the pool yesterday makes the sentiment authentic. Sonnet isn't hanging off me trying to seduce me. She's blushing and bashful as we move toward the third sculpture.

Hercules and Cacus was finished by the same man who designed *The Fountain of Neptune*. It features an unclothed man and a fire-belching monster that looks like a naked man. This one does not inspire strange reactions or compliments from Sonnet; however, we still have the statues displayed in the Loggia dei Lanzi.

She's unamused by *The Rape of the Sabine Women* due to the name, which may be a misnomer due to the translation from Latin.

"The same word in Latin is translated as rape, kidnapping, or abduction," I say to her in explanation.

She turns to me for the first time since her embarrassing confession and says, "Do you honestly believe that ancient Roman men abducted young women from other regions and didn't touch them in any way? Men who abduct women in present times rarely keep their hands to themselves, and they'll actually be punished if they're caught, unlike in centuries past."

I do not argue because she's right; history has not been kind to women. "From what I remember of the legend, they did marry the women," I say, though it doesn't forgive the incident. "The women were the ones who stopped their husbands and fathers from killing each other in battle and instead united them as one nation. Those Sabine women certainly weren't weak." Sonnet gives me a small smile to thank me for my effort, though futile.

Perseus with the Head of Medusa is a nude man killing Medusa. Because it's completely logical to kill a Gorgon without any sort of protective armor. I appreciate that her head faces three men made of stone, though. That was well thought out by whoever decided where the statues should be placed.

"No comment?" I ask Sonnet as she takes photos of the bronze sculpture.

"I would be killing the source of the snakes, too, if I had been in his shoes," she says and shrugs. "Your abs are better than his, though." I shake my head at her bluntness as we continue our rounds through the covered exterior gallery.

When we reach *The Rape of Polyxena*, I say, "Rape literally means kidnapping or abduction here. One of the key aspects of Polyxena's character was her virginity."

"Well, that's one way to die," she says as she turns her head to inspect all angles of the art piece. "At least we can't accuse the Romans or Florentines of censorship. And look, there are clothed statues and a few lions."

"Ready to go look at an old bridge?" I ask her as I pull her toward the Arno River.

Unamused, she says, "That was a terrible joke."

Sonnet

꘎

Ponte Vecchio sounds fancy to the English-speaking ear; however, literally translated, it means "old bridge." While it is that, it's a unique bridge because shops are built along it. It was the only bridge to survive World War II, so maybe "old bridge" is the proper name for it.

"It's a welcome reprieve after the bronze and marble erections in the piazza," I say before I realize the double entendre in my words. "No, that's not what I meant!"

Alex loses all composure and doubles over with laughter. At least one of us is getting entertainment out of my mortification. I may not be thrilled with my pun, but the sound of his laughter reduces the desire to run away. It's a laugh that reverberates through my own body like a siren's call beckoning me to my death. His laugh doesn't change who he is outside this fantasy. The tale of Alex De Luca is more likely to end in my broken heart than a happily ever after.

"I know it wasn't intentional, but that's the best pun either of us could have come up with," he says once he's caught his breath enough to talk again. "We should go back to the piazza and get lunch. Perhaps one of the restaurants on the opposite side of the statues. I'd rather not risk Medusa turning my food into stone."

As he leads me toward my next pizza with his hand in mine, I fight all the thoughts and hormones that want to make him a permanent fixture. My self-preservation reminds me of the boys I liked before the masquerade ball, the unrequited feelings. Ten days isn't long enough to fall in love or bet a lifetime on. It's over ten times longer than my time with the masquerade mystery man, but it doesn't scratch the surface compared to two years of dating. Despite the two years with Richard, I didn't see the red flags until we were engaged. Ten days isn't long enough.

The respite from the rain is temporary as the sun beats down on us. Alex requests a table with an umbrella to give us some shade. The male hostess has a ring on his left hand, so I know it isn't Alex's charming smile that gets us a good spot this time. In the States, he could walk into any restaurant, and they would be clamoring for his business. If not his face, his name is enough to incite special treatment. Here in the fantasy, he's just like every other patron.

"Let me guess, you're ordering pizza again," he says as I peruse each menu page. I know what I want, but I had to make sure it was something on their menu before ordering it.

"And you're not?" I ask with one eyebrow raised.

He makes a show of glancing at every page of their menu as I had before he closes it, sighs, and says, "You're a terrible influence on me."

"You can swim it off later if you're that concerned about preserving your physique," I say. "Plus, authentic Italian pizza isn't nearly as bad for you as the typical pizza in America."

"I work out so I can eat as much as I want of any pizza. Or any dessert that I want. I'm not concerned about my abs." He's teasing as he crosses his arms and smiles at me. I showed my hand with my confession earlier, and now he's using it as a joke at my expense. That's the last time I comment about his muscles. If only I could fully convince myself of that.

We both eat pizza because carbs are what give our bodies energy. Originally, we were supposed to be on an optional museum excursion, but the museum is closed for reasons I missed. Unfortunately, one of the cons to Alex's distracting presence is that I sometimes miss details. With two more free hours, we venture to some shops near the piazza. The leather trinkets I buy to add to the souvenirs may not be genuine, but my friends won't know the difference.

"You're not going to buy anything?" I ask Alex as he joins the checkout line empty-handed. What I want to ask is, *Are you only here to keep me company?*

"I found a nice purse for my mom at Peruzzi," he says as he inspects the leather bookmark on display. "None of my guy friends care much about souvenirs, so she's the only one I needed to find something for."

As nonchalant as his statement is, it makes me sad. It's been a while since I've had any close guy friends, so it's hard for me to say whether his assumption about his is correct. He hasn't mentioned any of them by name throughout this vacation. Is it because he keeps his friends at arm's length or because he's keeping me at arm's length?

My eyes need a few seconds to adjust to the sunlight outside the shop as Alex takes the bag from my hands to carry it for me. It's such a simple gesture, but it feels intimate. I ensure it's not heavy due to suitcase weight limits and the new shoes I bought at Peruzzi. Using some of my toiletries may free up space, but it'll be a close call. The disadvantage to traveling alone is not having someone else's suitcase to move things into if needed. Richard's capsule wardrobe would have left more space for me to fill.

"Do you live with your mom, or do you have your own mansion somewhere?" I ask Alex, despite how strange the question is. I try to imagine him in his own bachelor pad or penthouse apartment in whichever city he resides most of the time.

"That's one of those decisions that's been up in the air since my father passed away," Alex says, and I can see the door he's opened with that admission.

I mentally shuffle through multiple starting points before I settle on one. "Where were you living before your father died?"

"I have a penthouse apartment in a luxury apartment building, which you likely assumed," he says with resignation. Part of him must hate that he fits the stereotype in any way. "When my father passed away, I stayed at their

185

house with my mom until we flew here to Italy for the funeral. Having my own apartment has its perks, but it's also lonely. I needed time and space away from my dad since we worked together. Now that he's gone, nothing is keeping me from moving back so my mom isn't in the house alone. There's a separate suite on the property roughly the same size as my apartment but with more privacy."

"That sounds like a good arrangement then," I say in agreement. "I'm sure your mom would appreciate having you close given all you've been through. Plus, cooking for one takes as much time and effort as cooking for two or more."

Even if he decides to stay in his apartment, it feels like an accomplishment that I could be a listening ear and sounding board. Rich often informed me of decisions he made after the fact rather than discussing them with me beforehand. Throughout our engagement, I made a point to ask for his opinion on wedding details to show I valued his input. He never caught onto the hint.

"So, what about you? Do you live in an apartment or house with roommates?" Alex asks me as we round the corner back into the square of famous statues. Do the city residents get used to seeing this kind of art regularly?

"I live in a house that my grandmother left to me when she died," I say as Alex leads us toward a gelateria. "No roommates currently. Taylor lived with me for about two years before she got married. Dick was supposed to move in after the wedding, but since there was no wedding, I still have the house to myself. I've thought about fixing up the house and selling it, but I hate the idea of living in an apartment with loud neighbors again. Rent certainly hasn't gotten cheaper over the past few years either."

It's not until we're looking at gelato flavors that I remember yesterday's false alarm and the lack of any today. This time, the thought of using the restroom has nothing to do with possible bleeding and everything to do with the water we drank during lunch. I gesture to the restroom to let him know where I'm going.

"Everything good?" He asks me with poorly masked concern when I return to his side.

"Everything is good," I say with a nod and a smile as I give the gelato options the attention they deserve.

The shop has a basement with limited seating, but we take our chances as we venture down the wooden stairs. Raucous laughter echoes as we're greeted by Leo, Carlotta, Lawrence, and Jean. Leo has a glass of red wine in his hand. He drinks wine so often that his wineglass may as well be another appendage. I would tell him it doesn't turn into water once he drinks it, but I doubt that joke would go over well.

"Leo, you know that wine doesn't turn back into water when you drink it, right?" Alex says, and everyone laughs at the joke. He stole my joke that I hadn't even had the chance to share with him. I don't know whether to be angry or alarmed that he read my mind.

"Come, sit down," Jean orders as she gestures to the two open chairs at the small table next to theirs.

As we sit, I notice none of the others have wine or gelato in front of them. Depending on how long they've been sitting in this basement, any food they bought could be long eaten by now. Leo's wineglass is never a consistent way to measure how much time has passed.

I'm about to ask what was so funny earlier when Leo says, "I was just telling them that I got my niece a keychain replica of *Michelangelo's David* as a way to embarrass her. She's a lawyer in Chicago."

A keychain of a statue of a naked man. Am I the only one who finds it strange that someone thought to create that? Then again, Taylor is the sort of person to get a good laugh from a gag gift like that. She was an art major during her first semester at college before she switched to interior design. She's also Taylor, who told me to kiss an Italian while I'm here. Without her, I wouldn't break out of my comfort zone as often as needed. Taylor will flip when I get the chance to tell her about all my blunders today.

Alex and I might as well be bystanders as we eat gelato and observe the two couples interact. Leo and Carlotta are opposite that of Lawrence and Jean in that they met in high school and married shortly after. At nineteen, they were certain that they wouldn't find a better fit than each other. Decades later, it's worked out well for them. It could be that once they committed, they no longer gave themselves any other option. After what I've been through, the dream is to be someone's only choice.

Another fact about Alex is that his parents stayed married until his father's death. It's something we have in common, minus the dead father aspect. My parents have a marriage that fuels my desire to find the same.

"Are you ready to go get our things from Peruzzi?" Alex whispers in my ear as the clock on the wall signals twenty minutes until our group is expected at Piazza Santa Croce. Alex's shopping bag is noticeably larger than mine, but his mom could be one of those women who carry around large purses. I've gone through those phases myself.

Per Marisol's earlier warnings, the gypsies wander through the piazza as the others trickle in. Due to the absence of an afternoon excursion, Florence was more relaxed and low-key than the constant moving in Rome. Here, I don't need to see everything all at once. There aren't endless lines of cars fighting for limited spots or double parking when they can't find any.

None of us escape the city without a purchase made of leather. My eyes grow heavy as our coach journeys back to our hotel. I see the appeal of taking midday breaks as the Italians are known to do. Carbs, gelato, and walking in the sunshine all contribute to the desire for a nap. Peeking at Alex, I notice his eyes are already closed. He's beautiful when he sleeps, but not as beautiful as when he smiles.

Alex

With tonight's dinner arrangements taking place at the hotel, the afternoon of rest is extra long. After swimming a few laps in the pool, I jump out and lounge in the chair next to Sonnet's. The poolside is more crowded today, giving us little privacy. I remind myself that being alone with her in a swimsuit would be counterproductive to keeping my promise to her. Tomorrow's agenda includes hours of sitting on the bus with a stop in Pisa and likely another one for lunch.

Since I have a connection to the Wi-Fi out here, I type out a text to my mom.

> Would you be okay with my moving into the guest suite permanently? I don't think it makes sense for me to continue paying so much for rent when the suite is more than sufficient for just me.

I send it to get the ball rolling, not expecting a response right away. To my surprise, my phone lights up with a notification a few minutes later.

MAMMA

You and I both know it has nothing to do with saving money, but I would love it if you stayed with me longer. I'll ensure enough room in storage if you need to move anything in there. When are you coming home?

Home. It's been years since anywhere has felt like home, but it seems to fit as I think about my mother there waiting for me. Home is more about the people than the place. I mull over her question, unsure of the answer. I have yet to book the return ticket home. All I know is that I can't stay here indefinitely either. Next to me, Sonnet is submerged in another romance novel, oblivious to the inner turmoil I've hidden from her. While it's better now that one uncertainty has been settled, my soul remains restless when face to face with the future.

When I look into her eyes, I see the same fears that cloud my ability to move forward. It takes a considerable amount of my strength to hold back from her when my heart longs to be tethered to the real thing rather than a fading memory.

"Looks like I'll be moving out of my penthouse once I fly back to the States," I say to Sonnet to break her out of the literary reverie.

"I was hoping that would be the outcome," she says with a triumphant smile. "Family is important, and you two need each other as you go through the grief. It's not something that we're meant to go through alone."

"Now, when I create an online dating profile, I can add 'lives with mom' to my narrative," I say, but the joke falls flat. I don't want to try online dating any more than I want to say goodbye to Sonnet in less than a week.

She deserves so much more than a long-distance relationship with a workaholic. Sonnet is worthy of the moon and songs written about her from a husband who pampers her so much she stops arguing with him about it. Because there's no way she'll let a man spoil her without putting up a fight initially. Whether she's stubborn and fiery or vulnerable and broken, she deserves a man who will love all the pieces that fit together into the most captivating woman I've ever encountered.

Once she's past the awkwardness of my failed one-liner, she says, "As common as online dating has become in our culture, to me, it still feels like a last desperate resort. My problem with it is that someone can look perfect on paper or in text, but in person, there's either no chemistry, or he turns out to be a cheating ex-fiancé after two years. A connection is more than a list of common interests and goals. A person is more than their profile picture."

In one sentence, she summarized why I've distanced myself from all dating apps. The other unspoken reason is the irrational fear of coming across the girl from over seven years ago. If she were on an app, would we match or pass each other unknowingly like ships in the night? I've always assumed I would recognize her right away or vice versa, but every year that passes, my mind becomes fuzzier as I attempt to recall the details.

"I certainly hear more horror stories than success stories where online dating is concerned," I say. "My friends are fairly decent guys ninety percent of the time, and they've gone on dates with women who could inspire characters for psychological thrillers. Dating can fairly be compared to the Hunger Games."

"Because women are thirsty or because they treat men like a piece of meat?" She says, pulling out all the puns.

"Because you'll be lucky to come out alive, let alone with someone from your district. You have to be wary of both serial daters and serial killers just to find someone that you might be able to consider a lifetime with. You and I are too old-school for that mad world."

She takes a breath and releases the air slowly as she lies back in the lounger. "Too many options on our screens and not enough opportunities for organic meetings. Being an introvert doesn't help the situation at all."

I lie back to mirror her posture. "Being an extrovert isn't much easier when you're looking for something long-term and stable."

Her stomach growls—the first sign that it's later than either of us realized. I glance at my watch, noting there's just enough time to shower before dinner. She notices the time as well and grabs her book and unused towel.

"Why did you bring a towel if you weren't planning to swim?" I ask her as we walk back inside the hotel.

"In case you decide to stop playing nice," she says with a smile I can't quite decipher. Did she want me to pull her into

193

the water with me? She either has too much or too little faith in my self-control.

I hop in the shower while the water is still cold because the sun and Sonnet are hot. Is this what women mean when they call someone a "hot mess"? I feel like a hot mess who can't think straight. The solid black line between want and need is fading with every passing day around her. I want to be the good guy who lets her go and doesn't upend her life for my selfish desire to make her my everything for the rest of my life.

During dinner, others in our group discuss the possibility of exchanging contact information to keep in touch after the tour. My schedule is often so packed that I hardly remember to keep in touch with my friends, let alone strangers who will be strangers again. I glance at Sonnet to read her reaction, to gauge whether giving her my phone number at the end of this is inviting the worst possible anxiety. It would be torture waiting to see if she calls or texts. Absolute, beautiful torture. It's fairly reasonable compared to the idea of escorting her home before flying back to my own city.

Some go as far as to suggest we all go on another European tour together next summer. Sonnet meets my eyes and gives me a sad smile, knowing it would be impossible for me. Work and increased notoriety will make many things difficult or impossible for me once I become the official face of De Luca Enterprises. It's pure luck that Sonnet is the only one among us who has figured out who I am, given that my face is on a billboard in Rome. And it wasn't even the billboard that tipped her off.

"What about you?" I ask her quietly. When her expression turns to one of confusion, I clarify, "What will be your next vacation or adventure?"

Sonnet is taken aback by the question. Surely, she has an extensive travel list that only planning and budgeting can accomplish.

"It's not that I don't have places that I want to see," she says, "but most are places that I don't want to travel to alone. I wasn't supposed to come here by myself, but it was nonrefundable, and with it being a travel group, I'm only alone at night. My best friend is married with a baby on the way, and my other friends are also moving in the same direction. I assumed my husband would be my travel companion starting with the honeymoon, but alas."

Hearing her mention the honeymoon turned Italian escape, I'm hit with another curiosity. "Since this was your original idea for a honeymoon destination, where would you go for your honeymoon if you were to get married a year from now?"

The gears in her head turn as they cycle through the options on her list. "Definitely something less exhausting than this tour. I'm unsure what I thought when I looked at the itinerary, but I certainly didn't consider the honeymoon activities. Jet lag and early morning wake-up calls are not the ideal environment for newlyweds." I nearly spit out my drink at her statement.

"But this tour does include plenty of wine and the romantic atmosphere," I say to play devil's advocate.

"I don't know if you've noticed, but I don't really care for the wine," she says, dripped in sarcasm but as if it were a big secret. We've all noticed that she prefers water and coffee.

"Fine, but your future husband might enjoy the wine before he enjoys you," I say. Her face flushes red at the insinuation. I'm struggling to keep my body language neutral as my mind fights to keep from imagining myself in the scenario with her. A tour like this would be a terrible honeymoon.

She takes a few bites of her food and a few sips of water. Finally, she asks, "Where would you go on a honeymoon then, since you seem to have a better idea than me?"

"Southern Italy is gorgeous," I say as I remember a weekend trip with my cousin for his bachelor party. "I would spend at least three or four days on the island of Capri off the coast near Napoli. Mornings sleeping in and lazy days on the beach or swimming. Then, after we're adjusted to the time difference, we can venture onto the mainland and explore Napoli and Pompeii and maybe a few other places at our own pace."

"That sounds perfect," she says as another round of tiramisu is dispersed among us. Neither of us seem to be tired of the dessert yet as we savor the taste. After the dessert, we are physically tired from our time spent in the Tuscan sun.

Sonnet

> Code red. I repeat, code red.

I measure how long it takes for Taylor to call. One minute. My best friend is impressive regularly and excessive when I'm in need.

"Did you kiss him?" She asks when I accept the call.

"No, but it's worse," I groan as I fall onto my bed. I had the foresight to shower and change into pajamas before lighting the Batman signal.

"Well, if you didn't kiss him, I'm assuming you didn't do *other* things with him," she says as she tries to piece together the source of my distress. "Did you tell him that you're in love with him?"

I pause at her inquiry. "What makes you think that I'm in love with him?"

"Because the last time you used a code red, it was when you thought you were in love with Nate, the guy you liked before you went to that masquerade ball," she says in one long sentence without taking a breath. "You didn't even use code red when Dick cheated on you three months before your wedding. It's always an emergency signal that you're falling for someone, even though all you want when you're not in love is to be in love. I love you, but you're a walking contradiction in your love life."

"I forgot about Nate. Whatever happened to him?" The memory of a past unrequited attraction sidetracks me from the immediate panic.

"Sonnet, Nate is gay," Taylor says. Right, what an embarrassing way to find out I was entirely wrong in reading that situation. "Back to code red. I need you to spill everything going through your head, no filters and no holding back on me. Give me all the mess to sort through."

I take a deep breath and begin, "He's thoughtful—"

"And hot," she interrupts.

"Taylor, if I'm going to do this, you can't interrupt me. Just because I didn't start with hot doesn't mean it wasn't on the list. Of course, he's hot. It's worse when we're by the pool, and his shirt is off. He looks like a male model; he *is* a male model, so no touching up or editing is needed. He makes me laugh a lot since we have a similar sense of humor. He can somehow sense when to push me to open up or when to give me space. Sometimes, when we talk, it's as if we're the same person even though so much in our lives is as opposite as it could be. He loves to read books. And—"

I stop mid-sentence as my eyes catch the blue leather jacket hanging over the chair at the small desk. Someone else has been in this room. Ignoring Taylor's objections to my sudden silence, I peel myself off the bed to further inspect the foreign object. It's the same blue leather jacket I had unwillingly put back on the rack at Peruzzi this morning. Five hundred euros of gorgeous azure. Alex.

"He bought me the jacket," I say with mixed feelings. "I told him I didn't want him buying me anything, but he bought it for me anyway."

"Good, I like him," Taylor says, and I roll my eyes and shake my head despite this being an audio-only call.

"Taylor, I didn't want any gifts from him. If there's no future for us, I don't want physical reminders of him. It only makes it harder to move on. I need to confront him about this so that he doesn't think this is okay. Sorry, but I have to go before he falls asleep." I hang up, grab the leather jacket and my key card, and make a beeline for Alex's room.

I knock firmly, but not too loudly in case others on the floor are already sleeping. If he's out too, I might not be able to hold onto this fury until morning. I know I won't be able to muster this much determination after a night of sleep. When Alex opens the door, he's in his pajama pants, shirtless chest exposed. I must stay angry. I lift the leather jacket to his line of sight to explain my sudden appearance at his door.

"Consider it a thank you for helping me talk out my living situation," he says nonchalantly as if he weren't ignoring my wishes with this purchase.

"I asked you not to buy me anything," I say a little louder than I mean to. Alex holds up a finger and disappears back

199

into his room. A few seconds later, he's wearing a shirt and slippers. He gently grabs my elbow, and I follow him through the hallway. We walk down the stairs to a dimly lit lounging area on the main floor of the hotel away from possible sleeping guests or eavesdroppers. This area is deserted due to the time of night.

He sits in one of the armchairs and says, "Would you like to take a seat so we can talk this out?"

I cross my arms in defiance but sit in the other armchair. "Why couldn't you follow this one request?"

"Because I saw how you looked at that jacket after checking the price tag. I understand that the money is a big deal to you, but—"

"Alex, it's not about the money," I interrupt. "The jacket could have cost a tenth of that price or ten times that price, and I would still be upset that you bought it for me. I didn't want you to buy me anything because it'll remind me of you every time I see it." I stand since I'm too worked up to remain seated. Seconds later, he's standing and pulling me against his chest in a hug.

"Sonnet, I know. I understand. I'm terrified, too." His voice is near a whisper as he temporarily soothes my worries. "This is uncharted territory for both of us, and you're not the only one in this."

Though all he says and does as he holds me screams, "I'm falling for you too," he doesn't confirm the suspicion with his words. While the last thing I want or need is empty words, I long to hear him say what my heart insists with every beat. I long for a promise of a possibility beyond this vacation.

Wordlessly, we walk back up the stairs and toward our rooms. I keep the jacket and watch him unlock his door and walk in before crawling into my bed. Taylor sent me a final text in the time I was with Alex.

TAYLOR

Love is worth being brave for.

AFTER A DEEP, dreamless sleep, I'm confronted by another morning of packing for the next destination. The advantage and disadvantage of having a maximum of two nights in any hotel is that you never truly settle in. I neatly fold the blue leather jacket and place it in my suitcase knowing that I won't get the chance to wear it while I'm here. It's a jacket meant for a crisp autumn day with a hot vanilla latte.

On cue, Alex knocks on my door to walk me to breakfast. I open the door to let him know I need another minute or two, but my brain short-circuits when I see him. I'm not sure what I'll miss more—the spread of pastries with automatic espresso machines or the mouthwatering man who keeps me company.

"I can wait a few minutes so you can finish getting your suitcase packed," he says as he sees the pile of toiletries sitting on the bed behind me.

"As much as I love traveling, I'm not a fan of living out of a suitcase," I say as I rearrange my shoes to fit the toiletry bag among my clothes. Years of loading the dishwasher as a teenager prepared me for moments like this.

Alex silently watches me from the door with a soft smile. It's butterfly-inducing to see him look at me like that. I can't help but smile back and grab the hand he holds out for me after I've rolled my suitcase to the hallway. Rich never made me feel like I was floating. Why did I say yes to his proposal if it didn't make me feel like this?

I limit myself to one cappuccino this morning due to the long bus ride on today's schedule. While there will be at least two stops, I'd rather not have to use the bathroom on the bus.

"Do you want to go up to the Tower of Pisa?" Alex asks me as he sips his second macchiato. "There's not much else to do there apart from walking around the Piazza dei Meracoli and going inside the Duomo. If you want my opinion, this is the one tower we should climb."

"Then let's do it," I say, glad that he made the decision this time. "As long as I get my conventional selfie with the tower in the background before or after we go up, I'm good with whatever."

He teases, "So easy to please as long as you've had coffee and food."

"And an excellent book. You can't forget the book. I'm not good company if I'm bored." I could never be bored when I'm around Alex.

"You don't need a book when you have me as your travel buddy and places to explore," he says with complete confidence. That's what makes him so attractive; he doesn't feel the need to compensate for anything. Some guys are loud and obnoxious to try to attract attention. Others flaunt their money to seem wealthy. When Rich felt threatened by another guy, he was a combination of both those extremes. I ignored it because I could see right through it, but it didn't increase my respect for him.

For the first few minutes of the ride to Pisa, I watch the town as it flashes past and disappears. There won't be any poolside afternoons for the remainder of this vacation, but it's a small sacrifice. When I reach to pull my book out of my backpack, Alex stops me.

He asks, "Instead of reading, why don't we play a game?"

"Go on," I say as I lean back in my chair sans romance novel.

"We ask the other five questions that must be answered, alternating back and forth. We each get one pass, but then another question can be asked in its place." It's the perfect opportunity to better gauge whether this connection has a chance of survival in the wild.

"Who gets to go first?" I ask. "That's not one of the questions, obviously."

"Obviously," he says with a smile. "You can go first."

I start with the one that has popped into my mind the most over this trip. "If you weren't the heir and future CEO of De Luca Enterprises, what would you want to do with your life?"

The corner of his mouth quirks into a smirk as he thinks through his response. "Maybe marketing or a literary agent. I enjoy books, and I think I would enjoy promoting authors and marketing their books. Or I could start my own publishing house and sign you as an author. De Luca

Publishing. Honestly, I'd probably be happy working in a library or bookstore, assuming money isn't an issue."

"Ah, yes, the world of marketing," I say with slight sarcasm. "Marketing books could be fun, though. The publishing houses in the books I read always sound like fun places to work, even if it's also crazy busy."

"Okay, my turn. Why haven't you been doing any writing while on this vacation?"

His question catches me off guard, though it shouldn't have. I've asked myself the same thing each time I open my tablet and keyboard. Why haven't I been writing?

"I haven't written anything since the engagement. With all the planning and the doctor's appointments followed by the wedding cancellations, I didn't have time to spare to sit down. Even if I had the time, I didn't feel particularly inspired. Then, when the dust of the breakup settled, I didn't know what to write. It can be difficult to write romance while recovering from a failed relationship. I brought my tablet and keyboard with me in case Italy sparked a good story. My mind has been so busy trying to process that it hasn't quite calmed enough for me to get down anything useful."

He raises one eyebrow and says, "Perhaps you should be writing to process and organize what's going through your head. If you waited until your mind was clear and you felt inspired, you would never accomplish anything. Even if you write and your first idea is terrible, you're at least doing something."

"Fine," I say with a sigh. "After we've completed our five questions, I will force myself to write while you return to reading. I can't imagine the drive from Pisa to Venice will be brief."

"We have ourselves a deal. Hit me with your second question whenever you're ready."

It doesn't take me long to fabricate one that could be revealing. "What is your biggest regret?"

Alex

I'm tempted to use my pass on this question, but it feels too early to risk it. Unlike some, my biggest regret is something I think about at least once a day, even if it stings less than it did immediately after.

"My biggest regret is not pursuing the girl I was in love with. I had told myself that walking away was the selfless thing to do, but I was afraid of trying and failing to make it work. So, I walked away. By the time I realized what a big mistake I had made, it was too late. I have no way of finding her; otherwise, I might have tried years ago. The only thing I can do now is try to not make the same mistake." As I say the words aloud, my heart screams that letting Sonnet go would be the equivalent of making the same mistake.

"Sounds like your younger self missed out on an epic rom-com moment," she says with a hint of teasing.

I shrug and say, "A big gesture followed by a potentially difficult relationship. It certainly would not have been a precursor to the 'happily ever after.' More like the first page

206

or chapter of the story in the grand scheme. There's no guarantees that it wouldn't have been a tragedy in the end."

"There's never a guarantee in life, though. Sometimes engagements end or shortly after the wedding, one of them is diagnosed with a terminal disease. Or a child dies, and it drives them apart. Any number of things can happen, but at least they tried. Half of marriages might end in divorce, but half of them still survive until one of them dies. That's a bigger chance at growing old with someone than you get if you walk away before the end of the prologue."

I look at her as she gives her speech, and I don't see a heartbroken woman who would have been married by now had circumstances been different. I see someone who tried and failed but is willing to try again if it means finding what she's looking for.

Remembering it's my turn again, I fish around my head through the numerous options. I settle on one and ask, "If I were to talk to your friend Taylor, how would she describe you?"

It's unnerving how much I want to kiss the smile that spreads across her face at the question. I imagine it would taste how it looks, a mix of sweet and savory, like eating maple bacon crepes. There's no doubt that she would be addicting to my poor emotions that are wrapped up in her. My heart is close to surrendering any willpower it has left to keep me from falling head-over-heels for her.

"If I had to guess, I think she would describe me as cautious but stable and loyal. I won't always be the one to initiate or join in on the spontaneous plans. When I do, though, I'm a lot of fun. It's just hard for me to be fully present if I know there are things I need to get done at home. Responsibilities first, entertainment later."

"I believe that's called being an adult," I say tongue-in-cheek. "But seriously, it sounds like you're the one people can count on. Without responsible people, no one would have what they need when they need it. It's a sign of maturity when someone chooses delayed gratification over what's fun now. When there are kids and pets in the picture, a guy would rather be with the responsible girl than the spontaneous one." Or at least, I would rather be married to someone stable and dependable.

She shrugs as she says, "It is what it is. It's who I am, and I don't see any reason to change it. I'm getting too old to go out every night and be functional the next day at work."

I laugh because I refuse to plan any social activities during the week for the same reason. Usually, I'm at the office so late my bed is the only place I want to be afterward. Now that I'll be moving home again, dinner with my mom will likely lure me out of the office earlier in the evening.

As her third question, she asks, "Since you mentioned that you never pursued the girl you were in love with, how many serious relationships have you had?"

"None," I say and then decide to elaborate, "none of my relationships have been serious. My last girlfriend was in college before the girl I was in love with. Losing out on the chance with her made me picky with relationships. Since then, I haven't gone on more than one or two dates with the same girl. I know I told you that I don't remember the last time I kissed a girl, but that was a lie. The last girl I kissed was the one that got away."

She seems flabbergasted when she says, "But you're you. Most guys would have more than kissed several girls by now just to try to get the heartbreak 'out of their systems.' You're a billionaire male model who could have his pick of any girl out there—"

"But I only wanted her. Sonnet, I might be irresistibly hot and stupid rich, but I'm also the guy who reads tragic romance novels and looks forward to every time I get to hold your hand. I'm a big romantic who wants the once-in-a-lifetime, happily-ever-after love I can tell my grandkids about when they ask how I met their grandmother."

"Alex, are you a virgin?" Her voice is almost a whisper as she asks the question.

"Sonnet, it's my turn to ask a question," I say in response, earning myself her unamused expression. "When it comes to brownies, do you choose the center or the edge?"

Her lips quirk into a smile as she shakes her head at me. "Center."

"Perfect, because I love the edges," I say. She shoots me a look that likely means *you know my next question.* "Yes, Sonnet, you and I are the same in that. I've always believed that it's a big deal and means something. Given my lack of serious relationships, I've never felt enough of a connection to any of my past girlfriends to consider it. My parents kinda taught me to be old-fashioned."

"Incredible. I don't know if I would have believed it if I hadn't heard it straight from you."

I use my fourth question on the one I've been saving. "Do you believe in love at first sight?"

"Yes," she says without hesitation. She uses her final turn to return the question. "Do you believe in love at first sight?"

I lock eyes with her as I say, "Yes. Are you willing to give this a chance when this vacation ends?"

"I am if you are."

The bus parks a short walk from the Piazza dei Miracoli. Well, I thought it was a short walk. The trip to the Tower of Pisa involves a ride on a tram as if we're going to an amusement park rather than an internationally renowned monument. As if my feelings for Sonnet weren't enough to make me feel like a teenager again. I hold her hand and have flashbacks of holding hands with my first girlfriend on something similar.

We pause to take photos of the piazza from the outer archway. The square is walled-in on the perimeter with four buildings in the large expanse. Marisol leads our group to a building on the outer edge where tickets for the tower are sold. We arrive early enough that any of us in the group can get a time slot. Sonnet doesn't argue when I pay for her ticket.

Two hundred fifty-one steps to climb to the top. Looking down, I count the bells that line the circle. Ironically, they would choose to install the bells on a tower that was already leaning considerably by the time they reached the top during construction. The bells have remained dormant for over a century now, though. Discreetly, I pull out my phone and snap a photo of Sonnet framed by the birds-eye view of Pisa —a breathtaking moment digitally eternalized for me to pine over later.

The descent back to ground level is almost more nerve-wracking than the trip going up, mostly because I remember when Sonnet's sandals slipped on the Spanish Steps. She's wearing her sneakers today, which eases my anxiety to half of what it would be. When her feet reach the bottom step, I release a breath I didn't realize I was holding. After the obligatory Tower of Pisa selfies and a quick tour of the Duomo, we're back on the bus heading east toward Venice.

"I know this is going to sound terrible," Sonnet says quietly because she's slightly ashamed of whatever is about to come out of her mouth, "but part of me thinks Venice is overrated."

A laugh escapes before I can stop it. "Is this based on movies you've seen?"

"Yeah," she says with a shrug.

"Those movies don't give you the full effect of the magic of Venice," I say, though she's unconvinced. By tonight, she'll experience it for herself. "Someone promised me she would use this long driving day to stop avoiding her writing."

She writes as I read my book. Occasionally, I glance at her tablet screen, but I can only catch snippets of the manuscript at her fingertips. Out the window, the landscape shifts from vineyards and villas to mountains as we travel through the northern Apennines. At the end of our stint through the mountain range, we pause for lunch in Bologna at a rest stop with a full-service cafeteria and gas station. Sonnet doesn't object when I pay for our meals together at the checkout. Her only complaint comes when I steal a bite of her pesto lasagna without her permission.

"If I recall, I'm the one who paid for that lasagna," I tease because flirting with her is preferable to arguing.

"I let you pay for it," she says as her rebuttal. "You would get argumentative if I tried to pay for my food. I prefer to choose my battles where that's concerned. You don't listen to me anyway when I tell you not to spend money on me."

With full stomachs and empty bladders, our group boards the bus for the second half of our journey. I fall asleep to the rhythmic sound of Sonnet's typing on her keyboard. A few hours later, she nudges me awake as the coach pulls into the parking lot of our hotel outside the main city. I attempt to shake off the grogginess before we walk into the lobby where servers are handing out flutes of Prosecco. Sonnet eyes the bubbling white wine in my glass.

"It's Prosecco, not champagne," I say to her as I sip the complimentary drink. She scrunches her nose before politely declining the flute the server offers her. "Wait, you're telling me you don't want to try Prosecco, but you'll try champagne? Prosecco is usually the sweeter of the two."

"I'll try some at dinner if they serve it," she says as she claims her room key from Marisol.

I finish off my glass before following her lead to the elevator. Similar to our room assignments in the other hotels, our rooms are on the same floor. This is the second to last hotel in our tour and our resting place for two nights. We stop by her room first and plan to walk down together ten minutes before tonight's departure time. In the lobby, I overheard our travel companions discussing how they were dressing up tonight. Dinner near Piazza San Marco is a good excuse to pull out the sports coat and get a reaction from Sonnet.

After a quick scan of the hotel room and bathroom setup, I connect to the hotel Wi-Fi and send my mom the photos of Sonnet I took while we were on top of the Tower of Pisa. She immediately likes the photos and sends a red heart emoji in response. I half expect her to call me demanding an update, but she seems to be respecting my space. My request to move back home may have convinced her that she'll hear the whole story eventually.

An hour after leaving her, I knock on her door. Wearing a sports coat and cologne makes this feel like a date. The way my heart stops before racing full speed at the sight of her makes this feel like a date. The butterflies in my stomach and the low-key electric buzz between us make this feel like a date. It's not a date, technically speaking, but my lungs don't seem to know that as they struggle to breathe normally. I want to remember this moment forever.

"Think this is too much or not enough?" Sonnet asks me as she does a full spin in her knee-length black dress. The classy fit accentuates the small of her waist and her curves. It's a grenade to my self-control. As if her dress weren't enough to drive me crazy, she paired her outfit with bright red lipstick. The color subconsciously pulls my gaze to her lips. Absolute torture, and she knows it. Bella donna pazza.

"You look perfect," I say in honesty. My voice is gravely, inciting an eyebrow raise from her. I clear my throat and gesture out the door to prompt our walk to our waiting transportation. Neither of us speaks during our descent down the flight of stairs. I use the opportunity to observe the details I had missed a few minutes ago. Her pearl necklace is likely fake given how symmetrical each bead is, but it still adds a timeless element to her ensemble. My mom has always loved pearls.

The voyage to Piazza San Marco from our hotel involves a bus ride to Tronchetto where we park and depart to board a rented private boat that transports us to the island known as Venezia—Venice to English speakers. Sonnet stares out the window with her phone camera raised and takes photos as we slowly pass other islands in the Venetian Lagoon.

Without breaking her gaze fixated on something miles away across the water, she asks me, "If I tell you something, can you promise not to laugh or make fun of me?"

"I can promise that I'll try my hardest not to," I say in compromise. I know better than to guarantee my reaction without context for what's coming.

"Close enough," she says as she turns toward me. My heart rate picks up as her dark chocolate eyes meet mine. "I didn't realize that Venice is an island. I knew it had canals and gondolas and was along the shoreline, but it never occurred to me that there weren't any cars. In the movies I've seen set in Venice, the characters travel by train to get to most places in Europe, so the island aspect of it is unclear."

My mouth lifts in a gentle smile. Her former assumptions are far from silly for someone who has never seen the city. "At least you knew which city is famous for canals and gondolas. Besides, there are other cities with creeks and rivers that run through it, despite being landlocked. The fact that it's an island with so many canals running through is amazing."

I point out the window toward the monuments I recognize as we grow nearer Piazza San Marco. Saint Mark's

Campanile looms tall as an easy way to locate the square from a distance. Marisol will likely give us the official history and background tonight and tomorrow morning, but I share what I can recall with Sonnet. Fortunately, none of our group is showing signs of seasickness. Our walk from the dock to the square involves crossing over four canals, the last of which gives us a view of the Bridge of Sighs. Sonnet is mesmerized by the arches and columns of Palazzo Ducale and how the current position of the sun gives her the ideal angle for creative photography. I'm more mesmerized by how she finds and uses the light to capture the image she's aiming for.

Piazza San Marco is just as I remember it. The Columns of San Marco and San Todaro welcome the hoards of tourists that overtake the city in the summer. It's no wonder that the restaurants along the piazza charge a premium. Once we round the corner and enter the piazza, Sonnet is torn between taking photos of the Clocktower and Saint Mark's Basilica. She has more than enough time to get a few pictures of both before we continue toward the restaurant. We'll also be coming back here tomorrow.

"You don't have to try to get everything right now," I say to her as she rushes with her finger on the red button of her touchscreen.

"The sun won't be in this same position later this evening or tomorrow morning," she says, and I take her word for it. Although my family has been here many times, my mom will still appreciate it if I take a few photos. I sneak another photo of Sonnet in the mix before Marisol ushers our group to the left of the Basilica to the Piazzetta dei Leoni and through the maze of streets to Antico Pignolo, a restaurant near Saint

Mark's Square. It's a short enough walk with few enough turns that I could find my way back without a map if needed.

As promised, Sonnet tries the Prosecco the waiter pours into our wine glasses. Though subtle, I can read the displeasure on her face. At this rate, I'm not likely to find a wine she likes while we're on this particular tour. However, the others in our group are fans of the Venetian specialty. When Sonnet excuses herself to go to the restroom between courses, I choose the same given my bladder situation. Finding a restroom is typically easier as a group activity, a fact that women take advantage of frequently.

"I'll wait here when I'm done so we can walk back together," I say to Sonnet as we depart toward our respective restrooms.

"You assume that you'll be done first," she says as she disappears through the door to the women's toilet to get a head start.

When I emerge back into the hallway less than two minutes later, she's discovered the back door that leads directly to the Rio di San Zulian. Directly, as in if she kept walking and didn't pay attention, she would fall into the canal. The usually closed door is the only barrier marking where the building ends and the water begins. She's a few steps from the edge with her phone capturing an image of the picturesque bridge within swimming distance of this edge. Hidden spots like the one she's found are one of the reasons I adore this city.

I gently touch the small of her back to alert her to my awareness without startling her. The last thing I want is to scare her over the precarious edge when we haven't had dessert yet. "Venice is decidedly not overrated," she says with admiration. I take my photo of the sight before we return to our table inside the main restaurant.

"Tired of tiramisu yet?" I ask her as they serve plates of the popular dessert. I've lost count of how many times I've eaten various versions of the same dish while on this trip to Italy. She shakes her head as a satisfied grin stretches across her face. Not too sweet and not too heavy—the perfect way to end a meal.

When we leave the restaurant, the sky is darkening. String lights line the exterior walls, and the archway has a large light hanging from the center, creating a romantic ambiance. *Una bella notte con la bella donna pazza.* Our hands meet in the middle as we instinctively reach for each other like plants to sunlight or magnets of opposite poles. The atmosphere is alive with energy and something I can't quite pinpoint but have felt before. Marisol reiterates the time we're supposed to meet at the dock and the four bridges we need to cross to find the right one before she lets us loose into the fading day.

During the two hours we were eating dinner, the Piazza San Marco has transformed from the historic tourist-overrun square to one of near-magic. The windows and arches of Ala Napolenica are illuminated as the moon shines brightly in the azure backdrop. With the sky devoid of clouds, the stars will soon join the half-moon as guardians of the night. The restaurants along the square are at full occupancy. With the sun below the horizon, the day's heat has lifted and welcomed the coolness of the slight breeze. An ensemble of musicians with various classical instruments is stationed under a tent and playing a song from *The Sound of Music*. If a fragment of time could feel like magic, this would be it.

Mesmerized by the sights and sounds, Sonnet releases my hand to pull out her phone. Within a few seconds, she recognizes what I already know to be true—beauty like this is nearly impossible to replicate. This is a feeling in the soul just as much as what we see and hear. She slips her hand back in mine, and we walk around without the need to start a conversation. We drift toward the shops on the north side to glance through the windows at the display items. Murano, another island in the lagoon, is famous for handmade glass, a popular commodity in these stores. Sculptures, vases, and jewelry in various colors reflect the light as we walk past.

"Can we go inside to look?" She asks as if I wouldn't grant her any request. I smile as I lead her toward the entrance. One glance at the price tags confirms that she's likely to walk out of here without purchasing anything. Most of the glass items would need to be shipped internationally on top of the sticker price. She doesn't linger long before smiling at me and gesturing to the exit.

"The store we're going to tomorrow should have a good range of glass items," I say to break her out of whatever is going through her head. "Plus, things tend to be marked up at shops and restaurants on the square. We can stop at a few places on the walk back to the dock."

Sonnet glances at the Clocktower before nodding in agreement. "We should start walking in that direction to ensure we're on time. I don't want to think about how much hotels cost per night here compared to the city's outskirts."

The change in lighting warrants another round of photos as we meander our way over the four bridges. After the fourth bridge, there's a stretch of stores and restaurants, a deviation from the cluster of hotels we passed. With twenty minutes left before our departure, Sonnet discovers a shop with hundreds of Venetian masks for sale. The last time I wore a mask was over seven years ago and on a different continent. She rifles through piles, avoiding any that contain feathers, and hands me a simple black and gray mask of the same style as what I wore at that masquerade. While I'm preoccupied with putting on the mask to humor her, she finds what she's been searching for.

Time stops and rewinds as my eyes meet hers framed by a gold glitter mask. I'm transported back to memories of a girl with those same dark chocolate irises and a gold mask, the glitter a lingering reminder. That suit jacket still has a few flecks I refuse to shake away. The unshakable, magnetic pull to her that I constantly feel isn't a coincidence. Years ago, I kissed those same perfect lips that tempt me multiple times a day. The straightened, sleek hair is now soft curls that suit the woman she's become over the last seven years. I recognize the shock of realization on her face as she arrives at the same epiphany. She's my mystery girl from the masquerade ball.

Sonnet

O n the boat ride back to Tronchetto, we sit in separate rows. Our bus affords us the same luxury since tonight is an optional excursion. By some unspoken agreement, we're giving the other space to process. A day hasn't passed in the last seven years that I didn't think about the boy who made me believe in love at first sight. Yet, the memory had faded enough that neither of us recognized the other until tonight.

"What if we meet again in the future and somehow figure out who the other is?"

"If you and I meet and know it's not the first time, then we'll just have to admit that it's fate."

We never put an expiration date on the hypothetical situation because neither of us thought it a possibility. Prince Charming isn't supposed to find Cinderella seven and a half years later. Surprisingly, neither of us recognized the other on that first day in Rome, but then again, maybe that's what the instant connection was trying to tell us. Part of Alex has been pining for a girl he let go of without giving it a real chance. He couldn't have been talking about me. I mean, I had a hard time moving on from him after that night. However, my lack of dating experience puts that night and that kiss at a very high standard.

Lawrence and Jean sit across the aisle from me, their eyes heavy with exhaustion. Tiredness doesn't prevent Jean from noticing the distance between me and Alex. She mouths, "Is everything okay?"

I give her a small smile and nod to reassure her. The shift in the dynamic between Alex and me isn't due to anything bad, but rather an added element. Ironically, it took both of us putting on a mask again to see the truth. Once the bus reaches the hotel, our whole group trails off to our respective rooms without much word from anyone except Marisol reminding us of tomorrow's departure time.

With my mind still occupied, I go through the routine of showering and getting ready for bed. I ignore the buzzing of incoming notifications from my phone connecting to the hotel's Wi-Fi. Chances are, Taylor sent a day's worth of texts in the few hours I was unreachable. Which is to be expected considering I had texted her to tell her about Alex's final question from this morning. It's not that I don't want to tell her about tonight; I need more time to wrap my head around it before I talk to her. Better yet, I need to know where his mind is on all of this before involving anyone else's opinions.

The knock I hear at my door seems like a trick of the mind, but my heart skips a beat at the possibility that it's him. My thoughts are too occupied to sleep anytime soon, so if it isn't him, I might find myself knocking at his room. I pull the door open to Alex pacing in the hallway outside my door. When he turns and sees me, he strides toward me with desperation and hunger in his eyes. His hands cradle either side of my face milliseconds before he breaks his promise.

For over seven years, I relived that electric midnight kiss in my memory. Memories are incapable of accurate recollection. Alex's lips on mine shatter every unrealistic expectation that Dick failed to live up to. It's fire and butterflies and shivers and absolute bliss. In fairytales, this is the kiss that breaks the spell or lifts the curse. I try to pull him closer to deepen and prolong the kiss, but Alex gently pulls away to catch his breath.

"That was better than the first kiss," I say with heavy breathing that matches his.

"It really is you," he says with wonder as his eyes skate over my face as if seeing me again for the first time.

Although he's the same Alex I've spent every day with since arriving in Italy, it's as if this is the first time I've seen him in years. Before a few seconds ago, the last person he had kissed was a younger version of me, assuming my math added up. "Does it count as love at first sight if it took until the second time to be sure? Love at second sight might be more accurate."

He smirks as his eyes drift to my lips again. Since I've somehow become a quick addict, I close the distance to taste that smirk. He ends the kiss prematurely again and steps back toward the hallway.

"Goodnight, Sonnet," he says as he slowly continues to put distance between us. "We'll talk at breakfast." Like the gentleman he is, he returns to his room for the night, leaving me flustered and floating. Despite the emotions and revelations of the day, my body's exhaustion overrides my brain as I crawl into bed.

THE GIRL in the mirror looks happy, happier than she looked when her boyfriend of two years proposed to her. If I didn't know her and had to guess, I would assume she's in love. She's also a few shades darker from spending time in the Italian sun. Any foundation I own will be too light until the vacation glow fades. I'm ready when Alex knocks on my door to walk me down to breakfast.

Before saying anything, he leans in to kiss me. It's more effective than caffeine at this point. If I weren't starving, I would stay here and kiss him for the next hour until we need to join the others on the bus, but my stomach protests. I feel his laugh as he breaks the kiss.

"Is it just me, or is that getting better every time?" he asks as we walk toward the stairs while holding hands.

"I'm trying to figure out how that's even possible," I say as I brave a glance at his lips again. As much as I enjoy kissing him, he was right to hold back on doing so for the majority of this tour. I would have completely missed all the Italian beauty around me with that kind of distraction. "I thought our first kiss was as perfect as it could get, but I'm starting to think every kiss with you is like that."

"I'm going to need you to be a little more resistible so we can have a conversation without interruptions," he teases as we round the corner to the dining room. I'll miss the full spread of breakfast food when I have to go back to my life of grocery shopping and cooking.

"Do you cook for yourself, or do you have all your groceries and food ordered and delivered?" I ask Alex as we each grab a plate at the start of the buffet.

His eyes shimmer with amusement as he places a croissant on his plate. "Haven't you learned by now that I'm not your stereotypical billionaire bachelor? If I have an early morning or late night at the office, I'll order in, but I prefer to do my grocery shopping and cooking when I can. Once my new role as CEO is announced, I may have to switch to grocery delivery since it'll be harder to keep a low profile."

I picture Alex in a baseball hat and disguise to hide his identity while walking through store aisles and again in a penthouse apartment kitchen with the city skyline in the background. The Kansas City skyline. The main office and headquarters of De Luca Enterprises is in the heart of downtown Kansas City. Realizing that we live in the same city—that we've been living in the same city for years—makes this real.

"How long was that extended trip after the masquerade ball?" I ask to fill in the gaps. "Was it here in Italy?"

"I lived in Italy with my extended family for a year before returning," he says as he motions toward an empty table.

Alex sets his plate on the table and heads to the automatic espresso machine to grab our coffee. I don't try to hide that I'm watching him from across the dining room. Jean catches my gaze and winks, clearly having witnessed Alex and I walking in together. For all I know, any of our travel companions could have glimpsed one of our kisses. I lose all ability to pay attention to our surroundings when his lips are on mine.

We both take sips of our coffee simultaneously, our movements mirroring the other. Despite all that we need to discuss, we eat in comfortable silence. After today, we'll only have two more mornings like this.

"On a practical level, what do you think everyday life looks like in giving this a chance?" I ask him when my plate and cup are empty. It's the question I've been mulling over since I suspected I was falling for him. The difference between a vacation fling and a relationship that started on vacation is how we transition and plan for longevity. Does he feel as strongly for me as I feel for him?

Alex reaches across the table to hold my hand in his. "I'm not sure what my life will look like once I step into the CEO position. I'll have to figure out how to carve out time, but it's my problem to solve. I'm not running away from this again."

It's not romantic, but it's honest. With how my engagement ended, I would rather Alex be open with me about what he wants and how he's feeling. Knowing that he's the same boy as the one at the masquerade ball doesn't erase the fear I have about this ending in a broken heart. If anything, the connection leaves my heart more vulnerable to becoming entirely his.

Venice in the bright daylight is beautiful, though not quite as magical as Venice in the early hours of twilight. Lines of tourists crowd the Piazza San Marco around the main entrance to the Basilica. In many ways, sightseeing in Italy is similar to going to Disney World if you exchange the themed rides and roller coasters with ancient churches and landmarks and remove the crying children. Marisol leads us over a bridge near the restaurant where we dined last night.

While most of us are focused on the glass-blowing demonstration, Alex slips his arm around my waist, his fingers lightly dancing near my tickle spot. I fight to keep a straight face as sparks ignite where I can feel his hand through my blouse. I don't have to turn my head to see the smirk plastered across his face. Once the demonstration is over, we walk up the stairs to the main store where thousands of glass items are displayed for sale. Goblets, plates, sculptures, jewelry, ornaments—if it's something you can form with glass, it's likely available for purchase. This store is not meant for those with small children.

Alex releases my hand to pick up and inspect a few items. His mom would love the decorative glassware. I inch toward the jewelry display with options in my price range that are small enough to pack when flying home. A bracelet for my mom and a pair of earrings for each of my almost bridesmaids add up, but I have extra due to Alex's insistence on paying for my gelato and meals. When he's preoccupied with asking about a particular set of wine glasses, I pay the cashier for the gifts.

After making an order and setting up the delivery details, he finally spots the shopping bag in my hands. He leans in and whispers in my ear, "I find it extremely attractive that you don't expect or want me to pay for everything. It's how I know you're not just with me for my money."

"Have you looked in a mirror? Clearly, I'm with you for your looks," I quietly tease.

"And here I thought it was my charming personality that won you over," he says in mock offense while returning his hand to its place holding mine.

He holds on as Marisol ushers our group out of the store and back into the maze of Venetian streets and canal bridges. He only lets go for the few seconds it takes us to board the precariously rocking gondola. The gondoliers seem unfazed by the constant change in weight distribution as they shift and maneuver as one who lives on the water. They would likely pick up surfing easily given their ability to balance on the waves. The gondola next to us has an extra passenger, a man playing the accordion and singing classical Italian songs.

Lawrence and Jean claim the two remaining seats on our gondola before our gondolier unties the small boat and pushes off the dock toward the mouth of the Canal Grande.

"You two seem to have resolved whatever misunderstanding you had last night," Jean says as she glances at our intertwined fingers.

"It was less a misunderstanding and more of an... understanding," Alex says, trying to explain the situation while remaining vague about the details. While I feel completely comfortable with and around him, the shift in the seriousness of what we're pursuing still seems new and fragile, much like a glass slipper.

Lawrence snorts at Alex's response before saying, "Sometimes the truth takes more time to process than whatever misbelief or delusion we previously held."

Whether anyone else was aware of it or not, the truth is that falling for Alex while on this trip to Italy isn't coincidental; part of me has been in love with him for over seven years.

Alex

My ego gets the best of me once again. Ten minutes ago, I insisted I could navigate us through the labyrinthian streets from Piazza San Marco to Ponte di Rialto over Canal Grande. Now, I'm unsure if I'm leading her in the right direction. The words, *I told you so*, are written across her expression, though she keeps her mouth shut. Before my pride spoke up, she had offered to pull up a map on her phone. I stop to survey our surroundings, debating whether we should turn back the way we came or look at the map.

When I see her free hand reach for her phone, I grab it and pull her in for a kiss. We might be lost, but I know we're a few streets away from the crowds of tourists and locals. My hands release hers before I place them on either side of her waist, consumed by the crackling air around us. Even if we weren't alone, I wouldn't notice anyone else nearby. Her arms snake up my shoulders as her hands find the back of my head to pull me closer. I need to create some distance before things become too heated.

"You were right," I say when I find the will to end the kiss. "Let's look at that map and find somewhere to eat."

Her face is smug as she unlocks her phone and navigates to the app. Sonnet slips her hand back in mine and pulls me toward the crowded streets lined with stores. I willingly let her lead as she checks her phone every thirty seconds or so to ensure we're heading toward our destination. Before long, I see the large covered bridge lined with shops along the interior walkway and steps leading to the center peak. She puts her phone away and lets me resume leading us toward a restaurant for lunch.

The further from the bridge we walk, the less crowded the restaurants are. We find a table with a view of the river and a fan nearby.

"Does this count as our first date if I pay for your food?" I ask her as she flips through the menu.

"You've been paying for my food for days now, but we can count it as the first if you want," she says while reading through the pizza options. "It sets a fairly high bar, though, if a lunch date in Venice is the first date. Are you sure you're up for the challenge to compete with this in the future?"

I chuckle and wait for her to look at me before I say, "You're not the only one who reads romance novels. I have so many ideas that it'll be years before I run out of ways to impress you."

Years. I could only dream of years, decades, a lifetime with her. We've thrown around cliché sayings about love, but is it as serious for her as it is for me? I want to tell her I'm all in without looking back, but I'm concerned that might scare her away or cause her to step away. I'm doing what I can to avoid too much too fast until we've agreed on the pace.

Walking back to Piazza San Marco is less eventful with Sonnet at the helm, giving us an extra ten minutes before our meeting time for the boat tour of the Venetian Lagoon with an extended stop at Burano. Given her indifference, I suspect Sonnet either hasn't heard of Burano, or she hasn't realized we're spending a few hours on the iconic island. Not only is it famous for its lace work, but the brightly colored houses are featured as a popular photo for many Pinterest users.

We pass Marisol and climb onto the boat, where half the group patiently waits. Per our usual arrangement, I offer her the window seat. She gets an unobstructed view to take photos while I admire her and the landscape simultaneously. The combination of a full stomach and the low hum of the boat engine would lull me to sleep if Sonnet weren't here to capture my attention and act as a second tour guide. Some islands are nearly submerged beneath the water level, while others are identified by their abandoned buildings. Due to the vivid colors of the houses, Burano is recognizable from a distance. Sonnet gasps as she mentally puts together the pieces.

"I've wanted to see this place, but I hadn't recognized the name when I looked at the itinerary," she says with contagious excitement. I want to kiss her when her eyes glimmer like that, but I also don't want to be the guy oblivious to his public displays of affection. I also don't want our physical chemistry to interfere with our ability to discern the strength of other aspects of our connection.

With feet on solid earth again, we wander to the square with the leaning campanile. From there, the colored buildings are the main architecture. The legend says the colors helped the fisherman find their way home when the weather was foggy. Now, the government approves any color changes and ensures the paint's maintenance.

"Last night, we were walking through a fairytale, and now we're walking through a box of crayons," I quietly comment as Sonnet pulls me toward a lacemaking shop. Next thing I know, she's admiring hand-crafted lace while Italian women try to convince me to "buy her something nice." If I could without inciting her wrath, I would, but I've already pushed my luck with the leather jacket. My best strategy moving forward is to remove the price tag from any gifts.

"These are so beautiful," Sonnet says to the women as they show her the various patterns. For someone who doesn't want me to spend money on her, she has expensive taste. Although I'm the one who was dragged into the store, I leave with yet another souvenir for my mother.

Sonnet stops to give me a questioning look. "Why the face?"

"You insist that I don't spend any money on you, but you have no problem convincing me to spend hundreds on my mother who already has everything she could need." I didn't intend to sound exasperated, but this woman is puzzling to me at moments like this.

"When you tell her that I helped you choose the gift, she'll see that I have good taste, and it'll help ensure that she likes me," she says without eye contact.

This time, I'm the one who stops her to encourage her to look at me. "My mother will love you. I can guarantee that. She wants me to be happy, and you make me happier than I've ever been. Plus, you're smart, and you understand Italian. As soon as she meets you, she will be on my case about proposing."

The reference to marriage is followed by an awkward silence. It's entirely too soon to bring up something so serious, and yet...she's endgame for me. The seven-year gap with failed attempts at dating makes her reappearance a miracle in my book. Knowing that I want a lifetime with her doesn't erase the reality that we don't know each other well enough to take that step. Pining for someone is not the same as talking to or spending time with them. How much of Sonnet is truly who she is versus the faded memories and skewed perceptions?

Every few buildings or so, Sonnet pauses to take a photo of the picturesque colors. An island like this is small and secluded enough that I might be able to risk returning once I step into the CEO position. The biggest issue would likely be reliable internet in case of an emergency.

"We should ask someone to take a photo of us together with the houses in the background," Sonnet says, interrupting my thoughts.

I scan the people around us for someone who seems trustworthy. An elderly woman who reminds me of my grandmother sees my searching eyes and walks over to us. In Italian, I ask her to take a photo of Sonnet and me on the bridge. She looks at us and smiles as she takes my phone and gestures for us to stand closer together.

"Vi baciate!" She says in command, and I lean to kiss Sonnet's cheek. As much as the woman might scare me, I'm not about to let a stranger take photos of me kissing Sonnet without discussing it with Sonnet beforehand. Once I have my phone back and we've both admired the photos, I grab Sonnet's hand and lead her toward an alley between two houses.

"What are you doing?" she asks with laughter.

I kiss her smile, smothering her laughter with my mouth on hers. I need to get a grip on my self-control again, but part of me feels as if I'm trying to make up for seven years of lost time with her.

We both pull away and stand on opposite sides of the narrow walkway. "We need to stop doing that so much. I can't think straight when you kiss me like that," she says as she shakes her head.

She's right, of course. If she weren't waiting until marriage—if we both weren't waiting until marriage—this would have already become much messier. Other couples who don't have this standard would have spent last night in tangled limbs and sheets. Last night, I walked away to catch my breath and further process all the possibilities.

"By the way, I love the naturally curly hair," I say to her as we peruse a gift shop on one side of the canal. "Your hair was beautiful before, but this fits you better. It goes with the whole 'Bella donna pazza' theme you have going."

Sonnet rolls her eyes when I wink at her. Then, she convinces me that it's the perfect time for gelato, which she lets me pay for without comment or complaint. Right now, it's convenient to believe that life won't interfere with this perfect moment.

Sonnet

"I was beginning to worry when I didn't hear from you for a full twenty-four hours," Taylor says, her voice close to yelling over the phone.

"That's one way to greet your best friend who is in another hemisphere and several time zones ahead, might I remind you," I say as I plop down on my bed. Upon arrival at the hotel for the evening, Alex and I decided that the best way to keep from kissing each other too much was to go our separate ways until dinner. That way, I could finally call my best friend, and he could call his mom and check in.

Taylor says, "You texted me that lover boy wants to extend this vacation fling into a real relationship and didn't respond to any of my questions following that confession."

"I'm calling you back now, aren't I?" I ask as I prepare to share the earth-shattering developments that will make her current fixation seem minuscule in comparison. "I have both sappy and steamy news. Which do you want first?"

"Since I suspect the chronological order of events is sappy and then steamy, I'm going to choose sappy to save us both the trouble of confusing time jumps."

I brace myself for Taylor's possible reactions while taking a deep breath. "Alex is the boy from the masquerade ball."

Silence. She's so silent that I check to ensure the call hasn't dropped. Taylor is rarely speechless, often speaking before thinking about what she's saying. This time, though, I know she's letting her mind wrap around the repercussions. "As surprising as this is, it really isn't. You were obsessed with that boy in a way I haven't seen again until you got to Italy and met Alex. It makes sense that you could fall in love with him so quickly. I'm guessing the steamy means he finally kissed you...again?"

"Seven years has not lessened the effect his kiss has on me," I confess.

"Which is why you're in your room talking to me rather than spending every minute with him. You've probably been making out like teenagers to make up for seven years of lost time. If you hadn't lost touch after the ball, you two would have either broken up or been married with kids by now."

I roll my eyes and say, "I don't know about the kids part."

"When you're married to someone that attractive, kissing always leads to more. Both of you are very good-looking and share top-notch chemistry. No birth control is completely guaranteed. It's math."

But that math can't account for possible infertility. I push the worst-case scenarios out of my mind. "We live very different

237

lives when not on vacation. Do you really think this is something that can go the distance?"

"I believe that two people who want to make it work and are willing to do the work can figure those things out. Yes, he's a super wealthy, soon-to-be CEO of a huge company, but when you take away the details, you two are very similar. You both work hard to grow your careers. You both love your families and want to be married and have your own family. If you want the same things and share the same priorities, the rest will figure itself out with time. Just have a conversation with him without the distraction of kissing each other. Do it somewhere you're around people but can have privacy without interruption."

The tour bus would be the ideal location for such a discussion. It's where we've had a large part of our serious moments. No one could join our section of two seats the way they could join our table during meals. This hotel doesn't have a fitness room or a pool to distance us from other guests, and distance involving walls would result in more kissing than talking.

With my game plan decided, Taylor and I spend the remainder of our phone call reviewing details for her baby shower. Our friend Maggie is finishing up the decorations she took home after leaving my house the morning following our "dodged a bullet" slumber party. The big things are handled, and the small things can wait until I return in a few days. Still, thoughts of my best friend's impending motherhood break me out of the vacation love bubble that must be a side effect of the Italian air. Now, it seems impossible to come here single and leave without falling in love with someone or something. The coffee alone evokes a strong emotional response.

When Taylor finally hangs up, I plug my phone into its charger and set an alarm to wake me up from the nap that's overtaking my other plans for the afternoon. I'm still half asleep when I hear knocking through the fogginess of my fading dreams. As my mind sharpens, it pieces together Alex's muffled voice through the door. The red numbers on the bedside clock indicate an hour until dinner and fifteen minutes until my alarm is supposed to wake me.

"Don't you know that if someone doesn't respond right away, they're probably trying to sleep?" I yell toward the door without making any moves to get out of bed.

"I'm bored, and I miss you," he says as the knocking stops. "Plus, I made some arrangements for our second date. I'm giving you fifteen minutes to get ready before I start knocking again."

I smile as I roll myself out of bed and to my suitcase. Dick would have made comments about how many days' worth of clothes I packed for this trip, but I'm continually grateful for the options as I pull a white midi dress from my remaining clean dresses. In a flurry, I change and inspect my appearance in the bathroom mirror. I swish some mouthwash around even though we'll be eating dinner soon.

Precisely fifteen minutes after his declaration, the knocking resumes. He manages a few knocks before I open the door to his smirk. I inwardly melt as he slips his hand in mine and leads me to the hallway stairs. The concierge at the front desk greets Alex and gestures for us to follow him outside to a garden on the backside of the hotel property. The sun casts hues of tangerine and magenta across the horizon. Candles illuminate the simple plate setting at a table for two.

Once we're seated, the concierge disappears and is replaced by our waiter. Two of the three glasses are filled with water, and the waiter pours wine into the remaining glass on Alex's side. The glow of candles and pavilion lights on his sun-tanned skin is an image too perfect for a camera to capture.

Over the dinner courses, we exchange stories from childhood. His are devoid of siblings to annoy him or blame him for any shenanigans. Despite that, he shares fond memories of holidays and celebrations with his cousins. Some live in Italy, while others have migrated to the United States like his parents did. The distance doesn't keep them from gathering together at least once a year.

"This year, my father's funeral is what brought all of us back to Italy," Alex says with a sad smile. "Usually, it's a wedding or new baby, though. Nonna worries about me because I don't have a wife yet." We both shake our heads and smile at the notion.

The warmth I feel during this second date is more a smoldering coal than an all-consuming fame. He's taking every opportunity to touch my hand or arm, but none of my senses are overwhelmed by him. The spark of electricity hums between us as we laugh and flirt like a normal couple would on a second date. After our tiramisu with espresso, he walks me back to my room inside. Our goodnight kiss is sweet and the perfect way to end our last evening before returning to Rome.

As he walks away, Alex says, "Sleep well. I'll see you in the morning."

"Goodnight."

I text Taylor a quick update about the date before hopping in the shower to rinse away the sweat from a full day in the sun. Once my skin and teeth are clean, the tiredness convinces me to go to bed without looking at Taylor's response.

ON MY LAST full day in Italy, I wake up in a bittersweet mood. I'm sad to leave this piece of paradise, but I'm excited to be done with living out of a suitcase. Today is when I'll have a conversation with Alex about how we move forward. Scanning the bathroom and bedroom, I ensure all my belongings are packed in my suitcase and backpack. Alex knocks at my door as I double-check all the drawers and crevices.

After he rolls my suitcase to the hallway for me, despite my insistence that I could do it myself, he kisses my forehead and gently tugs me toward the breakfast buffet. Rather than sit by ourselves, we join the others from our group as Lawrence recounts his meal at his favorite restaurant in Florence.

"It's my favorite restaurant in the world," he says to end the story. Alex pulls out his phone to look up Il Latini to add to his favorites. Someone like him could probably talk his way into the best table there without a reservation. Someone like him would make a reservation and insist on being treated like every other patron.

I'll miss Lawrence and Jean when we go our separate ways tomorrow. I'll miss Marisol and how she sometimes flutters around like a mother hen to ensure we know when the coach is departing.

"Half an hour," Marisol says to our table with an espresso in her hand.

Half an hour to finish my cappuccino and run back to my room to brush my teeth. Half an hour to use the restroom a final time before the hours we'll be on the bus. Half an hour to descend the stairs and walk through the lobby to the tour bus waiting at the entrance with our luggage already loaded.

"At least we have a stop in Assisi and another for lunch on the drive back," Alex says as we settle into our seats for the final leg. With the drive split into three parts, I mentally debate the best time to start the needed conversation. "You're unusually quiet. What's on your mind?"

Looks like now is the best time. "What's the plan for us when I fly home tomorrow?"

His expression isn't surprised. Alex shrugs as he says, "I haven't booked my flight back yet, now that you bring it up. I haven't decided when I'll go back."

Though I have no claim to him, I'm disappointed he isn't jumping at the opportunity to fly back with me. After all this time together following all those years apart, shouldn't he want to spend every minute he can to prolong this fairytale the way he did when he offered to walk me to my car on the night of the masquerade ball? I know he'll choose me over his other dating options, but will he choose me over his dedication to work or his temporary escape from that same responsibility?

"Maybe we should just exchange phone numbers, and you can call me when you're back home," I say with all the nonchalance I can muster. "That way, it gives us both time and space to think about us and what we want beyond this."

"That sounds like a solid plan." Part of me wilts when he doesn't argue with the suggestion or fight for me because I don't need time and space to be sure about a future with him.

Alex

~~

I shouldn't feel gutted by her suggestion. It's reasonable since I have yet to decide when I'll return home. The time difference has made it difficult for both of us to stay in touch with friends and family, especially when we've spent most of our days walking through ancient cities and eating gelato. Missed calls and phone tag are why we didn't start a relationship the first night we met.

Assisi is another Italian town with an incline keeping me in shape on this vacation, the road leading to the Basilica of San Francesco d'Assisi. I recognize his name from the facts I can remember about church history, but the details are worth reading about again in the museum section of the grounds. There's a room where speaking is strongly discouraged. It's fitting that the first full tour day and the final full tour day would include a silent chapel. The art inside is nearly as beautiful as the outside view of the surrounding province of Perugia.

"I would suggest that we get some gelato once we're tired of looking at this countryside, but I think I'll die before that happens," Sonnet says, her soft voice jarring after the whispers and echoes of footsteps in the Basilica.

"Take some photos and look at them later," I say to her, my mouth watering at the mention of the Italian frozen dessert. "Gelato waits for no one."

"Tell that to the gelato shops that have been open for centuries," she says as she heads toward the road that led us up to this view.

In a few strides, I catch up to her. "The oldest gelateria opened in 1880. America is older than gelato. The Civil War is older than gelato. Compared to nearly everything else in Italy, gelato is a new invention."

As my last sentence hangs in the air, I know I've lost her attention. Her phone is open to the camera app with magenta flowers in focus. Everything in the background blurs—still present and necessary to give the image depth. Upon closer inspection, I recognize the flowers as the same type my nonna and mamma like to grow.

In the absence of stracciatella, Sonnet opts for the closest flavor to it—cookies and cream. The existence of cookies and cream gelato in a place like Assisi shows how prevalent tourism is for the whole country. I can't blame anyone for obsessing with this country and its culture.

"Give me your phone," I say to Sonnet once we're back on the bus.

She eyes me suspiciously and asks, "Why?"

"So I can save my phone number in your contacts," I say as I hold out my unlocked phone for her to do the same. "I need your number to call you, and you need my number so that you don't mistake my insistence for a spam call. I would rather you pick up the first time."

She accepts my phone and quickly unlocks hers using face recognition before handing it to me. When we exchange phones again, I open my contacts to search for her name to make sure it's there. She assigned herself the nickname "Masked Vacation Fling." I smile to myself as I change it to "The Love of My Life" for good measure. As if checking my contacts wasn't enough, I type a short text to her to ensure she'll be there when I need to find her.

> I'm going to call you. I promise.

THE LOVE OF MY LIFE

> I know. Just don't wait too long.

Relieved that things aren't awkward or strained between us, I read while she works on her novel. Though her typing patterns are as sporadic as the flow of the story in her head, the sound is soothing. I could fall asleep to the sound of her fingers flying across the keys every night for the rest of my life. My eyes grow heavy as the initial sugar rush from the gelato subsides.

As if sensing the gradual deceleration of the bus's speed, I open my eyes when we park for our lunch stop. Pretending to sleep, I peek at Sonnet's document and word count to gauge her progress during my nap. Five hundred words is a big accomplishment, especially since she's been wrestling through writer's block for months.

"I know you're awake," Sonnet says without looking away from her screen. Satisfied with the sentence she had just typed, she closes the tablet and slips it into her backpack for safekeeping.

"When will you let me read it?" I ask her with feigned nonchalance. I'm ridiculously curious to read her writing, but I don't want to seem desperate.

She thinks about her answer as we walk into the cafeteria. This one is similar to the food courts at the shopping malls I begged my parents to let me go to as a teenager. I'm old enough that the mall was cool when I was in high school. Whether I was allowed to go depended on who I was going with and whether they had been debriefed on our family's security protocols. All my close friends were vetted and approved by my father's advisors.

I follow Sonnet's lead as she scans the various food options. Mentally, I follow Sonnet's lead as she sets the speed and tempo of this dance on the edge of a cliff. The waters below are warm and inviting, but the safest way down is to jump willingly.

Ten minutes after the bus is back on the highway, Sonnet hands her tablet to me with her manuscript open. "Now is when I'll let you read it."

She sleeps with her head propped on my shoulder as I digest the way she crafts scenes into a masterpiece of attraction weaved with tension. Although she's not nearly finished with the draft, I can see the possible paths the characters may take to reach that resolution. In some ways, it seems obvious that a happy ending is the only way for it to end. The last paragraph she wrote before I had asked to read it introduces another twist—another wrench in the complicated puzzle.

I close her tablet and set it on my lap before I carefully fish my phone from the front pocket nearest Sonnet. I don't want to wake her until we're approaching Rome again. With my notes app open, I type out a to-do list of all the things I need to do in the next year.

The final hotel on this trip seems the most "Americanized" of our accommodations. The Internet is also more reliable once I ask the concierge for the password to input into my phone. My name—or my company's name—must reach the ears of someone in authority. Ten minutes after unpacking a few things in my room, the concierge from the front desk delivers a complimentary bottle of wine to my door. Sonnet emerges from her room across the hall as I accept the gift, and she shakes her head with a smile. Her wardrobe suggests that she's headed to the fitness room. I fight the temptation to change into a T-shirt and basketball shorts to join her.

Space. If she wanted me to go with her, she would have invited me. I need to give her time and space to miss me. To keep myself from caving, I revisit my to-do list and make a few phone calls to check things off my goals.

The bittersweetness of the tour's end covers our group as we sit in the same section of the dining room together. We exchange phone numbers and email addresses with promises to stay in touch—promises likely forgotten when the routine of everyday life takes over. Lawrence and Jean share a table with Sonnet and me, their sad smiles affecting me the most.

"Unlike the others, I have every intention of staying in touch with both of you if you want," Jean quietly says to us. "Where did you say you live again?"

Sonnet looks to me for my answer, which is when it truly hits me. We live in the same city. Part of me knew this, but it's not a detail I've let myself mull over. If I were ready to leave Italy tomorrow, I could accompany her to her doorstep with an extra day to change her mind about time and space. I could take her to dinner at all my favorite restaurants, starting with Lidia's in the Crossroads Arts District. We could watch football games in the front row at Arrowhead Stadium or from the comfort of a private suite. The place that feels like home is the same city where the people who feel like home live.

Noting that I've temporarily tuned out of the conversation, Sonnet says, "Kansas City. We're both in the Kansas City metro. Kansas City is in both Missouri and Kansas, but the parts most people know are on the Missouri side."

Jean's face lights up the way I imagine mine does when I see Sonnet for the first time every morning. "It must not have come up before because I would have remembered if either of you had told me that. Lawrence and I have lived in a suburb outside Kansas City for the last ten years. That will make it much easier to stay in touch."

The image in my mind morphs to include Lawrence and Jean sitting across from Sonnet and me at Lidia's. I can and will carve out time for moments like that. Sonnet beams at all of us, and I can't help but wonder about all the divine arrangements that took place to bring us all here together on the same tour in Italy. There's too much significance here for this to be coincidental; it has to be God-orchestrated. I signed up for this tour as a way to escape life long enough to process and grieve my father's passing and what it means for my future, and I've found so much more than I could have ever imagined.

When Sonnet excuses herself to go to the restroom, Jean says to me, "So, are you going to tell her that you're in love with her, or are you waiting for some grand gesture? Grand gestures don't just happen on their own, you know."

When our group dwindles to a few people left in the dining room, I walk Sonnet to her door the way I have every night since she's come back into my life. Rather than going to my room, I take the elevator to the ground floor to find someone at the front desk to help me solidify my next move.

Sonnet

〜〜〜

Rome's international airport is larger than I remember from my arrival. Then again, I had been jet-lagged and desperate for a shower and bed. Getting a layout for the airport was a low priority for this newly-landed American. Now, I appreciate the offerings beyond security. Ads for luxury brands go nearly unnoticed, though I can hardly miss the one featuring a grayscale image of a shirtless Alessandro De Luca. He really does look like that when he's coming out of a pool. The lack of color detracts from the depth of his blue irises, but the intensity accurately translates. Still, my mind can't equate that version with the one that is warmth and sunshine.

With an hour remaining before my flight boards, I wander around the terminal with a coffee cup in hand. I fill my water bottle before stepping into a gift store. When I walk closer to the shelves of books, I note that there are familiar titles translated into Italian. Alex would love to reread his favorites in another language. Admittedly, I'm sad that he's not flying back with me. He never bought his return tickets, and knowing him, he can book a private jet home with one text or phone call. His absence today is my fault for suggesting that we take some space.

I buy two books, one for me and one for him, assuming he follows through and calls me when he's back in town. Assuming this whole botched honeymoon-for-one isn't just a dream. The masquerade ball felt like a dream for months after that night. It might take seeing Alex in person a few times for this experience to feel solidly real.

After one final bathroom trip, I settle at my gate and pull out the Italian edition of *Twilight* that I bought for Alex. It's fitting that this series has been translated into Italian because the main character is named Bella and part of the second book takes place in Italy. The ruling vampires love this country as much as I do. It's not a bad place to spend your immortality.

As I stand in line to board the plane, I text my mom and Taylor to update them on my status. Because I opted for all the extra excursions on the trip, paying for Wi-Fi on the plane is an expense I'm not willing to break the budget for. I'll likely lose connection to the free airport internet once in the plane's cabin. Before I'm out of range, I send a text to update Alex.

I find my seat and watch as the other passengers trickle in and fill the rows of the large plane bound for Newark. Using the book to hide that I'm spying on those in my vicinity, I periodically shift my eyes between the page in front of me and the people around me. Most are too caught up in settling in their chairs to notice me.

A flight attendant making her rounds through the economy class section stops by my seat. I see her out of the corner of my eye, waiting to see where she'll go next. She asks me, "Excuse me, are you Sonnet Kincaid?"

"Yes?" I say to her uncertainly. My mind starts the downward spiral of worst-case scenarios where I'm stuck in Italy and have to wait for another flight. Not that being stuck in Italy is terrible. The worst-case scenario would be receiving news that a loved one died in a freak accident, and this was the best way to get ahold of me.

"I've been told that your seat has been upgraded to first class," she says, politely smiling. First class?

"There must be a mistake," I say, confused, "I didn't pay for an upgrade."

Her smile morphs into one more genuine as she says, "I can assure you that there's no mistake, Sonnet Kincaid. If you follow me, I'll show you to your seat."

I gather my things as my mind concludes that this must be Alex's doing. This is his sneaky way of giving me something nice in a way that I can't refuse. Or won't refuse. First-class tickets for an international flight might be expensive, but it's certainly an expense I'd be willing to splurge on if I had the means to do so.

I follow the flight attendant past the rows of Americans returning home from their vacations and trips. Most of them appear exhausted and ready to pass out after take-off. There's a stark difference in the size and comfort of the seats in first class. These seats were made for sleeping. As she gestures to the row of my newly assigned seat, my eyes meet familiar blue ones. Just like it has many times before, my heart somehow stops and then races at the sight of him. Alessandro De Luca.

Alex stands up to let me take the window seat in our two-seat row. I hurry over to get out of the way and to ensure the flight attendant can resume her other duties.

"You're here," I say with a smile that will hurt my cheeks before it fades away. He kisses me as seconds slow to feel like minutes. I know it's not minutes since we're far from alone on this plane where anyone could recognize him.

"I realized that I'm not letting you out of my sight until I've walked you to your front door," he says with his lips only inches from mine. "And then I'll know where you live, and we can avoid letting another seven years pass. I'm not making that mistake again."

"One, that's borderline stalker-ish, but I'll allow it since you're hot," I say as I lean back in my seat. "Two, I hope you plan to let me go to the restroom by myself, at least."

He intertwines our fingers in an all-too-familiar way and kisses the back of my hand. "I love you, Sonnet Kincaid. Part of me has been in love with you for over seven years, and I'll be in love with you for the rest of my life. I'm all in for whatever it takes to make this work and last."

I blink away the tears threatening to escape and say, "I love you too, Alessandro De Luca. I want to marry you one day." His smile melts away all the fear and confusion that previously clouded my emotions.

"Does that mean you'll keep me company back to Kansas City?"

"Alex, I'm surprised you're on a commercial airplane rather than in your private jet. First class is a high standard for me, but this must be slumming it for you." My voice is teasing; my words warrant his eye roll.

Then, after a few moments of silence, he admits, "My private jet is in the States, and it seemed like a waste to bring it back over the Atlantic when I'm perfectly content sitting here with you. Besides, the plane will be waiting for us at the airport in Newark for the last stint of our trip. One flight on that thing, and you'll never want to fly without me or my plane again."

I shake my head and let go of his hand to find the book I purchased for him while saying, "I bought this Italian edition because it reminded me of you." I hand him the translated *Twilight*. His laugh gives me enough satisfaction to justify the airport retail mark-up. Once the plane is in the air, he quietly reads the book out loud until I fall asleep with my head on his shoulder.

PART THREE

Together

Sonnet

~❧~

lex looks like he barely slept. He loads my suitcase into the car as I finish putting away the dishes that dried overnight on the drying rack. I mentally run through my checklist before turning off the lights. Alex waits in his car with his disposable cup of coffee in his hands. My nervousness overrides my jealousy that he can drink coffee right now, but given how late he worked last night to clear his schedule for today, I keep my coffee-related comments to myself.

The streets are nearly empty as the streetlights near the end of their night shift. Neither of us says anything on the short drive; neither of us is a morning person. When he shifts his car into park, the time on his dashboard confirms that we're a few minutes early, and I'm in no rush to go inside.

"Do you want me to stay in the waiting room, or are you comfortable with me coming to the back if they'll let me?" Alex asks, his first words to me today apart from, "Good morning."

"I wouldn't have asked you to be my ride this morning if I weren't comfortable with having you here for all of it," I tell him. My mom offered to be the one to pick me up and be my ride after the procedure, but I knew Alex would have a hard time sleeping or working if he weren't the one by my side. She doesn't seem to mind how eager he is to take care of me.

He slips his hand in mine before we walk through the automatic revolving doors at the front entrance of the main hospital. The halls are quiet this early in the morning, but a lady quickly waves us over to her office to check me in for my surgery.

She goes through the steps of confirming my date of birth, my primary care doctor, whether I would accept transfusions in a life-or-death situation, and other questions I never thought about before, including having a medical directive. No doubt, Alex and my mom will discuss what my medical directive should be in the future. Finally, she's reached the part where she tells me how much my copay is—a number I've memorized and had months to budget for.

I pull out my wallet to find my credit card, but Alex is faster than I am as he intercepts me and hands her his credit card. I want to punch him and kiss him, in that order. If we were alone, I would have done exactly that. Except that I remember the thing he doesn't yet know that I know—I know about the engagement ring he ordered. This doesn't count as spoiling me as much as it's an investment in my health and our future together.

We wait in the seats near the gift shop with a few others for about ten minutes before our whole group is moved to the waiting room designated for outpatient surgery. The TV displays a chart of patient numbers and their current status, reminding me of the flight status boards at airports. Patient 5011926 is currently in prep. Patient 7460082 has arrived. I wonder which patient number is my designation. One of the men in the group to our left is called in first, and he doesn't go without complaining. Deep in my gut, I know I'm next to be called.

When a nurse emerges and calls my name, Alex squeezes my hand that's linked with his before letting go. Just before the door closes behind us, I give him a brave smile of reassurance. The nurse leads me to the first prep room and gives me instructions. Pee in the urine sample cup, change into the hospital gown with the open part in the back, and put all my clothes in the bag provided in the bathroom. The most awkward part is going commando in the hospital gown. The best part is the socks and the warm blanket that waits for me on the hospital bed.

Once I'm settled on the bed and under the blanket, I answer questions about my date of birth, the last time I ate or drank anything (last night), the procedure in my own words, whether I want my belongings placed in a locker or given to my boyfriend in the waiting room. I nearly chuckle at the imagined response Alex would have if I chose the locker option over him. I choose him for my stuff, and I choose to let him come back here with me until they're ready for me in the operating room.

They check my blood pressure and temperature before sticking sensors across my bare chest to monitor me. One nurse struggles to find a vein in my right arm for the IV, so another brings in an ultrasound machine to give her the visual layout of the veins and arteries in my left arm. The needles are my least favorite part. I divert my eyes away from the process of the bloodwork and IV, catching Alex as he sits in the chair not occupied by my purse.

The anesthesiologist gives me options, but I opt for the stuff that'll knock me out. "I could use a nap," I joke to him, though it's not untrue. I've been more exhausted than usual this week.

"How long will she be out?" Alex asks him with masked concern.

"If everything goes according to plan, you should be out of here early enough to still get breakfast," he tells Alex with a reassuring smile.

My gynecologist comes by with many of the same questions I could answer in my sleep by this point. She introduces herself to Alex as she looks between the two of us. "I'll give you a booklet when we discharge you, but no tampons, baths, swimming, hot tubs, or sexual intercourse for two weeks after the procedure."

"Her quick recovery is the priority," Alex says as his face lightly flushes pink at the last item on the list.

One of the nurses in charge of my prep gives me a few pills to swallow in advance of the strong stuff that'll be administered through the IV. After she slides sleeves on my legs to prevent blood clots during surgery, she slips away, leaving me alone with Alex for the first time since we walked through the front door.

"I can see your heartbeat on the monitor," he says as he observes the machine to my left. "For some reason, the seriousness of this didn't hit me until I saw you in that hospital bed. I'm glad you let me be here for this."

"I'm glad you cleared your schedule to be here for this," I say as I wish the worry away from his eyes.

"I hope this is the only time you have to go through surgery for this." He doesn't say the worst-case unknowns of complications or the polyp growing back. Or even the possibility that it isn't benign. Some things could go wrong, but many things are more likely to go right.

Although I'm not yet on anesthesia, I feel as if I could fall asleep. "You look like you could use a nap," I say to Alex. The months since returning from Italy have been full of early mornings and late evenings as he's adjusted to his new role as CEO. Despite his constant sleep deprivation, he's thriving in the way his father trusted he would.

"I'll be able to sleep once I know you're better."

Before I can respond, the nurses collectively burst into the prep room, ready to wheel me to the operating room. Once again, I wordlessly attempt to reassure Alex with a smile as we're separated.

My surroundings are hazy as I wake from the blackness of unconsciousness. There are voices and activity around me as I attempt to read the clock, but without my glasses, it's a lost cause.

"Her boyfriend has her glasses. I'll go get them from him," one of the nurses says before disappearing through the curtains around us.

Another nurse asks, "Are you in any pain? Any burning?"

My nerves slowly come alive again as I feel the slight burning she mentioned. "Yes." My throat is dry, causing my voice to croak.

"We're going to give you pain medicine, but you need to eat something with it," she explains before listing options. I choose applesauce, the only one that sounds remotely appetizing at the moment. "Alex will take you to the pharmacy to pick up your prescriptions after this."

After eating applesauce, swallowing a pain pill, and putting on my glasses, the nurses help me off the bed. They leave me with my clothes and a pad to change out of the hospital gown in privacy. Though I'm a little unsteady, I get back in my clothes on my own, finally feeling like myself again rather than the out-of-body experience of the last hour. The bleeding is to be expected when tissue has been cut from my uterine lining.

I verbally confirm that I'm ready. The bright lights flood the space as the curtains part, and a nurse rolls a wheelchair for me to sit in. It's a slight relief that I'm not expected to do a long walk to navigate the halls to wherever the next stop is. She wheels me through various doors and hallways until we're outside, where Alex's car sits ready for me. He has my purse and the printed instructions from my doctor ready to go. He would have hopped out the driver's side to lift me from the wheelchair to the passenger seat of his car if I weren't too fast for his chivalry.

"We're going to get your breakfast while we wait for your pharmacy to fill the prescriptions," he says as his car slowly loops around the parking lot toward the hospital complex exit and entrance. "I'm assuming you want coffee as well."

"Can we go back to my house to eat the breakfast too?" I ask as we wait for a long enough break in traffic to turn right. "I'd like to go to the bathroom before we drive to your mom's house."

His face etches concernedly as he asks, "Are you feeling okay? Of course, we can stop by your place if that's what you need. It's close to the pharmacy, so we can hang out and eat until your medications are ready for pickup."

"Alex, I'm fine. I just want to change my pad because the free one they gave me doesn't have wings. I don't expect you to understand what that means right now, but you'll get it one day when we're married. I also forgot to pack my contacts. I'm used to already having them in rather than carrying the case with me."

"Change of plans," he says without further explanation. I'm content to sit and wait as he passes every open restaurant and fast food joint between the hospital and my house. He pulls into the garage and uses his key like he had a few hours ago, closing the garage door behind us.

While I slowly walk up to my room to grab my contact lenses and use the bathroom, I hear the clang of pots and pans and the whir of my automatic espresso maker from the kitchen. He's making me breakfast instead. While in the privacy of my master suite, I check my phone for the first time in hours. Multiple message notifications fill my screen. My mom Sylvia and Alex's mom Belinda started a group message with Alex and me to ask for updates. He last texted when he walked to his car to pick me up at the entrance overhang. The other set of messages is from another group message with Lawrence and Jean. Alex kept them in the loop as well.

In both text chains, I add to his reassurances with a message of my own.

> We stopped by my place to eat and wait for the pharmacy to fill my prescriptions. I think Alex is making me breakfast.

There's a flurry of responses singing my boyfriend's praises, but none of them require my response. I don't need them to tell me how wonderful he is when it's all I've experienced from him since the moment we met again in Rome. When I find Alex in the kitchen, he's flipping a pancake and singing Ed Sheeran. I climb into one of the barstools at the peninsula and watch the man I can't wait to marry one day.

WITH ALEX and both our moms around, I fight them to be able to do anything for myself. It's a relief when Alex returns to work the day after my procedure simply because it's one less person to fuss over me. The only reason I didn't try to go back to work was that Alex insisted that my mom stay in town to ensure I didn't push myself too hard. He knew I wouldn't go to the office while she was in town. Despite the overbearing mothering, it's nice seeing our moms get along. Both our families seem aware that a wedding—a marriage— joining us is inevitable.

The tissue sample taken during the hysteroscopy is sent to a clinic in Cleveland for further examination. I know I shouldn't be nervous since the probability of it being benign is high, but I fight back the anxiety. Alex reminds me over and over that if God can somehow put us in each other's path after seven years, He can get us through the worst thing the doctors could say. That man would marry me next week if that meant he could pay for any medical treatment required to get me back to full health.

Twelve days after my surgery, my phone lights up with a notification of a new test result in my health record. Benign. None of the cells are cancerous or precancerous. I immediately call Alex.

"Hey, is everything okay?" He answers after two rings with concern in his voice.

"It's benign," I say with tears of joy threatening to spill from my eyes.

"Thank God," he says with a sigh of unhindered relief. "I know this is what we expected and have been praying for, but it's a relief to have it confirmed. I'll call my mom, your parents, and Lawrence and Jean and plan a small celebration dinner."

"Alex, you don't need to do that," I say, though I'm thankful even for the intention. "I'm content with it being just the two of us since that's easier to plan."

I hear muffled voices in the background. "Hey, I need to hop in a meeting but keep your Saturday night open. I love you."

"I love you, too."

Despite the abnormalities in the tissue sample, my doctor isn't concerned. It's still benign. It'll take a cycle or two to know for sure if the procedure fixed the bleeding issue. She asks about Alex and whether or not birth control is something I even want in the foreseeable future. Five years ago, I would have jumped at the option of having Alex to myself for a few years. Going through this with uncertainty about my fertility erases those former notions.

Early Saturday evening, Alex drives me to Lidia's in the Crossroads and leads me to the sunroom filled with our close family and friends, all of whom know about the surgery and the good outcome. I'm more surprised that he could even rent this space on such short notice than I am that he could get everyone to come. When he gets down on one knee during dessert, the whole picture comes together. He made this reservation intending to propose in advance of knowing whether or not we would receive good news this week. Because Alex would have asked me to marry him no matter what.

In every scenario, I say yes.

Sonnet

The knock at my door is so quiet I question whether it was imagined. Taylor has already parted ways with Gabe and Belle for the night to keep me company on my final night as an unmarried woman. We're both in the guest house on the large estate, meaning no one could accidentally knock on our door. Thinking it could be Gabe having issues with his fussy daughter, I open the door to check. Alex pushes his way in before I can react to his presence.

"What are you doing here?" I ask as he closes the door. The dim lighting from the lamp paints dark shadows across his face and cheekbones. I'm tempted to trace the lines with my fingers—and then my lips. This is precisely why we're staying in two different buildings until tomorrow.

His arms pull me into an embrace as he says, "I wanted to see my bride. We have a big day tomorrow with little or no privacy for most of it."

"You're not supposed to see me the night before the wedding," I say to him with my arms crossed despite his tight hold around me. "Your nonna would kill you if she knew you sneaked out here."

"Seriously, Alex, you couldn't go one more night?" Taylor says from behind him, causing him to jump a little.

He releases his hold around me as he turns to face my matron of honor. "Taylor, I didn't realize you were here too."

She raises an eyebrow at him in a silent challenge he knows he can't win. Even if she weren't here, I know he's not here for more than a kiss. He's never complained or tried to talk me out of wanting to wait for sex until we're married the way Richard had. If I had to guess, I would think he's relieved by it. Often, he's the one who reminds others that we're waiting.

"Tomorrow night, I'm all yours," I say with promise before I kiss his cheek goodnight again. He obeys Taylor's silent warning and escapes back out the way he came.

THE FOLLOWING MORNING, the others in my bridal shower drive to the estate from the main city area of Treviso to join us for breakfast and wedding day preparations. When debating venues for the wedding, his family's Italian estate was thrown out as the option that would give us the most privacy. The venues in the Kansas City area were convenient, but convenience also meant the potential for unwanted guests crashing the wedding. There's a reason celebrities get married on private islands or in other countries.

I knew my friends and family would jump at the excuse to travel to Italy for a wedding, especially since my fiancé refused to let anyone pay for their plane tickets or accommodations. The other reason I knew the family estate was the perfect location is that his father is buried on this land. Here, it'll be like he's with us—his death was one of the unfortunate events that brought Alex and me back together after seven and a half years.

A late afternoon ceremony followed by a dinner reception gives us hours for hair and makeup before the photographer arrives. Much of the wedding details were decided over a group text chain between Taylor, Alex, and me. Not Alex's assistant or the famous wedding coordinator he hired. He was hands-on and involved, often communicating our preferences to the wedding coordinator faster than I could. It was the opposite experience of planning a wedding with Dick.

"Are you nervous?" My mom asks as she and Belinda join us in the large living area of the guest house. The two have been thick as thieves since we landed in Italy a week ago.

Our mothers were already familiar with each other after getting to know each other over the holidays and during my mom's short stay after my hysteroscopy. Despite it being a minor surgery with little recovery time, Alex refused to let me stay in my own house even though my mom came into town to stay with me. His argument was all the stairs in the split-level house weren't "surgery-friendly." To appease his worry, my mother and I stayed with his mom in her house. She appreciated the company for a few days, and he was a short enough distance away during the evenings that he could check up on me if needed. At least I have no worries about whether he'll take care of me when I need it. In sickness and in health.

I smile at the two mothers in my life and say, "About marrying Alex, not at all. About any surprises or shenanigans he might have up his sleeve—absolutely."

"I made him promise not to do anything too crazy," his mom says reassuringly. A promise to his mother isn't empty words coming from him. Although neither of our mothers has asked me our thoughts on a timeline for kids, I know they're scheming with each other. The joke's on them, though, because there is no set plan or timeline.

Time is fast and slow, stretching and thinning until Taylor leads me to the gazebo for the first look. She's still in her outfit from this morning due to the sleeping baby wrapped around her in a sling. Gabe passed Bella back to his wife this morning so he could resume his duties as Alex's best man. They became best friends when Alex brought Gabe to his private suite for a football game during the playoffs. And then the Super Bowl. If Gabe weren't married, he would probably try to steal Alex from me just for those perks.

Though I have yet to spot the photographer, I hear the distinct sound of a camera shutter. In the distance, I see Gabe leading my blindfolded groom toward me. My heart still doesn't know how to react to his presence, the pendulum swinging between racing and stopping altogether. Being his girlfriend meant accompanying him on the red carpet, but this suit somehow eclipses how he looked in the others. It could be the rose-colored bubble of my wedding day.

I stand wordlessly as Gabe removes the blindfold from Alex's face. Those familiar blue eyes blink as they adjust to the brightness of the afternoon sun before focusing on me. With his attention fixated on my eyes, the rest of the world disappears.

"Hi," he says as his mouth lifts into my favorite smile.

"Hi," I say because my brain can't formulate coherent thoughts when he looks at me like that. It's a good thing the officiant will tell us what words to repeat during the ceremony. Except for the part where we add our own vows.

"Took us long enough to get here," he says as his grin turns mischievous. The photographer interrupts us to instruct us on poses for photos. Because Alex insisted on arrangements for a famous designer to make my dress in exchange for a wedding photo on the front spread of a magazine, our photographer is one of the best in the wedding industry. It's a loophole in our agreement about how much money he can spend on me. Outside the necessities, I'm strict about gifts except for birthdays, anniversaries, Valentine's Day, and Christmas. Only time will tell whether he wears down my resolve in the years to come.

The afternoon is a whirlwind as we pose and smile and kiss for more photos than my mind can count with all the excitement swirling around. The boy from the masquerade ball is about to be my husband, and it's the furthest thing from settling. Today isn't happily ever after, but it's happier than I could have ever imagined. It's an ending to the longing and wondering and a beginning of mornings and nights next to those blue eyes. It's good days and bad days and days when we're both exhausted. We'll have each other through the best and worst moments for the rest of our lives.

When he looks at me as I walk down the aisle, the butterflies are relentless. The sparks are ever-present as he takes my hand in his. After our vows in both English and Italian and the exchange of rings, the officiant reaches the climactic finale of the ceremony. I nearly miss when he pronounces us Mr. and Mrs. Alessandro De Luca, but I don't miss the glint in Alex's eyes—the mischief he's hiding behind his stoic expression. It's the only warning I get before he dips me into a kiss fit for the Hollywood red carpet. I would swoon if I weren't otherwise engaged in my first kiss as his wife.

Given the presence of a string quartet on the night of the masquerade and the night in Piazza San Marco, we both wanted the same during our dinner reception. It's another night of near-magic surrounded by friends and family, including Lawrence and Jean. Our guests wave sparklers as we make our grand exit from the party to the guest house for the night. Tomorrow morning, we will take the train to southern Italy for our honeymoon. My husband carries me over the same threshold he sneaked through just last night.

"This isn't going to be like those steamy romance novels or the movies," Alex says as his lips trace my jawline. "I've been dreaming about this day for years."

"The couples in the books and movies usually aren't virgins," I say as I comb my fingers through his hair. "I don't expect perfection. That night at the masquerade ball and this day have already met the perfection quota. Being your wife will always be enough."

Alex

S onnet is frustrated and complaining about how none of her clothes fit, but I've been in awe of her baby bump from the moment she started showing. Just when I thought she couldn't get more beautiful, the pregnancy proved me wrong. After the wedding, she moved into the guest suite with me. After a few renovations, Gabe and Taylor started renting Sonnet's house from us at a discount. The location didn't offer us enough privacy, but it's perfect for their growing family. My mom and Sonnet are already painting and decorating a nursery in the main house on our family's property.

"Want me to take you shopping this afternoon?" I ask her as she continues to comb through her clothes in the closet. Her refusal to buy maternity clothes is less about the money and more about not wanting to go to the store by herself. "I have a lunch meeting with a client, but I can take off the rest of the day after if you want."

"I have a deadline at two, but I should be free once it's submitted," she says as she emerges from our shared closet space wearing a pair of my jeans, one of my motivations for taking an afternoon off. She may look good in my jeans, but it leaves me with fewer clothing options. Plus, in a few weeks, the waist of my jeans will be too tight for her pregnant belly.

I pull her into a chaste kiss before saying, "Bella donna pazza," with an amused shake of my head.

"Don't look at me like that and say those words," she says as she gently pushes me away. "That's how I got pregnant to begin with."

"It's not like I can get you pregnant again for another—" I say with my signature smirk, interrupted by her lips on mine for a final goodbye kiss. I watch her walk out of our room and toward the front door to leave for work. After checking a few more emails on my laptop, I brush my teeth and head to my morning in the office.

My lunch meeting ends five minutes before my wife calls me.

"Hey, where should I meet you?" She asks seconds after I accept the call.

"Let's meet at the house," I suggest as my phone transfers the call to my car's Bluetooth. "Makes it easier if I don't have to drop you off anywhere once we're done."

"You just want to trap me so you can insist on spending money on me," she teases. That's exactly why I prefer we travel in one car this afternoon. Sharing a vehicle guarantees I have leverage when she's hesitant to buy the things she needs or wants. I would much rather face the challenge of outsmarting that side of her than be married to someone who cares more about spending money than our relationship.

I smile as I shift my car into drive. "Am I that predictable?"

"You're the ideal level of predictable," she says because she knows I'm likely to surprise her if I think I'm being too predictable. I'll find a way to surprise her either way. When she hangs up, I dial her favorite restaurant to make a dinner reservation for tonight. Estimating that I have a ten-minute head start home compared to her, I swing by a flower shop on the way home.

By the time my wife walks through our front door to use the restroom, the fresh roses are in a vase on her bedside table. She smiles, and I'm tempted to cancel all plans and stay here all afternoon and evening. But she needs maternity clothes, and I need my jeans back.

I play the good husband by holding the clothes she wants to buy and telling her that everything she tries on and wants a second opinion for looks good. They all look good on her. She's the type of woman who knows what's likely to be flattering and is picky about what she'll try on. One pair of jeans that fits her turns into three pairs of the same brand and style in different denim washes. At the checkout, I block her view of the total price.

"Do you have to return to the office to make up for taking the afternoon off?" she asks as I buckle my seat belt. Missing a few hours in the afternoon often means playing catch-up in the evening.

"No, you're stuck with me for the rest of the day," I say as I drive home. "We have a dinner reservation tonight at seven. I'm giving you an excuse to dress up tonight."

"You're lucky some of my dresses still fit because otherwise, I would be angry that you gave me short notice." Any potential anger would have disappeared once the butternut squash ravioli was placed before her. I double-checked that it's on the menu for tonight when making the reservation. Dinner at Lidia's in the Crossroads Art District is a foolproof way to earn her affection for the night.

Late that night, I hold her as she drifts off to sleep. My hands rub circles on her bare stomach, eager for the day I'll feel our child kick for the first time. I have so much I'm thankful for, starting with an incredible wife and a healthy pregnancy.

"I can't wait to meet you," I whisper to my unborn child before letting myself fall asleep.

THIS PLANE CAN'T FLY FAST ENOUGH. My mom called as I was boarding my private jet en route home to Kansas City from New York. Sonnet has had Braxton Hicks contractions on and off for the last month, but this particular set of contractions has lasted longer than the others. Once we were up in the air, Sonnet texted that her water had broken. My mom is driving her to the hospital in my absence, but she knows the birth plan as well as we do. My mom likely memorized every detail due to her over-excitement for her first grandchild. Granddaughter, to be precise.

The half-hour remaining until landing leaves me antsy. I was minutes away from rescheduling this business trip when Sonnet insisted she would be fine for one weekend. She is fine, especially with my mother living in the same house. At the beginning of the third trimester, Sonnet and I moved into the main house where the nursery was almost ready for our first baby. My mother insisted she would rather move into the guest suite eventually than have her grandchildren living in any other house. My phone screen lights up with another text from my wife.

THE LOVE OF MY LIFE

> The nurse says I have at least another two hours before I'll be dilated enough. That should be enough time for you and my mom to get here.

Her parents have been on baby watch for the past two weeks, keeping an eye on their phones for a call or text from any of us. If Sonnet hadn't gone into labor today, her parents planned on driving up tomorrow.

> I'll be there in an hour or less. I'm never letting you convince me to go on a trip this far into any of your pregnancies ever again. You've proven it's too risky.

THE LOVE OF MY LIFE

> You assume I'm letting your sperm anywhere near me again. You'd better hope our daughter is cute and makes me forget how much this hurts. I thought pregnancy was the hard part, but labor is no joke.

> I love you. There's no way our daughter won't be as beautiful as you. We can always adopt if you want to be done after one labor.

And I mean it. I'm down for whatever she wants to do moving forward. If I have to get a vasectomy and fly to China or Africa to adopt the rest, I will do it willingly. Aware of the situation I'm flying home to, Derek watches me out of the corner of his eye.

"I'll handle tomorrow's meeting and the contracts," he says about the new clients we met in New York. "Just focus on being a good husband and a good father. Come back to the office when she gets tired of having you around all the time." I'm grateful for this business partner who has kept the company running like a well-oiled machine anytime I leave the reigns in his hands. The transition of leadership from my father to me was smooth because Derek and my father were equally responsible for the company's growth. He's why we could have a wedding and honeymoon in Italy and out of the public eye.

I can't seem to get to her fast enough as the plane lands at the downtown airport, the smaller and more private of the two airports owned by Kansas City. It's closer to the hospital, the office, and the house. As soon as I'm in my car, I call my mom through the stereo system.

"Alex, don't you dare get in an accident or get pulled over for speeding," my mother says when she answers the phone. "The last thing you want is to do something that could delay your arrival. You still have at least an hour to get here. Just breathe and drive safely."

With my mom calming my nerves over the phone, my thoughts slow down enough to keep my sanity. I hang up as I approach the valet parking and check in with the receptionist. My beautiful wife gives me a strained smile when I enter her room. It's the expression of someone attempting to hide pain. I kiss her forehead and let her strangle my hand through the waves of contractions. Periodically, I remind her that she's incredible and strong. By the time the final labor pushes arrive, both our mothers are coaching alongside the doctor.

My daughter isn't crying, but she's breathing and healthy and perfect. The nurses take her to clean off the fluids and record measurements while Sonnet's head rests on my shoulder in exhaustion. As quickly as they whisked her away, the nurse brings back the newborn wrapped in a blanket and hands the bundle to Sonnet. Blue eyes that resemble mine look at me from Sonnet's arms. My perfect daughter.

It's love at first sight.

Acknowledgments

THE STORIES BEHIND THE STORY

One night in early 2022, I drove in my Corolla while listening to the Taylor Swift Essentials playlist on Apple Music. Sometimes, I skip the unfamiliar songs, but on that evening, I let "Enchanted" keep playing. The lyrics in the first verse are so descriptive that I could easily imagine the scene as it played out.

From there, my imagination took over, and the idea for this book started to form. I knew I wanted the second part of the story to follow the tour of Italy that I got to experience with my family in 2019. I knew that Venice would be the turning point of the plot. I forced myself to wait until November to draft this during National Novel Writing Month in 2022.

On November 1, I picked up iron supplements at the store while getting my weekly groceries. I had been experiencing symptoms of iron deficiency from heavy bleeding, including shortness of breath after climbing up the stairs. Someone who exercises five to six days a week shouldn't have been struggling like I had. Sonnet's experiences with her endometrial polyp were written from my own journey as I was drafting this story.

In December 2022, I had a blood test followed by three iron infusions to get my hemoglobin back to normal. Then, I had an ultrasound scan, which confirmed the polyp. I drafted this novel while waiting for answers and dreaming about my next trip to Italy.

Unlike Sonnet, there was no boyfriend to accompany me to the minor outpatient surgical procedure to have it removed, but I wasn't without a support system. I also didn't put off having the surgery. Most people didn't know what was going on, though. Less than three months after my hysteroscopy, I climbed the hundreds of steps to the Palamidi Fortress in Nafplio, Greece, in under fifteen minutes. That accomplishment felt like a victory when compared to the struggles from months before.

Writing this allowed me to relive the memories from my first trip to Italy. While this book is obviously fiction, some events occurred in some shape or form. During our dinner in Rome, the waiter gave me three roses instead of only one. As of the publication of this book, I've been to Peruzzi twice and have been selected to model the leather jacket both times. I did not buy the jacket either time, but I did buy leather goods both times. I danced by myself at the dinner in the Tuscan countryside. Venice—Venezia—won me over. I didn't tell many people, if any, but one of my desires was to see Venice again before turning 30. At 29, I experienced Venice for a second time, and it felt just as enchanting as it had the first.

The bonus chapter (featured in the hardback edition) was partially written on my second visit to Italy. One evening, I wrote while sitting in the lobby of our hotel in Florence with the city street in view. I wrote on the coach as it transported us east from Florence toward Verona and Venice. During our day on the ferry to Greece, I even wrote a few sentences. There's something about writing it in the place that helped inspire that it makes this special.

While Alessandro is certainly a figment of my imagination, Lawrence and Jean were directly inspired by friends of mine, Kevin and Paula. Not only did I want to honor them for everything they have done for me and others, but I wanted to shine a spotlight on their story of second chances to supplement the main plot. I didn't know how much the characters needed them until I started drafting. I hope they are both surprised when they read this.

Without God, I wouldn't have gotten through drafting this book. It was physically one of the toughest seasons of my life so far, but I know I had His help. I'm thankful for the answers I got through modern medicine and doctors and for answered prayers.

Rachel, thank you for keeping me accountable and encouraging me to be consistent with my writing. I also couldn't have finished this and gotten it out so quickly without feedback from Erica and Ally.

Thank you, the reader, for going on this journey with me. If you never get to see Italy for yourself, I'm glad I could show you glimpses through the eyes of my characters.

Abridged Autobiography

As a second-generation American, I share a love for both my country and for all the places abroad that I haven't seen yet or that I want to see again. It doesn't help that I have enough nationalities mixed into my genetics that I have yet to see all the places my ancestors are from.

I love to read and write almost as much as I love all things Italian—the food, the language, the country, the leather, the coffee, the food, and the list goes on. The slight obsession with Italy is evident in my stories. My preferred schedule is that of a night owl, though I'm adaptable when necessary as long as I have caffeine. When I'm not lost in another world or country, Kansas City is home and the Chiefs are my NFL team.

Jesus is an essential part of my life and identity and a big reason why I keep on writing happy endings. Sometimes I write as a way to balance the power between my imagination and the logical part of my brain, the side that tries to remain tethered to reality.

lbethcampbell.com

For updates on future releases, sign up for my monthly email
newsletter through my website and follow me on Instagram

@L.BethCampbell